ECHOES
of the SEA

OTHER PROPER ROMANCES
BY SARAH M. EDEN

STORM TIDE ROMANCE
The Tides of Time
Echoes of the Sea

STAND-ALONES
Ashes on the Moor
Ashes on the Moor Collector's Edition

HOPE SPRINGS
Longing for Home
Longing for Home, vol. 2: Hope Springs

SAVAGE WELLS
The Sheriffs of Savage Wells
Healing Hearts
Wyoming Wild

THE DREAD PENNY SOCIETY
The Lady and the Highwayman
The Gentleman and the Thief
The Merchant and the Rogue
The Bachelor and the Bride
The Queen and the Knave
The Dread Penny Society:
The Complete Penny Dreadful Collection

ECHOES
of the SEA

A Storm Tide Romance

SARAH M. EDEN

SHADOW
MOUNTAIN
PUBLISHING

© 2025 Sarah M. Eden

All rights reserved. No part of this book may be reproduced in any form or by any means without permission in writing from the publisher, Shadow Mountain Publishing®, at permissions@shadowmountain.com. The views expressed herein are the responsibility of the author and do not necessarily represent the position of Shadow Mountain Publishing.

This is a work of fiction. Characters and events in this book are products of the author's imagination or are represented fictitiously.

PROPER ROMANCE is a registered trademark.

Visit us at ShadowMountain.com

Library of Congress Cataloging-in-Publication Data
Names: Eden, Sarah M., author.
Title: Echoes of the sea / Sarah M. Eden.
Description: Salt Lake City : Shadow Mountain Publishing, 2025. | Series: Proper Romance | Summary: "When actor Kipling Summerfield is swept two hundred years back in time, he meets Miss Amelia Archibald, bound by her grandfather's will to stay on England's Guilford Island or lose her inheritance. As Kip and Amelia work to secure her future, Kip realizes the truth of his situation and their growing bond-a love destined to endure, no matter where time takes them"—Provided by publisher.
Identifiers: LCCN 2025003282 (print) | LCCN 2025003283 (ebook) | ISBN 9781639934249 (trade paperback) | ISBN 9781649334626 (ebook)
Subjects: LCGFT: Romance fiction. | Novels.
Classification: LCC PS3605.D45365 E24 2025 (print) | LCC PS3605.D45365 (ebook) | DDC 813/.6—dc23/eng/20250207
LC record available at https://lccn.loc.gov/2025003282
LC ebook record available at https://lccn.loc.gov/2025003283

Printed in Canada
PubLitho

10 9 8 7 6 5 4 3 2 1

*To the film industry,
for crushing actors' dreams and, thus,
giving me a great foundation for this story*

Chapter 1

London
present day

Tennyson Lamont's death was proving increasingly inconvenient. That Kipling had lost his job as a result of that ill-timed demise was particularly annoying.

Negotiations with television producers weren't generally known for being effortless. And when someone had endured a streak of bad luck like Kip had, the bargaining was almost destined to go badly. He'd fully anticipated not getting the pay raise he'd asked for, perhaps even having less screen time in the next season of *The Beau* than he'd hoped for, but the result of his request had, by all counts, been far worse than that.

With one stroke of the pen, Tennyson—Kip's most iconic role—had died, and Kip's career had come to a screeching halt.

Half a year had passed, and he hadn't booked a single role. Even his agent had stopped passing along auditions. In fact, his agent had stopped communicating with him *at all*. That, he knew from years in the industry, didn't mean everything was awesome.

Still, he hadn't been entirely forgotten.

He arrived at the Dorchester for a post-awards-show party. An awards show at which he'd been a nominee. For the role he'd been fired from. He hadn't won.

It had been a stellar six months. Stellar.

He entered the party knowing he at least *looked* like a television star with potential. Five seasons on one of the world's biggest shows—a runaway hit set in England's Regency era and credited with resurrecting the historical romance genre of television—had gained him a lot of cachet, and he was depending on every bit of it tonight.

The Dorchester's largest ballroom was filled to the rafters with actors: some he'd worked with, some who'd wanted to work with him, and quite a few he hoped to work with at some point in the future. There would also be directors, casting directors, and producers. This was *the* place to see and be seen.

He needed this.

What he didn't need, though, was spotting Giselle Ridley the moment he stepped inside. They'd dated for a year, often being referred to as one of Hollywood's "it" couples. Giselle lived in LA, and Kip had visited a lot while she'd been working on a long list of impressive projects. She was from London, and he'd lived there while filming *The Beau*, so she had often visited him. So they were sometimes referred to as one of *London*'s "it" couples. But, they were now going in different directions and ought to go in those directions without each other. He knew that was the case because she'd told him so within a few hours of the announcement that his time on *The Beau* had come to an abrupt end. He hadn't had a lot of trouble reading between the lines.

"Going in different directions" was basically Giselle saying, "You are about to be nobody, and I don't have time for 'nobody.'"

Stellar.

Thankfully, Kip was an actor—a good one, despite his current lack of employment—and didn't let his surprise and discomfort show. He simply walked past Giselle, glancing in her direction with a brief look of indifference. If anyone noticed—and with the way things were going, probably no one did—they would think he wasn't bothered in the least. And the swiftness of his glance came with an additional benefit: he had no idea how she responded.

Willis Keaton, one of his costars from *The Beau*, stood nearby, so Kip stepped up to him with a friendly smile and, he hoped, a convincing lack of awkwardness. A few in the cast had reached out to Kip when his contract had not been renewed. Willis had been one of the few who'd stayed in touch. Barely, but still.

"Good to see you, Willis," Kip said.

"Kipling." Willis's smile was a little strained, a little uncomfortable. "How have you been? We don't hear much from you."

The first thing anyone had said to him all night, and it was, "We don't hear much from you." That was industry talk for, "You're on the brink of being a has-been."

"I have a few things in the works." That was a lie. "For the time being, I'm just enjoying my first time off in years." Even more of a lie. He hadn't been "enjoying" much of anything the last six months.

"I hope it is something where you can use your American accent," someone in the group said. "We're so used to hearing you speak like you're British. It would be novel to hear your real voice."

Though Kip couldn't pinpoint exactly what, there was an insult in there somewhere.

The conversation swirled around him, pulling farther from him until he was entirely excluded from it. They were speaking of people he knew and about shows he had guest-starred on, but now, he wasn't connected to any of it.

He wandered away from that group toward another, pausing just long enough at the bar to gather a spot of courage.

He recognized the casting director from *Red, Red Rose*, another historical drama, this one set in the 1600s rather than the 1800s.

Period dramas were his bread and butter. It wouldn't be a bad idea to garner some notice there.

When he slid himself into their group, the casting director asked the person standing next to her who he was. He'd auditioned for her before. She'd even cast him in a couple of gigs. Either she genuinely didn't remember him, which made him think they ought to be dialing up emergency services with instructions to deliver her to the nearest A&E to check for signs of a stroke, or she was pointedly letting him know that he was considered on the outs in the industry. If he hadn't already known that, *he* was likely the one needing to be checked for signs of a brain injury.

His negotiations on *The Beau* had ended badly, yes. And a decent amount of that was his own fault, yes. But this level of ostracism was excessive. It, however, was all part of the game.

When you're hot, you're hot; when you're not, you're not. That had likely first been said by a casting director.

Kip continued around the room. With each new encounter, people remembered him with an expression of disappointment because he "wasn't doing anything anymore," or they made a point of having forgotten him.

Salvation came in the form of Malcolm Winthrop. He was the star of *The Beau*, but they hadn't met on set. They'd been friends since their university days, when Kip had left America behind for what he'd anticipated as a career-making London arts education.

Recent high school graduates were often adorably naive.

While Kip's part on *The Beau* had never been as large as Malcolm's, getting to work together had been one of Kip's favorite things about doing the show. Malcolm had offered him a few tips here and there on making his British accent more authentic. Kip had introduced him to the woman who was now his wife. That made them more or less even, he'd often joked.

ECHOES OF THE SEA

Through everything that had happened in the last six months, through all the challenges no one knew had occurred in the year leading up to the worst days of Kip's life, Malcolm had been there to support him.

Kip didn't let his "I'm perfectly pleased with my career path because amazing things are happening for me" expression slip until he was standing next to Malcolm and facing away from everybody else.

"They are enjoying this," Malcolm said with a knowing smile.

"Apparently, I didn't earn enough good karma by choosing not to be a diva while I had the chance."

Malcolm shook his head. "Karma does not exist in this dojo." His expression remained perfectly laidback.

No one looking on would guess that they were having this conversation. But Kip knew his friend too well not to recognize the concern in his eyes. Of course, *Vanity Fair* had described those eyes as "hauntingly expressive pools of cerulean waters a person could drown in and die happy." *Vanity Fair* had never written any odes to Kip's eyes. If Kip didn't deeply like Malcolm, he would probably hate him.

"Have you managed to book anything?" Malcolm asked.

"Have you received any texts from me that weren't just GIFs of famous people crying?" Kip tossed back.

"Fair point."

"*Unfair* point, really. I was passed over for a dog food commercial. All I had to say was, 'Good boy.' The casting director said I wasn't articulate enough." Kip gave him a dry sidelong look. "I wasn't articulate enough to be having a conversation *with a dog*."

"Were you using your American accent or your British one?"

"Are you saying one of those accents would be better suited to a conversation with a canine?"

"Have you tried cat food commercials?" Malcolm asked. "I suspect cats actually prefer it when we sound like idiots."

For the first time since—well, since he had last been in company with Malcolm—Kip laughed.

Malcolm smiled more broadly. *Vanity Fair* had also said a lot of things about his smile, most of which Kipling refused to recall at the moment, knowing millions of people the world over had likely stitched them onto throw pillows. Should Malcolm do another interview with any major publication, it would probably turn needlepoint into the next crafting craze.

"I have suggested you a few times when I've heard of roles you'd be a good fit for," Malcolm said. "I think many directors and producers are waiting to see how you're going to pivot after *The Beau*."

"How am I supposed to pivot if no one will hire me?"

"I've worked in this industry since university, and I still don't understand it," Malcolm said.

"I've known you since university," Kip countered, "and I still don't understand why Jen married you."

"As that is, without question, the most remarkably lucky thing that's ever happened to me in my life, I have no intention of tempting fate by trying to make sense of it."

"What are the chances you'll toss some of that luck my way?" Kip asked.

"You're hoping to get married?" Malcolm eyed him narrowly. "I thought after Giselle, you wouldn't be anxious to dive into a relationship anytime soon."

"I'm looking for a different kind of match entirely: the perfect . . . role."

"How romantic," Malcolm drawled.

This banter between them was well-established. It came so naturally to them in real life that the writers of *The Beau* had almost immediately started weaving it into their characters' interactions. The now-deceased Tennyson Lamont had quickly become the very best friend and confidant of Royston, the character who had made Malcolm a household name.

The connection had made Kip's character more popular and more valuable to the show. But that still hadn't saved him in the end. Tennyson had drowned at sea. At first, Kip had thought that meant there was a chance his character would be revived, having been marooned on an island somewhere only to be recovered to make a triumphant return. He suspected he had said that out loud to someone at some point, because within three episodes, Tennyson's body was discovered.

Partially eaten by sharks.

Unless *The Beau* was making a shift toward a Jane Austen–era zombie story—which, quite frankly, had already been done—his time on the show was over.

"Before you get back to rubbing barbed elbows," Malcolm said, "I do have one idea for you."

Kip perked up. "You do?"

"It's likely not one you'll be excited about."

"I'm willing to try almost anything, provided I'll get to act, get paid, and possibly convince this fickle industry that I'm not done for."

"It is decidedly the first two, and there's a possibility of it being the third."

Kip didn't like the hesitant way Malcom had said *possibility*.

Malcolm motioned with his head for Kip to walk with him. "Do you remember the job I took during our university days for which I dressed as a Viking and vanquished Tesco as an in-person advert for tinned fish?"

"Please tell me this promising opportunity isn't vanquishing Tesco."

"A slight improvement over that."

Kip threw back the last of his courage, then set the glass on a table as they passed. "How slight is this improvement?"

Malcolm shrugged. "It's not carpentry."

All those years ago, while Malcolm had been booking in-person advertising jobs, Kip had been relying on his other life skill: carpentry. He hadn't disliked building sets, but he'd wanted to be *on* those sets far more. "I'm beginning to suspect you're desperate to soften the blow you're about to deal me," Kip said.

"Some blows can't truly be softened."

That was not a good sign.

"Michael Osbourne is rumored to be in talks to produce an adaptation of that Victorian-era novel that did so well last year, the one about the American who inherits a title and has to move to England."

He had Kip's full attention. "An American leading man?"

"Believe me, I have made certain your name has been whispered anywhere that production is being discussed."

He didn't know what he'd do without Malcolm.

"But Osbourne will have the final say," Malcolm said. "He always does."

Osbourne was overbearing, bullying, and obnoxious. If the legendary producer didn't produce hit after hit after hit, he would likely be drummed out of the industry, though he was also something of a genius.

"Osbourne discovered Beatrice Jennings a couple of years ago during his family's annual pilgrimage to a living history site on the coast of West Sussex," Malcolm said.

"You're from West Sussex."

Malcolm nodded. "We went to the living history site a lot when I was growing up. My family, apparently, was connected to the place back when the history there wasn't *history* at all."

"And what does all this have to do with the possibility you're dangling in front of me?"

Malcolm stopped walking and turned to face him directly again. "Consider this with an open mind."

"Telling me to keep an open mind makes me *more* nervous."

"When Osbourne discovered Beatrice, she was working at the site as one of their reenactors. During their summer season, they hire actors to live the lives they would have centuries ago. When people come on open days, they get to watch and experience life as it used to be." Malcolm eyed him nervously. "The site's director has been there for about fifteen years, and we've met a few times. The Guilford Historical Site is in need of, essentially, a leading man."

Kip's heart made a beeline for his toes. "You're suggesting I go work as a history reenactor for the summer season at a kitschy tourist destination?"

"It's not kitschy," Malcolm said. "It's actually a really amazing place, really authentic. It's why Osbourne was impressed enough with Beatrice to cast her. The actors have to be good. They have to feel *real*."

Was this really what Kip's career had come to? This was the sort of job students took when trying to make ends meet. Kip had been on *The Beau*. He was a multiaward nominee. He had been one-half of a two-continent "it" couple. He'd had steady work that he'd enjoyed and a future even his father couldn't have dismissed as "destined to be disappointing."

He'd had the world at his feet, and it had all been snatched away.

Chapter 2

Sussex

1803

Amelia Archibald had managed to find a degree of peace in her less-than-ideal life as a perpetual poor relation with an even more perpetual limp. But her grandfather had managed to reach out from beyond the grave and wreak havoc.

Infuriating man.

She told herself to be grateful Grandfather's mission of misery would be a very temporary one. She would return to the family's estate outside of Tunbridge Wells just as soon as the excursion required of them was completed.

She traveled with her aunt, uncle, and cousin, and one look at them would have convinced an even mildly curious onlooker that their current journey was, in fact, a pleasant one. All three of her companions looked out the windows of their carriage with expressions of awe and excitement.

Amelia was doing her best to ignore the view entirely.

Guilford Island was a very minor holding for the Stirlings, her late mother's family, and a place she had heard mentioned many times but had, blessedly, never before been required to visit. The uncle with whom Amelia was currently traveling and with whom she had lived for twenty of her twenty-five years was her mother's older brother. He had often spoken fondly of Guilford and the time he'd spent there as a child. And as if it weren't a horrifying prospect, he'd mentioned repeatedly in every retelling that Guilford sat in the embrace of the sea.

The house and estate sat on an island connected to the stability of the mainland by a long and narrow road surrounded on both sides by the ocean. When a storm passed through, the surge of waves and water buried that road entirely.

"Sometimes for weeks!" her uncle had once declared, sending shivers of horror through Amelia.

She would have been far more enthusiastic about Guilford if she'd spent a lifetime hearing her uncle declare that the house was home to well-organized wolves with a penchant for hunting red-headed women. Wolves could possibly be reasoned with. The ocean didn't believe in negotiation.

Amelia's grandfather had died six months earlier. His will had been opened and read, and to absolutely no one's surprise, Amelia had not been included in it, despite being the only child of his only daughter. At the time, she'd assumed Grandfather had considered that exclusion his way of having the last word in their mutual, if not outright stated, dislike of each other.

But she had, to her own annoyance, underestimated him.

He had left instructions that another portion of his will be read at Guilford six months after his passing, and he had required that Amelia be in attendance. He'd known she was afraid of water; *everyone* knew it.

At last, the ocean road reached the rocky shore of Guilford Island and began the ascent toward the house. Guilford was not used very often, it being not so large and impressive as the estate her uncle had inherited six months earlier or the one on which

Amelia had lived nearly all her life. Guilford was also impractical, isolated on an island, battered by storms . . .

This was no place for a house.

It was no place for *her*. But poor relations, especially those who had the unfortunate tendency to be female, had very little say in their lives.

The higher the carriage climbed, the more easily she breathed. The ocean was still far too near for her peace of mind, but they were getting farther from it, and the likelihood of a surge of water sweeping them away was decreasing.

"I haven't seen Guilford in years." Uncle looked more excited than he generally did.

Her uncle was not an unhappy person, but he could be very stern. And when interacting with her, he was often irritated. Not unkind, not hurtful, but moderately vexed. That had more to do with his having been saddled with a ward than any dislike of her specifically. Amelia, likewise, wasn't precisely overjoyed to be an orphan living in another family's home.

The island was visually intriguing, seeming to be made of dark rock—not quite black but approaching it. In places, thickets of shrubbery and trees grew, apparently having found soil among the rocks. All around the house itself were what appeared to have once been well-maintained lawns and, if the walls she spotted were not deceptive, perhaps even an enclosed garden.

Amelia loved gardens, provided one acknowledged that the word *loved* could also mean "being so engrossed that she likely ought to be marginally concerned about her mental state." But as a tragic orphan, she thought herself entitled to a smidge of eccentricity, especially as it had arisen directly from that early tragedy.

The garden at her aunt and uncle's home had been her escape from almost the moment she'd arrived at the tender age of five years old. No one bothered her there, and she'd found she could easily make friends with plants and birds and the occasional fox that scampered through. It would have been precisely the sort of thing written in a tale for children, provided they'd left out the part where she'd cried through most of the first year she'd lived there and the fact that as she'd grown older and had been required to be a companion to her cousin, Susanna, five years her junior, she'd had little say in her comings and goings and no prospects for her own future.

Her grandfather's death had brought a vague sense of relief but very little other emotional reaction.

Eccentric, she acknowledged to herself, was not as accurate a descriptor of her as *lonely*. But that was hardly her fault. When a person didn't belong anywhere, a person was lonely everywhere.

The carriage stopped under a portico at the side of Guilford House. A boy opened the door, serving as footman, despite being nowhere near old enough to serve in that capacity. He didn't seem to entirely know what to do but appeared eager to attempt it.

"I guess you can come out, then," the boy said. That earned him raised eyebrows from Aunt and Uncle Stirling and a hint of a giggle from Amelia's cousin.

For her part, Amelia's heart went out to the boy. Filling roles one was ill-suited to and ill-prepared for was a very accurate way of describing most of her existence.

Despite the boy's inexpert service, they had all soon alighted from the carriage and were standing on the ground, looking at the house.

"It's not quite as well maintained as it once was." Uncle eyed the facade with a critical expression. "Not falling to pieces, mind you, but clearly in need of attention."

Despite its location in the worst possible of places, Amelia found herself feeling an odd kinship to the place. She knew how it felt to be in need of some attention.

"The grounds are rather lovely. Or were years ago, at least," Uncle said. "I will go inside and see if the solicitor is here while you girls walk around the island."

Walk around the island? Was he daft? "Could we not explore the *interior* of the house?" Amelia asked.

"This is likely to be a difficult day for your uncle," her aunt said. "One does not like to be reminded of the death of a parent, after all. Don't argue with him today."

In the six months since Grandfather had passed, Amelia had been extensively lectured on what it feels like to lose a parent. How fortunate for her that she had someone to explain that to her after two decades of being an orphan.

"Take a walk about the grounds," Uncle said again, shooing Amelia and Susanna away before he and Aunt stepped inside.

The house was large enough that Amelia likely could have slipped in a moment later and avoided them long enough not to reveal the fact that she had disobeyed. But she didn't know the space terribly well, and a lady with a limp didn't precisely navigate even familiar spaces clandestinely. There was nothing for it but to obey the directive and spend time out on the island, with the menacing sea staring her down.

Amelia turned to ask Susanna where she would like to wander off to first only to discover that her cousin had already left to explore on her own. Abandonment, yes. But also freedom, which Amelia didn't mean to scoff at or waste.

She would go see if the wall she had spotted toward the interior of the small island did, indeed, surround a garden. Nothing could stop her from hearing the waves, but perhaps in that space, she wouldn't be able to see them. And she would be in a garden, which always made her happier.

ECHOES OF THE SEA

With her trusty cane for added stability, she made her way along a path edging an overgrown lawn. Her wool cloak was buttoned firmly in place, but the robust sea wind sent it billowing all about her. She snatched hold of the edges with her free hand, attempting to wrap it more tightly around herself. It was not designed to be in such a place. *She* was not designed to be in such a place.

One wasn't supposed to think ill of the dead, but Grandfather was impossible to think well of. And it was, in all honesty, his fault that she was currently having to think about him at all. So, really, she could be excused for silently declaring him a curmudgeonly old grubber. *Silently.* Poor relations had to be very, very careful to appear very, very meek. And always grateful.

"In this moment, I am grateful that . . ." It was a game she played with herself, finding something to be grateful for, even if she sometimes did so with a heavy dose of irony. "I'm grateful that I don't actually live on this island."

Upon reaching that mysterious wall, she followed it, looking for a gate. All the while, the crash and pull of waves bombarded her senses with a rhythmic reminder that she was, for the time being, in what amounted to a living nightmare imposed on her by a no-longer-living nightmare.

She didn't like water. Nothing frightened her the way it did. Nothing left her more shaken than feeling surrounded and closed in by it. Nothing.

At last, she found the gate, but it was locked. She peered through the iron posts keeping her on the wrong side of the one place she thought she might be able to pass a few pleasant moments. The garden appeared to have once been a rather formal and traditional English knot garden, but now, it was in a state of complete overgrowth. And yet she suspected it wouldn't take much to put it to rights again. Someone with know-how and a degree of time could do it. Or that someone could just accept the inevitable: that the sea would swallow this entire island whole at any moment.

"Amelia!" Her cousin reached her, out of breath. Susanna had always liked to run, a tendency she didn't seem likely to outgrow. "The solicitor is already here. We are to go to the drawing room."

"Did he give you any indication of where the drawing room is?" Amelia asked.

Her cousin shrugged. "Inside the house?"

Inside the house. Amelia, as had been required of her for twenty years, kept to herself the response that had sprung to her lips. Even when her cousin had been no more than two years old, babbling in the way children of that age did, and Amelia had been a seven-year-old, perfectly capable of conversation and intellect and discovery, she had been required to interact with Susanna without interrupting or putting herself forward. In time, Susanna had decided she had little interest in spending time with her older cousin. Sometimes, days would go by without Amelia having a conversation of any sort with anyone.

Yes, she understood this house. Neglected. Lonely. A little rickety.

Just as Amelia had expected it would be, the sound of the ocean was far, far quieter inside the house. Not gone entirely, because that would have been far too pleasant an experience to be something her grandfather required of her—but softer and easier to ignore. Though *ignore* didn't actually feel possible. "Pretend she couldn't hear" hit closer to the mark.

They were able to find the drawing room. Susanna glided gracefully to a chair beside her parents. Amelia clunked in with the help of her cane and found a seat on the periphery of the room.

"You're meant to be sitting up here, Miss Archibald." The solicitor indicated an empty chair directly beside her uncle. She couldn't remember the last time she had sat in a place of any significance. Even at meals, she was placed a few seats removed from the family. When guests ate at the house, Amelia took her meal in her room.

Amelia rose with her usual difficulty and crossed to the chair that was apparently going to be hers. She lowered herself with a degree of hesitation that likely was felt all the way back on the mainland, where she wished she were.

"This will not take long," the solicitor said. "I was instructed that once Miss Stirling and Miss Archibald's periods of mourning for the late Mr. Stirling were complete, we were to meet here at this residence for the reading of the last portion of the late Mr. Stirling's will."

"And he specified that Amelia had to come?" Her aunt had been hung up on that requirement from the moment it had been revealed.

Far from offended, Amelia thought the requirement every bit as ridiculous as her aunt clearly did.

The solicitor nodded. "Other than Mr. Stirling"—he motioned to Uncle—"Miss Archibald was the *only* person required to be here."

That was strange, indeed.

"And this last portion of the will is addressed to the two of them, beginning with the late Mr. Stirling's oldest granddaughter." The solicitor picked up a piece of very fine linen parchment, cleared his throat, and read its contents to Amelia.

In the matter of my granddaughter, Amelia Archibald, only child of my late daughter: there is a portion of my estate which I am required to set aside for any heirs or heiresses which might have been produced by my daughter.

That was unexpected.

> *While I cannot directly refuse to leave the sum to Miss Archibald, I am permitted to attach caveats to the inheritance.*

Now, that sounded like her grandfather.

> *I have been in deep consultation with solicitors and barristers and have made absolutely certain that the following requirements are both legal and binding.*

It was such an odd combination of very direct legal formalities and vaguely barbed insults.

> *The amount that I have been required to set aside for the inheritance of Miss Amelia Archibald is not insignificant. It is enough, in fact, that she could claim a degree of ease that most young ladies would envy. She would no longer need to live as a perpetual guest in the home of her aunt and uncle. As this is not a pittance, I feel it wise to make certain she is capable of seeing to her own affairs. Thus, the following requirements must be met before she can inherit.*

> *To prove herself able to look after an inheritance, one which might lead to the purchase of an estate of her own, I am requiring her to look after* this *estate for six months.*

"*This* estate," Uncle repeated. "He means Guilford?"

The solicitor nodded. He continued reading.

> *I recognize how easy it would be for her to simply hire someone to do all the work and coordination in exchange for a portion of her significant inheritance. Therefore, she will be required to live here, on Guilford Island, in this house, attend to it, see to any restorations that need to be made, and do so in person for the entire six months.*

"Live here?" Amelia didn't often let herself speak in public unless invited to do so, but her shock and horror pulled the question from her.

Again, the solicitor nodded and continued on.

For the entirety of those six months, Miss Amelia Archibald must never leave Guilford Island.

The small lighthouse on the island is manned. There is staff on the estate. There is a village that must be passed through after taking the sea road back to the mainland. Should she violate these terms, it would most certainly be noted and reported. In fact, I have set up in this will a certain monetary reward should any infractions of these requirements be both reported and proven. There is incentive to make certain she fulfills what is required of her.

She was to be held captive on this island, with spies all around, anxious to collect a reward should they catch her attempting to flee. It was a nightmare.

My solicitor as well as my son, Woodrow Stirling, will make regular unannounced inspections of the estate, to make certain it is being cared for, its needs are being met, and Miss Archibald has not left.

Uncle Stirling nodded but in that absent-minded way that indicated a person had heard something but only vaguely comprehended it. His mind was spinning, too, Amelia would wager.

Should Miss Archibald meet these requirements, at the end of her six-month sojourn on Guilford Island, she will be granted the entirety of her inheritance and the freedom to live her life in the way she chooses with the generous windfall she has been provided.

Should she fail, the entirety of her inheritance will be reverted back to the Stirling estate, with a portion of it designated as a dowry for her cousin Susanna Stirling. Further, in light of this inarguable indication that Miss Archibald is incapable of looking after herself, a second equal portion of the inheritance will be set aside for Miss Archibald's dowry to be delivered to a suitor of her uncle's choosing after a marriage of his arranging takes place.

These are my instructions, and these are the terms of her inheritance. Miss Archibald must choose within thirty minutes of the reading of this will whether she wishes to accept the challenge and remain on Guilford Island for six months, knowing that success means she has her full independence and failure means losing her inheritance and marrying a man of her uncle's choosing, or forego the challenge altogether and return to being a poor relation with whatever future should happen to play out. My solicitor will begin the thirty-minute contemplation period now.

The solicitor set down the paper and took up his pocket watch.

Thirty minutes to make a decision that would change the course of Amelia's entire life. *A curmudgeonly old grubber* felt too generous for her selfish rotter of a grandfather.

She had an inheritance, one that, by her grandfather's own reluctant admission, would give her freedom, give her control over her future. She would have enough to live on, not just in comfort but with a degree of ease. This was an opportunity she had never dreamed would come her way. But attempting to claim it also meant taking the risk of making her situation worse than it already was.

Being a poor relation in the home of her aunt and uncle was not necessarily a joyous experience, but it was not entirely miserable either. However, when her uncle undoubtedly collected "evidence" of her "lack of judgment," he would feel it unnecessary to consider her wishes, and he would match her with someone horrendous. And that someone would likely be marrying her for the dowry that would be bestowed upon her after losing her actual fortune.

Amelia might have gotten to her feet and paced, but her cane would have clicked loudly in the uncomfortably silent room. She wasn't ashamed of her walking stick nor of the twisted foot that necessitated it. Her aunt, uncle, and cousin had never expressed annoyance or disgust over it. But for reasons she never dug deeply into, the sound of her cane tended to put her more on edge when she was frustrated by other things.

And she was decidedly frustrated.

Her grandfather was dangling freedom in front of her but requiring that she torture herself in order to grab at it.

Six months on Guilford Island, surrounded by water, by an ocean. Six months in which the road back to land could disappear for hours, days, or even weeks at a time. Six months in which she was not allowed to leave.

Torture, pure and simple.

Her grandfather couldn't have simply withheld her inheritance, which he most certainly would have preferred to do. Tormenting her under the guise of making her prove that she could be trusted with an estate and income was a very fitting thing for the miserly scoundrel.

So what was she to do?

Chapter 3

West Sussex coast
present day

After a lot of frustration and raging against the fickleness of fate, Kip had finally acknowledged to himself that working as a reenactor for the summer season was a comedown but probably about the only chance he had to revitalize his career.

Rather than require him to hop on a train and make his way to the living history site, Malcolm had taken him there on the yacht he'd bought with his *The Beau* money. It wasn't a super yacht of the ultrawealthy, but it was his own boat and well taken care of and finer digs than Kip could boast of, especially as he'd had to sell his London flat after his television money had dried up.

They'd reached the coastal inlet where he would be passing the summer, and they were spending the morning walking along the beach while Kip waited out the time remaining until he was supposed to report to his self-inflicted humiliation. A breeze off the sea tousled Malcolm's hair and tugged flatteringly at his clothes but chose to do nothing for Kip except fling sprays of saltwater up his nose.

To Jen, Kip said in mock tones of umbrage, "I suspect if I didn't like Malcolm, I'd hate him." It was a common thing to toss at his friend and one that never failed to make Malcolm laugh.

Jen always did too. "Unfortunately, there are people who have decided they do hate him because things have gone well these past years. That hurts him more than he's ever let on."

Kip knew Malcolm well enough to have seen that firsthand. "He's the sort who would always be happy for someone who's had success, so I think it's probably baffling when other people aren't."

"And it bothers him that he can't keep in touch with everyone. He's having success, yes, but he's also overwhelmed and stretched to his limit, and plenty of people are peeved with him for not being able to stay on top of everything." Jen shot Kip a grateful smile. "Thank you for being the sort of friend who gives him grace and is genuinely happy for the person he is rather than the name he is."

"If the situation were reversed, he would be even better about it than I am."

Jen looked fondly up ahead of them, where Malcolm was standing on the rocky beach, looking out over the bay at an island not terribly far distant. He looked peaceful in a way Kip hadn't seen in a while. Kip hadn't pieced it together until Jen had hinted at it, but he suspected Malcolm was lonely. Once this summer was over, they needed to find time to just hang out. They'd both enjoy that, and they both needed it.

Jen slipped her arms around her husband once she was at his side, and he held her in return. They were quite possibly the happiest couple Kip had ever known. Having been the one who had set them up, he figured he was the modern-day Merlin of Matchmakers. If only there were a career in that.

"I know I'm biased," Malcolm said, "but I think this is my favorite part of the entire country."

"How far from here did you grow up?" Kip asked.

"About twenty miles inland, but we came out this way regularly."

"Big fans of the living history site?" Kip asked, dryly.

Malcolm tossed him one of his signature grins. "We came to the shore *for* the shore. The living history site was an occasional bonus."

Kip could appreciate his attachment to the spot. It really was beautiful. Even with storm clouds gathering in the distance, it was peaceful. Kip twitched his chin out toward the island. "What's that?"

"Guilford House, an old estate from, I think, the 1700s. It's called the Little Sister of Mont-Saint-Michel, that commune in France that gets cut off from the mainland when the tide comes in."

"Mont-Saint-Michel isn't an island." Kip knew that much about it.

"Neither is Guilford, technically. There's a road on the other side that connects it to the mainland. But when there's a storm surge or a particularly high tide, water covers the road until the sea recedes again."

"Is it abandoned?"

Jen shot him a confused look that matched Malcolm's.

"Ah, the return of your 'Americans Are Stupid' expressions," Kip said.

"Not *all* Americans," Malcolm said.

"Just this one." Kip feigned offense.

"I didn't say that."

Kip shook his head. "Your judgmental British eyebrow said it, Malcolm. Screamed it in a very posh accent."

Malcolm laughed. His character was often scripted as laughing because, again, publications had a lot to say about his devilishly alluring laugh. But there hadn't been nearly as much joking in the most recent Kip-free season, which Kip sincerely hoped the writers and producers were being torn to shreds for.

"Guilford House is part of the living history site," Malcolm said. "Not the entirety of it but an important portion."

He hadn't realized that. "Can I call this a search engine failure? Because I did look the place up."

"Did you actually read anything that came up in the search?" Malcolm asked doubtfully.

"Skimmed."

Jen gave him the all-too-familiar you're-an-idiot look. "You took a job you hardly knew anything about?"

"Let that serve as testament to my desperation," he said, assuming the lordly British accent he had always used on *The Beau*.

That set them to smiling again. It was going to be a long summer without Malcom and Jen around.

"I'd invite you two to come spend a day living history," he said, "but I suspect you would simply cause a stampede, and the whole place would fall to bits.".

"I'm not entirely certain your presence isn't going to prove more of an issue than they're expecting," Jen said.

A hint of mischief entered Malcolm's eyes, which Kip found incredibly intriguing.

"Why," Kip asked, "do I suspect there's something you aren't telling me, oldest and dearest friend, who certainly wouldn't keep an important secret from me?"

Malcolm's much-praised smile broadened. "Osbourne will, without question, visit the site this summer, which will be incredibly helpful for you. But I have my suspicions that the first time someone realizes who you are and posts about it, there will be a, as you so Americanly put it, 'stampede' of fluttery tourists flocking here to get their picture taken with the ghost of Tennyson Lamont."

"The ghost of a man who was half eaten by a shark," Kip reminded him. "I don't know that Mont-Saint-Michel's Baby Sister has access to the special effects needed to pull that off."

Malcolm just laughed. "I know this job isn't ideal, and I can't imagine you are at all excited about it, but if you look at it as doing something fun and enjoying a casual summer, you can lean into the fame you do have, impress Osbourne, and emerge in the autumn ready to conquer again."

"You may be the only person in the entire world who thinks I'm even capable of that." Kip looked back out over the water, pushing his father's voice out of his mind and pretending he'd never met Giselle or had the disastrous contract meeting six months earlier. If he could lie to himself about how wrong things had gone, maybe he could believe they would soon go extremely right.

"I know you, Kipling Summerfield. You're discouraged now, understandably so. This industry is never fair, which only adds to the frustration. But you're not a quitter. You never have been." Malcolm's eyes drifted back out over the ocean, the island, and the distant sky. "Change is coming for you, I know it. And I hope it brings you everything this world owes you."

There really were few people in the world as honestly good as Malcolm Winthrop. He was one of the few people who, upon hearing more of the details of Kip's growing up years and home life, had reacted not with pity but with encouragement.

He'd become family to Kip, and that had helped more than Malcolm would ever know, mostly because Kip had no plans to ever tell him. There were some things a person didn't tell even best friends who could probably qualify for sainthood but would be too . . . *saintly* to accept the honorific.

"Before I make my way to my summer home"—Kip used the phrase with a heavy degree of arrogance and his assumed British accent—"what can you tell me about the history of this place? Might be fun to have a nugget to toss in here and there."

ECHOES OF THE SEA

All three of them began walking in the direction of a small pier, one far too small to have docked Malcolm's relatively humble yacht. It likely couldn't have accommodated much more than a dinghy.

"Guilford Island holds Guilford House," Malcolm said. "Right across the bay from it, connected by the sea road, is Guilford Village. It dates back to the Domesday Book and is also part of the history site. From the island, looking west, you can see glimpses of Loftstone Island, which is bigger than Guilford but a lot smaller than the Isle of Wight, which is west of Loftstone."

Kip shook his head and rolled his eyes. "Say what you will about Americans' grasp of the English language, but most of us know the difference between 'history' and 'geography.'"

Jen thumped Malcolm with her hip, a variety of playful teasing that Kip had seen the two employ often enough to know what it was.

"History." Malcolm nodded. "There's a small lighthouse on Guilford that dates back even further than the house. The lighthouse on Loftstone is a dual light. The three made a triangle that sailing ships used to navigate this area. The water here is legendary for how quickly it grows rough and difficult to navigate. Historically, there have been more shipwrecks in this section of the southern coast than almost anywhere else. Storms brew quickly and fiercely. A lot of the history of this little bay is centered around shipwrecks and hauntings and otherworldly explanations for why it's so deadly."

Now that was interesting. Kip could weave tales around this all day and keep visitors to the site enthralled. Indeed, his character on *The Beau* was known for being able to tell a good story. Leaning into that wouldn't be a bad idea.

"And then there's the lightning." A moment passed without Malcolm offering any further explanation. Another moment passed. And another. Malcolm simply stood in contented silence as his gaze took in the view.

"You, my friend, are not a storyteller," Kip finally said.

"What do you mean?" Malcolm looked genuinely confused.

Jen laughed. "You can't simply say, 'And then there's the lightning' and end the tale there."

"This is what happens when I don't have a script." Malcolm shot Kip a laughing look. "'Improvisation won't be tolerated.'"

It was a good impression of the director who'd shot most of the second season of *The Beau*. They'd both decided within two episodes that the man was convinced that all actors were both arrogant and stupid.

"So skip the improvisation and go straight to the interpretive dance," Kip suggested. "Might not be very informative, but it will be entertaining."

Malcolm started doing a stupid kick-and-shuffle dance.

"You two are trouble when you're together," Jen said.

"Fine." Kip pretended to be annoyed by the objection implied in Jen's observation. "Just *tell* us about the lightning, Malcolm."

His friend wrapped his arm around Jen once more, and they kept walking. "This is one of the few places in all the world that is known to have green lightning over the water. Our ancestors insisted it was spirits or sprites or things like that. The consensus in modern day has far more to do with the way the bay catches weather patterns and water temperatures and swirls things around. But two hundred years ago, they would have considered it very otherworldly."

"I can use this for my character this summer."

"The dancing?" Malcolm started the routine again, but Jen tugged him out of it.

With a laugh, Malcolm slapped a hand on Kip's shoulder. Their characters had done it a lot in *The Beau*, and the gesture had tiptoed its way into their actual friendship. "Text now and then. Let me know how things are going."

Kip nodded. "More GIFs of famous people crying."

"You're too good an actor and too good a person not to have things turn around for you," Malcolm insisted.

"Maybe just text me that once in a while," Kip suggested. "Eventually, it might feel true."

Jen gave Kip a quick hug. "We don't want Malcolm to cause a mob before you even have a chance to get started, so we'll let you wander to your new place on your own."

Kip shifted to Malcolm and gave him a quick hug too. "Thanks, mate. I owe you for this. Well . . . for this and a lot of other things too."

Malcolm shook his head. "Friends don't need to keep score."

"Well, our indebtedness score is currently seven hundred twenty-three to probably about ten," Kip said.

"Who has ten?" Jen asked.

"Who do you think?" Kip answered.

She nodded knowingly. "According to your self-deprecating American eyebrow: Malcolm."

"Think of me and my poor American eyebrow this summer, languishing away in the 1800s."

"Were there even Americans in the 1800s?" Malcolm made a show of pretending to doubt it.

"According to my research, yes."

"And that research would be . . . ?"

Kip shrugged. "Five years on *The Beau*. It's basically the equivalent of earning a degree in English history."

"Good luck to you, Professor Summerfield." Malcolm took Jen's hand and started walking down the beach. A couple of steps away, he turned back. "We'll drop your things off so you don't need to come back to the boat for them. And we'll see you soon. Real soon."

"Thanks. For everything."

Kip wasn't a pessimistic person in general, but he wasn't feeling nearly as upbeat about this change as he was trying to appear. He would need to fake it soon enough, so he decided to offer himself thirty minutes of feeling pathetically sorry for himself before summoning those award-nominated-but-not-yet-award-winning acting skills once more.

The rickety old pier that they'd nearly reached was not terribly far off and felt an appropriate place to sit and sulk. He made his way there and walked out farther and farther down the boards until he reached the edge and plopped down, his legs dangling off the end.

It really was a beautiful place. A storm was brewing out on the sea, and the wind from it was whipping the trees around on Guilford Island. The house itself stood firm and stalwart against the gale. He wouldn't mind the view over the summer.

Over the summer. He had a summer job, like he was just out of high school. He really was a tad pathetic.

But as far as summer jobs went, he supposed it wasn't terrible. Spending time at the Little Sister of Mont-Saint-Michel wasn't the worst thing. And essentially reprising his most famous role for a summer and making it seem as though everything were great in the world while hoping to catch the eye of a well-known producer was just odd enough to be challenging.

He could do that.

And since his dad's number was blocked on his phone, he wouldn't have to spend the summer hearing the variations on "I told you so" that had started flowing in six months earlier. Dad never said it quite that bluntly, but the sentiment was there. Kip's older brother and his older sister had their lives figured out: an attorney and a real estate developer. They were stable; they were successful. They had families of their own and lives Dad was proud of. And Kip was the failure Dad had been predicting ever since Kip had discovered he enjoyed drama club as a high school freshman.

He'd actually unblocked his dad's number briefly after having been announced for the award he didn't end up winning, thinking maybe Dad would hear about it and acknowledge that Kip had some talent and some ability. But that hadn't happened.

He didn't plan to tell his dad how he was spending the summer. But the first time his presence at the living history site was posted about, Kip would have to hold his breath, knowing that eventually, Dad would hear and would have plenty to say.

If only he'd negotiated into the sixth season of *The Beau*. He'd suspected his character was about to have a significant arc that would make him a bigger name and open more doors.

Life wasn't supposed to be like a burrito, falling apart just as it got full.

Kip pulled out his phone and glanced at the text icon. No new messages. Dad wouldn't have texted even if his number weren't blocked, and Kip didn't really want him to. But somehow, it was still disappointing.

A sudden spray of water pulled Kip out of his distraction. Only then did he realize that while he'd been pondering dear ol' dad, the sea had grown miserable too.

The storm had reached the bay. Water angrily slapped the pier he sat on. He was going to arrive at his first day on the job soaked and scraggly. It wasn't exactly the 1995-*Pride-and-Prejudice*-Mr.-Darcy-emerging-from-the-water moment, but it felt fitting to be undertaking the slapstick version of that.

He jumped to his feet, but that proved a mistake. He slipped on the very slick pier and hit the boards hard. The impact knocked his phone from his hand. Before he could pull himself back to his feet, a wave crashed against him, sending him shifting to one side. Only by grabbing hard to a pylon was he able to keep himself on the pier.

Malcolm had said that storms in this bay were fierce, but this was ridiculous.

He tried to stand again but was pummeled again. And again. And again.

The next wave that hit knocked him into the water. He swam back up to the surface, gulping air while he could, knowing angry, choppy waters didn't always afford a person many opportunities to take in a lungful of air. Twice more, he undertook the same cycle only to realize he was being pulled farther and farther from the shoreline.

He was a good swimmer—he'd appeased his father's dislike of acting by also being on the swim team—and pushed hard for the shore, but it wasn't much use. The pull of the sea was too unrelenting. He was able to catch glimpses of land between crests of waves in the angry sea. He felt almost certain he was closer to Guilford Island now than he was to the shore of the bay. Perhaps he ought to swim there instead. The water seemed to be pulling him that way anyway. He changed course and did his utmost to reach the island.

Though he didn't think he was fighting as hard against the push and pull of the angry Channel, he was still losing strength and energy. Thunder rumbled overhead, the flashes of lightning punctuating the seriousness of his situation.

He wasn't staying above the water quite as easily as he had been, but he felt he was making some progress.

A flash of lightning lit the sky in an eerie green, and he swore the water crackled with it.

Another wave pushed him under, and he fought his way to the surface once more. The same pattern repeated more times than he could keep track of. And the angry water made it nearly impossible to see the shore or the island.

Then he heard a voice.

He was able to twist just enough, even in the surge, to see a dinghy, a lot like he'd pictured would have been tied to that pier, approaching him from nearby. Someone inside reached out a hand.

Almost before he could contemplate what had happened, Kip was in the boat, out of the angry sea, and being rowed toward Guilford Island.

Chapter 4

Kip followed his thus-far-silent rescuer out of the rowboat and up the rocky coast. The storm hadn't abated entirely, and the battering of the wind was still miserable against his soaked skin. He opted to blame his struggle to keep pace with the man on how cold he was, though he knew that had little to do with it. If he could still have afforded to pay his personal trainer, he would have fired him.

The land leveled out for only a single step before reaching the door of a stone lighthouse. Kip was no expert, but the lighthouse seemed small. The man pulled open the door and motioned him inside. They'd be really good friends in no time with both of them inside, but getting out of the wind was an exceptionally good idea, so Kip didn't argue or hesitate. Arguing wasn't an option anyway. His teeth were chattering so hard that he couldn't manage a single word.

He felt around the interior wall for a light switch but didn't find one. Maybe it was in a weird spot. Or maybe shivering made finding light switches more difficult.

A moment later, a click, like the sound of rocks smacking into each other, sounded, and a quick spark popped up in the darkness.

That repeated again. Once more, then a small fire started in what Kip guessed was a fireplace. The man added some wood to it. He still hadn't spoken, even though his teeth *weren't* chattering, which was proving kind of creepy. What were the chances that the living history site had accidentally hired a serial killer?

As the fire slowly grew and the room became less dark, Kip was able to get a better look. It *was* small. It was also, as far as he could tell, very authentic. None of the furniture looked at all modern. It was worn out and humble, the way a lighthouse of a couple hundred years ago would have looked. If this attention to detail was adhered to in the dinky lighthouse, then this gig might not actually be a terrible thing. Osbourne would easily be able to picture Kip in a big-budget historical film if he saw him against such an accurate backdrop.

The still-silent man lifted the lid of a small chest and moved around a few things before pulling out some folded items. He stood once more, turned back to Kip, and shoved the pile into his arms.

A quick glance revealed his armful to be clothes. Dry clothes. *Thank you, potential serial killer.*

The man added one more bit of wood to the fire, then tucked his hands into his pockets and stood with his back pointedly toward Kip. He didn't seem at all likely to walk away. Or turn around.

The six weeks Kip had been in a way-away-from-the-West-End production of *Much Ado About Nothing* had cured him of any squeamishness surrounding costume changes in crowded dressing rooms. And he hadn't even been dripping seawater everywhere back then.

He quickly pulled off his Thomas Pink button-down shirt. It was not likely salvageable, which was a pity because "summer player at a historical site" was not the sort of job that earned people wages sufficient to replace it. His trousers hadn't fared much better. He'd bought them at Primark, so it wasn't as much of a loss. Thankfully, he'd tossed the boots he'd worn for a good part of his time on *The Beau*—something the producers almost certainly didn't know he'd taken with him—into his suitcase, and those would be waiting for him in his room, wherever that was.

He flicked open the slightly grayed shirt. It was the same style they'd worn on *The Beau*. But the fabric was rougher. The trousers were of that Jane-Austen-would-think-this-was-hot variety and were also made of scratchy fabric that screamed "authentic." Did the people running this place make the actors portraying poorer people actually wear miserable clothes? No one on *The Beau* had been relegated to total discomfort. There was accuracy, and then there was sadism.

Freshly attired in his dry sandpaper, he folded up the wet clothes he'd pulled off, giving them a quick squeeze to get out more water.

"Be'st wise for we to take you up to the main 'ouse." The man spoke English but an odd version of it. "Us hasn't room for another who."

Odder still. Kip would guess he was "in character."

Kip could play along.

He channeled pre-shark Tennyson, leaning on his widely praised British accent and fine mannerisms. "I would be greatly appreciative to you."

The man looked over at him. "You aren't from this corner of the kingdom."

Kip dipped his head. "I am not."

Whether that met with the man's approval, Kip couldn't say. His rescuer simply jerked his head toward the door, then moved in that direction himself. He snatched up a wool blanket from the back of a chair and held it out to Kip with one hand as he opened the door with the other.

Kip accepted the makeshift cloak and wrapped it around his shoulders as they stepped back out into the sea spray and wind-whipped drizzle. He followed the hopefully-not-a-serial-killer back along the rocky outcropping. "In character" seemed more and more likely. The man was dressed precisely as Kip would have predicted a nineteenth-century lighthouse keeper would be: heavy coat over an equally heavy sweater. Thick trousers, well-worn but sturdy boots. His flat cap even appeared encrusted with salt from years of use near the sea.

Attention to detail, for sure.

The rocks gave way none too soon, and Kip was walking on an uneven but no longer ridiculous path around the island. As the path turned and began passing a clump of trees, the house came into view. He'd seen it from the rickety pier but could see it better now. It looked a lot like those they'd used for exteriors in *The Beau*.

"Is that the main house?" Kip asked, doing so in character still.

In response, he was offered a single, quick nod. And nothing else.

Unless there was another fine house located on the shore, where the rest of the historic site stretched, he was likely to be playing the role of the gentleman who owned this house. His character on the show had been a younger son without a house of his own. This could be a nice change.

Lightning flashed overhead. It wasn't green this time, which somehow made it feel less threatening. It did not, however, make the wind less cold. Or the clothes he'd been provided any less itchy.

Or his companion any less creepily quiet.

"Do you live at the lighthouse?" Kip asked.

The man shook his head.

"*Near* the lighthouse?" Kip tried again.

The man nodded but still didn't say anything. Attempting a conversation seemed slightly pointless.

They reached the house and made their way around the side. In *The Beau*, the side and back entrances of places were reserved for servants and tradesmen. It was likely now being used for the people employed at the historic site. During operating hours, he'd use the door his Regency-era counterpart would have.

The lighthouse keeper knocked at the door they came to, then waited. Not surprisingly, he did so without talking. Kip had worked with an actor who was intensely quiet like this, but he'd been that way only in the moments before the cameras had started rolling. Kip eyed the back entrance. No signs of a camera. There weren't even any lights. Or a doorbell.

Someone opened the door from the inside. Kip shouldn't have been surprised to see the woman in full costume, but he was.

"Found this'n in the water," the lighthouse keeper said to the woman Kip suspected was playing the role of the housekeeper. "Him's hands are too delicate for being anything but Quality."

Delicate? Kip eyed his hands. They weren't small or dainty. Was it just an insult for the sake of an insult?

The "housekeeper" eyed Kip critically. "Holds heself like Quality."

"I shiver like Quality as well." Kip tossed a grin along with the quip, hoping to convince his coworkers to drop their act and let him get settled into this new job.

The housekeeper's eyes narrowed. "You aren't from this corner of the kingdom."

Kip tipped his head toward the lighthouse keeper. "He already used that line."

His companions exchanged confused looks. He'd have expected there to be more of an "off the clock" vibe at the actors' entrance. This was going to be an exhausting few months.

"Best ask Miss what her wants done." The lighthouse keeper dipped his head, then walked away, leaving Kip on the doorstep, unsure if he ought to simply let himself in or go along with the nineteenth-century protocol. Until he knew more about the feel of the place, he'd probably do best not to rock the boat, even if that boat felt a little too much like a log ride in a shady theme park.

After a moment, during which he started shivering ever more violently, the housekeeper motioned him inside. "I'm Mrs. Jagger."

"Mick's mum, by any chance?"

Her expression was as surprised as it was confused. "I have no children, sir."

Mick Jagger. It wasn't a difficult joke to understand. Not necessarily funny but not confusing.

Actual candles lit the narrow hallway he followed her through. They passed rooms that, even glancing as quickly as he had, looked completely accurate. He was granted a tiny glimpse of a kitchen that didn't look modernized *at all*. Were tourists invited to visit the kitchen as well? Surely there was an updated place for the actors and staff to make their own meals.

They climbed a tight, winding set of stairs, again only dimly lit but, this time, exclusively by small windows at regular intervals. A door at the top opened into a far more impressive space. Once closed behind them, the door blended perfectly into the wall, almost impossible to spot.

Kudos to the set designer. Well, the *house* designer three hundred years ago.

They crossed paths with a man dressed in a costume that didn't merely resemble that of the butler characters in *The Beau* but also far surpassed them. Impressive. This must be a privately owned historic site, one that was receiving a tremendous amount of donations.

"Where's Miss?" the housekeeper asked the probably butler.

"Her's in the book room."

The housekeeper nodded in that way that said she ought to have been able to guess. "Quieter in there."

Quiet*er*? This place was as silent as the man he still wasn't certain *wasn't* a serial killer. Every step any of them took echoed. The site's season hadn't started yet. Once tourists flocked here, he would probably miss the reverberations. And everyone's insistence on being in character might not be so annoying.

He followed the housekeeper up a grand staircase, then down another hallway, this one far more impressive than the servants' hallway belowstairs.

Mrs. Jagger took him to an open door and stepped inside. "Pardon the interruption, Miss Archibald, but Mr. Ivers fished somewho out of the water and us is certain him's Quality."

"Good heavens." A woman's voice, sounding more like the hoity-toity accent the leads in *The Beau* had used. "Is he injured?"

Mrs. Jagger eyed him quickly, then shook her head. "Looks to be cold though."

"Please, show him in."

The housekeeper stepped aside, assuming a very deferential posture. They truly were adhering to protocol.

He knew his part. He made certain his posture was impeccable and his expression filled with a mixture of gratitude, self-assurance, and just enough humility to make him endurable. And because Tennyson had specialized in it, he kept a laugh in his eyes as well.

He entered the room, shelves of books explaining why Not-Mick-Jagger's-Mom and Probably-the-Butler had called this the "book room." Kip was ready to greet the person running the historical site. Malcolm had said he knew her and that she had overseen the running of the place for at least fifteen years.

This woman, though, looked to be in her mid-twenties. And it was more than her unexpected youth that rendered him shocked.

She was . . . stunning. Ethereal. There was a wispiness to her that, coupled with her amber hair and haunting eyes, made her seem almost magical. For her sake, he hoped Osbourne was also planning to cast a fairy tale sometime soon. She could play a sprite or fairy or any number of beautiful, otherworldly, enthralling creatures.

And she was watching him from her chair with a look of such concern that he worried that she thought he was going to die at any moment.

"Why were you in the water?" she asked.

He smiled. "I assure you, Miss Archibald, that decision was made by the sea and not at all by me."

Her light-amber brows pulled. "Where are you from? You speak oddly."

One hundred percent of the people he'd encountered since being fished out of the water had mentioned how he talked. Yes, it was only three people out of three, but that was still one hundred percent. His British accent was good enough that people often thought he *was* British. But no one here seemed to think so.

"I am originally from"—was America called America in 1800-whenever? In season two of *The Beau*, they'd made a reference to his home country, and the wording of it had felt kind of ridiculous—"the former colonies."

That seemed to explain things neatly to Miss Archibald. An "Ah" from the housekeeper told him she was satisfied as well.

Kip wasn't a big enough name as an actor to be offended that these two women hadn't recognized him, though he was beginning to wonder if they actually had and were making a point of cutting him down a hair.

"What has brought you to this area of the kingdom?" Miss Archibald asked.

"I am not entirely certain." He hadn't received any information about his character, after all.

"You do not know where you were bound for or why?" She didn't actually seem to doubt that explanation, which made him think she might have been informing him of his story line but doing so like everything else on this island—*in character*.

He could play along. There'd been an amnesia storyline in season three, though it had involved a character other than his. "I will confess, I find myself a tad befuddled. It seems my time in the water has mildly addled my wits."

Miss Archibald turned to Mrs. Jagger. "We cannot toss him out into the storm while his mind is struggling."

"The Iverses haven't room for anywho in their tiny house," Mrs. Jagger said.

"And the sea road is currently underwater," Miss Archibald said, "so he can't leave the island."

This was helpful narration, though why they were resorting to it, he didn't know. There was literally no one there but the three of them. They could just *tell* him what his part was.

"He'll have to stay here," Miss Archibald said. "If my uncle learns of this, though . . ." She clutched her hands tightly on her lap.

A bit dramatic. Still, this was additional, helpful information. There was a likely villainous uncle character who, apparently, would play a role in all this. It was, admittedly, a more intricate story than he'd thought they'd be enacting. Did visitors return repeatedly to get updates on the drama playing out at Guilford? That wasn't a bad idea, really. Repeat customers meant more revenue.

"Us'll keep a weather eye out for Mr. Stirling," Mrs. Jagger assured Miss Archibald. "Him'll not be able to surprise you."

For that bit of fierce defense, the older woman received an entirely convincing look of gratitude. "And perhaps by the time I see Uncle Stirling next, Mr.—" She turned to Kip. "I am sorry, I do not know your name."

Was he meant to have a character name? If so, he didn't know what it was. He'd rather his coworkers call him by *his* name. "Kipling Summerfield." He dipped a very nineteenth-century bow, minus the doffed hat since he hadn't been provided with one yet.

"I do hope you are able to recover more of your wits very soon, Mr. Summerfield," she said.

"A bit of rest might help he manage that," Mrs. Jagger said. "The blue bedchamber, perhaps?"

Miss Archibald nodded, though she did give him a questioning look. "That room looks out over the sea. Will that be uncomfortable for you?"

"It's an island. Can there even be a room without an ocean view?"

He swore she actually shuddered. But she'd managed it with impressive subtlety. *Well done.* "Some rooms have an obstructed view of the water."

"But that is not the case with the blue bedchamber?"

She shook her head. "It looks out over the Channel. Water everywhere."

"Despite my frigid dip in the water earlier, I am not aghast at the prospect of seeing the ocean out of my window."

"How fortunate." Miss Archibald turned to Mrs. Jagger. "Perhaps a meal could be brought to him so he needn't interrupt his rest."

Room service? That was both unexpected and exceptionally welcome. He doubted it was a daily occurrence, but it would explain the lack of a modern kitchen.

"I thank you for your hospitality, Miss Archibald." He bowed once more, bestowing on her one of the Tennyson Lamont smiles that had been written into a shocking number of episodes, even if they hadn't received the attention in the press that Malcolm's grins did.

Not all redheads blushed prettily, but she did. More than pretty, the effect was a little breathtaking. Osbourne might be on the verge of a truly enormous discovery.

Miss Archibald remained in the book room while Kip walked with Mrs. Jagger out into the hallway, then up yet more stairs and down another hallway. He was brought to a bedroom that was, indeed, decorated with pops of blue. Mrs. Jagger lit the fire using what looked like steel and flint. Authenticity didn't have to be this inconvenient.

"You can lay your clothes out near the fire when it gets more roaring." Mrs. Jagger crossed back to the door. "The maid'll knock at the door when her brings food up for you."

"Thank you, Mrs. Jagger," he said. "And thank Miss Archibald for me once more. Her hospitality is greatly appreciated."

That must not have quite been the right line; he received a look that bordered on suspicion. He hadn't received any information about his role. What did she expect of him? Magic?

She pulled the door closed, and Kip let his posture return to the more comfortable twenty-first-century version he was accustomed to. He laid his pile of wet clothes, unfolded, near the fireplace to dry. It wasn't "roaring" yet, but he didn't particularly want to keep holding the sodden pile.

He pulled the wool blanket he'd been lent by the potential serial killer more firmly around himself and wandered to the windows. The room did overlook the Channel. He could also see the small stone lighthouse at the other end of the island. He hoped that in the morning, someone would tell him more about his role, his hours, and the site's expectations.

In the meantime, he was exhausted. Convincing the ocean that he didn't want to drown had really taken it out of him.

He looked around the room but didn't find his suitcase. Maybe Malcolm hadn't had a chance to get it there. The storm might have delayed things. He wanted to lie down and sleep while he had the chance, but his clothes were too wet, and his costume was too uncomfortable. That meant sleeping in "the altogether," as his grandma used to call it.

At some point, someone would be bringing up some food. He'd simply have to pull the itchy trousers back on or, if enough time had passed to dry them out, *his* trousers. In the meantime, the bed was calling his name, and he didn't intend to ignore it.

Chapter 5

A sudden scream tore through the silence of Guilford House the next morning. Amelia jumped, anxious, worried. The unnerving sound had come from the direction of the blue bedchamber.

Amelia snatched up her cane and rushed—rushed *for her*—toward the noise. She didn't know enough about the mysterious Mr. Summerfield to predict what might be happening. Canes were handy tools for a person with a twisted foot wishing for a touch more stability but also for a person needing to fend off a strange American who'd been mysteriously plucked from the sea.

Amelia reached the room and its wide-open door. She switched her cane from walking-stick duty to makeshift sword duty. Holding it like an épée, she stepped inside Mr. Summerfield's room ready to go to battle, if need be.

The scene she found inside was so odd that she lowered her "weapon" and simply stared. The maid, Jane, stood by the fireplace with her ash brush and can in her hand, facing the bed, where Mr. Summerfield was sitting up. From the waist down, he was under his blankets, and from the waist up, he wasn't wearing a thing.

"What did you do to her?" Amelia demanded.

"What did *I* do to *her*?" he scoffed. "I woke up, and there she was. I asked her what she was doing in my room. She turned around, took one look at me, and screamed."

Amelia eyed the ash brush and can in Jane's hand. "She was seeing to the fire, obviously."

"And I should have locked my door, *obviously*." He rubbed at his eyes, then blinked a few times. He still looked half asleep.

And he was still half dressed and fully distracting. It was more than the fact that he was handsome, tousled, and bare-chested, which would have been stupefying enough. There was something drawn on his shoulder, as if someone had taken a quill and sketched a pattern there.

"I'm sorry I screamed," Jane said. "Quality's not supposed to have tattoos. I thought maybe a pirate had burst in and us were all going to be murdered in our beds."

"You can't be murdered in your bed if you aren't still in it." Amelia was attempting to remain calm in the hopes that the girl would manage it as well, but she had also never seen a tattoo. Like Jane, she had only heard of them in the context of seafarers of questionable repute.

Who was this man she'd let stay in her temporary home?

"You've never seen a tattoo?" Mr. Summerfield asked the question as if he not only didn't believe it but also thought it a rather ridiculous lie.

"Of course not," Amelia said. "I don't spend time lingering in seedy dockside taverns."

"I'm guessing I don't either," Kip said drily.

She gripped her cane tighter. "You're *guessing*. Are your wits still addled?"

"I've just awoken. I can't be expected to be witty yet." He pushed out a breath. "I'll make sure the tattoo is covered up."

"I should certainly hope so. It would only be *un*covered if you weren't wearing a—"

Amelia was hit with the remembrance of just how excessively inappropriate it was for her to still be looking at him in his state of undress. She turned around, her back to him, facing the fireplace. Hanging over the fireplace screen were the most odd assortment of clothes. They bore enough of a resemblance to what she was familiar with for her to guess at their function, but the fabric was odd and the cut odder still. Was there anything about this stranger that wasn't confusing?

"Was your sleep restorative enough that you've pieced together more of who you are?" she asked.

"I thought someone here might know," he said. "Kipling Summerfield? Tennyson Lamont?"

He was Kipling Summerfield; he'd said so the evening before.

"There is no Tennyson Lamont at Guilford," she said.

"I'm not looking for Tennyson Lamont. I *am*—" He stopped abruptly with a short sigh. "I'm Kipling Summerfield, but what that means, I haven't yet been told."

Did tattoos impact the functioning of the mind? That seemed unlikely, yet he was clearly very confused.

"Am I to stoke the fire or not, Miss?" Jane asked, having turned around as well. The two of them were speaking, standing shoulder to shoulder, facing the cold fireplace.

"I have no idea. He didn't seem particularly keen to have it built up, did he?"

"No, Miss."

"Perhaps Americans don't like to be warm."

"Is that what Americans sound like? Him speaks so strange."

"I feel I should interject," the American said from behind them, "and let you know that I can hear you."

Amelia further leaned on her cane. She wasn't in pain or feeling unsteady; it was simply her habit when feeling overwhelmed. "Tattoos don't impact hearing, obviously," she muttered.

"I heard that," he added.

"American clothes"—she pointed to the items hanging on the fire screen—"are very strange. Did you hear that as well?"

"Loud and clear."

Loud? She hadn't spoken loudly at all. Was Mr. Summerfield truly softheaded? It seemed more and more likely.

"Are these clothing items common or fashionable in America?"

"Thomas Pink isn't as popular in America."

A third name? "There is also no Thomas Pink at Guilford."

"Obviously."

Strange clothing. Nonsensical answers. A tattoo. Two people he claimed to be looking for whom he knew weren't at Guilford. He was either mad or hiding something, and she didn't know which possibility she disliked more.

Here was another reason to never live in a place entirely surrounded by the sea: she couldn't simply toss him out.

With her back to him still, she said, "After you've dressed, will you come speak with me in the book room?"

This was her home, and he was an interloper, so she would have been well within her rights to simply *tell* him to do so rather than request it, but old habits were difficult to shake. She had been the interloper for twenty years. She had needed permission for almost everything she did, and ladies were taught not to be bold, not to put themselves forward. Until she knew better how to approach this stranger, she would lean on what had worked in difficult situations in the past.

"I'd be happy to," he said, "but I'd recommend that both of you vacate the room first, or my tattoo will be the least shocking thing you encounter in here today."

It was a rather uncouth way to speak to a lady, yet she didn't detect any actual insult or malice in it. He grew stranger all the time.

Amelia pushed the swirling thoughts from her mind as she stepped into the corridor and closed the door to the blue bedchamber.

"Him's a strange one, isn't him?" Jane said with a quick shake of her head.

"Yes. But he is an American. Some patience must be shown on account of that."

Jane acknowledged the truth of the situation before moving away, no doubt to see to more of her work. The house was understaffed, and everyone had to work hard and work long, but she hoped it was, at least, not an unhappy place for them all to spend their day.

Amelia spared a quick glance at the closed door, pondering the man inside. He spoke strangely, dressed oddly, had arrived under suspicious circumstances, sported a tattoo, of all things, and couldn't seem to decide whom he was looking for. He was also handsome and intriguing, and despite his insistence that he was too tired for being witty, she had seen more than a few hints that he was, in fact, clever.

She put those thoughts firmly from her head and made her way directly to the book room. She was one month into her six-month imprisonment on Guilford. She was meant to prove she had a good head on her shoulders and could be trusted with her inheritance. That meant running Guilford well and comporting herself appropriately. More than anything, it meant not leaving the island.

The first two weeks had been the hardest thus far. She'd wanted so desperately to flee, to run with every ounce of strength she had down the narrow road back to the mainland. She'd managed to endure that desperation and was now firmly in a daily rhythm that helped her forget where she was and the water that surrounded her. Except the sound of the water never stopped. Even when the Channel was calm, the water lapped against the rocks, reminding her that she was never free of it.

She sat at the small writing desk in the book room, leaning her cane against it as she always did. This had become a favorite place of hers, as it was the spot inside the house that was the least disturbed by the sounds of the sea. And the garden she had spied on her first day was her favorite place out of doors. The sea was impossible not to hear when she was in the garden, but the walls were sufficient that she didn't have to see it. If she could keep to those two places as much as possible, she could last another five months.

She had to.

She looked over the list she had been working on in the past few days. Her uncle and her late grandfather's solicitor had made one of their surprise visits, checking to see that she was still on the island, that there had been no reports of her leaving, and that she was fulfilling her assignments in looking after the estate. They'd not been there more than a few minutes when they'd begun pointing out things that appeared to be neglected and in need of attention. When she had countered that those things were that way when she'd been given the keeping of the place, they'd looked at her with pity rather than understanding.

They'd had a conversation with each other that she had clearly been meant to overhear, in which they had talked about what a shame it was when those given the overseeing of an estate chose to blame its problems on others rather than take responsibility. The message had been clear. She was meant to fix everything that others had done wrong here before her arrival, and she had six months of forced isolation in which to do it.

Formulating a plan for addressing those repairs was proving difficult. She had the funds with which to do it—that much had been accounted for by the solicitor. But her staff was so small that sending any one of them into the village to try to find workers would create too much of a burden. To be without their housekeeper or butler or Jane would put them behind on the absolutely necessary tasks of each day. They could have sent Mick, the little boy who wandered about the island, but he was so young. The Iverses couldn't leave the lighthouse unattended, except to see to their own needs in the village. She was in a difficult spot and wasn't certain what to do about it.

But she currently had an able-bodied man in the house whose time was not already claimed elsewhere. For at least a few more days, he couldn't take the sea road off the island. As of the night before, he didn't seem to have any pressing business pulling him elsewhere.

On the heels of those thoughts, the now-clothed man arrived at the door of the book room. He offered a well-executed bow before stepping inside.

"I would like to formally request a cancellation of my wakeup service," he said.

What in heaven's name did that mean? "I beg your pardon?"

"We're doing this 'in character,' are we?"

"I beg—"

He held his hand up to dismiss the question as unnecessary. "My apologies, Miss Archibald, for the upheaval of this morning. I had not expected anyone to come into my bedchamber unannounced and, thus, was ill-prepared to soften the shock of both my state of undress and my now-infamous tattoo." There was something almost like sarcasm in his tone.

He was so very confusing. And distractedly handsome, blasted man. If she was to keep her wits about her, she was going to have to either not look at him or . . . or something.

"Your name is Kipling Summerfield. Did I remember that correctly?" That much needed to be cleared up before anything else.

"Yes, indeed." He offered another quick smile. His teeth were perfect. Quite literally perfect. One didn't often see such a thing.

"And you are searching for Tennyson Lamont?"

He shook his head slowly. "No." It was almost a question.

"You asked for him."

"I was curious if you knew him, but you have indicated that you don't."

"I also do not know Thomas Pink, whom you said you were looking for as well."

"No, I said my shirt was from Thomas Pink."

"You stole Mr. Pink's shirt?"

He looked at her like she was the one talking nonsense. "He made the shirt."

"Your tailor is Thomas Pink?"

"Not anymore," he grumbled.

This level of confusion was quickly growing exhausting. "And you are not expecting Mr. Tennyson Lamont to come here looking for you?"

"For copyright purposes, I don't think Tennyson Lamont will make any appearances this summer."

"*Copyright?*" What was he talking about?

"Unless you want to go nose-to-nose with a team of network lawyers."

"Lawyers?"

"Solicitors."

Was he in trouble with the law? That would explain having multiple names. It could also explain his tattoo. And yet the explanation didn't feel right.

"Who are you?" she asked. "I suspect the full story was not laid out last night."

He looked almost relieved. "I didn't think so either."

"What does that mean?"

Mr. Summerfield smiled, even gave the hint of a laugh. "How about we approach this in a far easier manner: you tell me what it is I am to do while we wait for the sea road to emerge from the water, and I will nod in agreement and do it."

He truly wanted her to simply tell him what she needed him to do? He appeared to be in earnest, and he didn't seem upset about needing to remain on the island for a time. She was not ever deferred to in this way. Mrs. Jagger and Mr. Marsh had treated her with incredulity at first, though they had warmed to her. Jane acknowledged her as the mistress of the house but had a tendency toward a bit of cheek. Little Mick simply did as he pleased.

Dare she take advantage of the rare bit of luck in finding this man who was proving so amenable, even if he remained mysterious?

She didn't know him well. She didn't know him at all. Yet without help, she was going to fail.

"This house has endured neglect in recent years," she said hesitantly. "When I first arrived here a few weeks ago, I was not expecting to be assigned the running and upkeep of it, but that is my role now."

"The role of mistress of the house." He nodded his understanding. "That is a significant one."

Significant and overwhelming but, she hoped, fruitful in the end.

"Have you skills as a laborer of any kind?" she asked.

That she asked didn't offend him, which she was grateful for. He did, however, seem confused. "I have done some work in carpentry."

Here was another spot of luck. At last, it seemed fate was going to be kind.

"That is tremendously fortuitous," she said. "Guilford is in particular need of repairs."

"That is to be my role? Laborer and carpenter?" He seemed a little disappointed but still not offended.

He gave every indication of being a gentleman yet also had carpentry skills. Who knew Americans could be so useful.

"You are also a gentleman." She didn't need to phrase it as a question, as she was certain she already knew the answer. "In the evenings, you could certainly dedicate yourself to that role."

"In the evenings? You mean after hours?"

She wasn't at all certain what that meant, though she could guess at the definition. Not knowing how things were done in America and not wanting to lose the help that she needed, she felt she could be accommodating. "Afternoons *and* evenings," she amended her offer of a moment earlier. "Though I will need you to spend the mornings undertaking carpentry and repair work."

"Do you have the appropriate tools and materials?" he asked.

She nodded. "There is an outbuilding on the island, not far from the house."

"This was planned for, then."

She supposed so. Most homes had to have access to such things. "The sea road might remain covered for days yet," she said. "If you would help while waiting for it to be passable, that would be tremendously appreciated."

"I'm just glad to know what my role is going to be," he said, "even if it didn't prove to be quite what I anticipated."

The sea had brought him here by accident; anticipation could not have played any role in it at all.

Kipling Summerfield merited watching. And she would watch him while he helped her secure her inheritance, while doing her best not to remember that she'd watched him rather longer than she ought to have that very morning.

"None of my belongings seem to have arrived here with me," he said. "And the lighthouse keeper's very generously supplied wardrobe doesn't fit particularly well." He motioned to the trousers that ended short and his shirtsleeves that seemed ready to burst across the shoulders. If they did that, his unsettling and intriguing tattoo would be obvious again. She wasn't certain she was ready for a repeat appearance.

"I had an opportunity upon first arriving to look through the attic," she said. "There is a trunk there with men's clothing inside. They will be partially outmoded and might not fit you perfectly, but there's a chance you'll find something in there that might suit your needs."

"Outmoded?" he repeated. "Great word. I wonder why it was never used on set."

On set. An Americanism, no doubt.

"I'll go rummage through the attic and see if I can find that very convenient trunk. Then I'll go explore this outbuilding and see what kind of ancient tools I might have to learn how to use." He offered another bow.

His eyes met hers again as he straightened once more. There was a genuine joy in his expression. Joy. It was so wholly unexpected that she didn't know at all what to think. He'd been washed here by the sea, was in many ways trapped on the island like she was, and was hiding something. Yet he seemed truly and genuinely happy.

Perhaps among his other tasks, he could teach her the trick of that.

Chapter 6

"What are the chances 'attic' is code for 'green room'?" Kip asked the man portraying the butler upon crossing paths with him in the corridor.

"I beg your pardon, sir?" He managed to look genuinely confused, though he must have understood the question. No one in the industry *wouldn't* have known what Kip was asking. "The attic is quite different from Miss Archibald's bedchamber, which you oughtn't be asking about as it is."

"Her bedchamber is the green room?" That couldn't be correct.

"The green bedchamber, yes. And it's no place for you, no matter how things might be done in the former colonies."

Kip arched his brow. "We're leaning this heavily into character, are we?"

"I hope I am a person of character." The butler's eyes narrowed. "Mrs. Jagger and I are hopeful that you are as well."

"Isn't the 'What are your intentions?' lecture usually delivered by a lady's father or brother?" That was still sometimes the way it happened nowadays, but it had *always* happened that way on *The Beau*.

"*Do* you have intentions?" That seemed to alarm the man. "You've only just arrived. Us know nothing of you; *her* knows nothing of you."

Did that mean Kip was supposed to play the role of eventual suitor who had to earn the approval of his chosen lady's protectors? Or was Kip being warned that he *wasn't* supposed to take on that role? Making an actor guess at his part was an annoying way to run a production or site or however he was supposed to refer to this gig.

"Miss Archibald instructed me to fetch a trunk of clothing from the attic," Kip said, leaning into what he did know of his assignment and his accent, which he thought quite good, despite the repeated criticisms he'd received since arriving. His fellow actors, he was certain, were all British, yet they didn't sound the way he would have expected. "As this is my first day at Guilford, I do not know how to access the attic." Or if "the attic" was, in fact, an actual attic.

The butler motioned for him to follow as he made his way to the stairs and began climbing upward. That bit of the journey Kip could have predicted.

"What am I to call you?" Kip asked him.

"Call me?" More drawn brows. More admittedly convincing expressions of confusion. "My name, sir."

"I would be happy to do so once I know what your name is."

"Ah." The man continued onward, up yet another flight of stairs. "Marsh, sir."

On *The Beau*, butlers had generally been called by their surnames, without including the "Mr."

Marsh walked with him down the uppermost corridor, one far plainer than any of the others below, directly to an equally plain door. He opened it. "The attic is at the top of these stairs."

"Thank you, Marsh," Kip said. "And allow me to reassure you, I have no designs upon Miss Archibald, nor do I have any intention of creating chaos at Guilford. I understand the rules and expectations."

He'd been in enough productions to know perfectly well that being demanding and difficult was reserved for those who were too valuable to a show to be let go, and that casual romantic entanglements in a cast were usually more trouble than they were worth.

The stairwell was dim but not nearly as poorly lit as the attic, which turned out to be an actual attic. A sliver of light peeked through a partially opened curtain. Kip navigated to it and pulled the curtain fully open.

Even the attic was historically accurate. Though all the furnishings and paintings in the dusty space had the look of furniture from centuries ago, they weren't worn enough to be actual antiques. Still, why go to the trouble of filling an attic with such precise replicas?

And again, there was no light switch. He hadn't spotted a single one in the entire place. No light switches. No outlets. And as his body was beginning to very urgently remind him, no toilets. If his phone hadn't been knocked out of his hand in the moments before the storm had knocked him into the sea for an afternoon of forced swimming, he would have texted Malcolm a few thoughts about this "opportunity."

There were three trunks in the attic. He couldn't believe the costumes were literally kept in trunks in an attic. This was, by far, the strangest job he'd ever had, and he'd had a few doozies in his time. He opened the smallest of the trunks. It had some papers and odd bits and baubles. Another one, closer in size to what he'd expect, had clothes inside, but they appeared to be women's clothes. The third one, then, was the one Miss Archibald had, with annoying subtlety, told him his "character" needed to go grab.

He pulled out a shirt. It was slightly more ruffled than what he'd worn on *The Beau*, certainly more than the lighthouse keeper's shirt that he was wearing at the moment, but it was close to the right thing. The trousers were knee breeches, like they'd worn for balls and more formal scenes, but the knee breeches weren't his favorite of the costumes. There were also very thick stockings, which would help with the cold.

He dug through and found jackets and neck cloths, even a pair of buckled shoes. They were unlikely to be a perfect fit, but it looked like they'd at least be kind of close. There was a nightshirt tossed in with it all, which should keep people from screaming when they broke into his room in the mornings. He knew that it had been common practice for the staff of a home to slip into a bedchamber in the morning to relight the fire and make things cozy and comfortable for the people who had money. And he recognized he was portraying, at least for half the day, someone of that station back in history. But actually busting into his room without so much as knocking, in the name of historical accuracy, felt like overkill.

And the way both the maid and Miss Archibald had enacted early nineteenth-century panic over the idea of a tattoo would have been entertaining if he hadn't been left wondering if he was going to lose this job that he didn't overly want but desperately needed. Makeup had just covered his tattoos in *The Beau* when he'd needed to be shirtless, which had happened a lot. A whole lot.

Among the trunk of clothing, he found something wrapped in burlap. He unrolled it. Inside was a book of some sort: parchment sewn together and hand stitched into a cover of leather, tied closed with a leather strap. Kip opened it.

A journal. There was already writing inside, so his character wasn't meant to be the one writing in it during his summer at

Guilford. It was specifically in *his* trunk of costumes, so he must have been meant to read it. Was his character supposed to read it, or was he, *Kip*, supposed to read it in order to get an idea of who and what his character actually was?

He'd been given so few instructions that he was guessing his way through this first day. The tourists weren't even there yet. Why not simply hand over his character description, give him a garment bag or suitcase of costumes, and explain to him how the summer was going to play out? This adherence to being in character and living in uncomfortable historical accuracy before it was even necessary was already starting to annoy him. And it was messing with how he talked, even in his own mind. He was leaning into old-timey Britishisms like *corridor* instead of hallway, *bedchamber* instead of bedroom, "I have no designs upon Miss Archibald" instead of "Nah, not feelin' it."

Michael Osbourne would visit at some point in the summer, he reminded himself. One of the biggest names in the industry. And he would visit Guilford knowing he'd discovered talent before.

Kip could endure some irritation in exchange for a chance to get back in the game. He would, of course, make sure Malcolm heard about every single even marginally annoying thing that happened.

He set the journal back inside the trunk and closed it once more. Thankfully, the trunk wasn't very heavy. He was able to pick it up and carry it out of the attic and down the stairs to the corridor below. Marsh hadn't hung around waiting for him, which was kind of a relief. It was too early in the morning and too early in the job to be dealing with drama.

He returned to the blue bedchamber and set the trunk at the foot of his bed. His suitcase still hadn't arrived.

Kip changed from his current clothes into the ones in the trunk. Again, the costume designer had gone for authenticity over comfort. This was going to be a long summer.

Kip pulled out the journal. He might as well get a start on solving the entirely unnecessary mystery of who he was supposed to be this summer.

12 May 1692

Something is decidedly odd in this place. I feel myself obligated to anyone else who might, in time to come, find himself here. As such, I will record what I have seen and experienced.

"Decidedly odd." That was certainly what Kip was feeling. And though the entry was dated 1692, he'd guess the time they were re-creating at Guilford was somewhere closer to 1810. Miss Archibald's clothes were pretty similar to what the women had worn on *The Beau*, and it was set in the 1810s. The writer of the journal had said it was written for people who would come there later.

Why was he being required to figure out his part by solving riddles?

This estate lies isolated from cities and people, from universities and advancements, and yet I find here extraordinary things I have not experienced at home. I feel in many ways as though I have left behind a comparatively primitive existence to arrive in a place which far surpasses even the grandest dreams my compatriots have of what might lie in the future.

If Kip was reading it correctly, he was supposed to view Guilford as a technologically advanced house. Perhaps during this summer season, the focus of the historical site was going to be inventions of the very early 1800s, common things that were considered new and state of the art for that era.

The fictitious keeper of this journal declared that his experiences before Guilford were comparatively simplistic. Perhaps at this time, America was less advanced than England. It fit his dual role of laboring carpenter and gentleman of leisure.

He wasn't willing to play the part of an idiot simply to satisfy some American stereotype, but he could certainly acknowledge, when tourists were around, things that were considered state of the art in the early 1800s. Hopefully those things would be pointed out to him. Maybe they were recorded in the journal.

Why did the people running this place think they had to do things the hard way?

> *The people here are clearly surprised at my lack of understanding of these new and novel things. It is both frustrating and concerning.*
>
> *I hold to my initial impression that something decidedly odd and, I begin to fear, a little duplicitous is occurring here. I hope, by continuing to record my thoughts and experiences, I will be able to sort out what it is and find either my place here or my escape.*

It was not the tone Kip would have expected the entry to end on. The man made it sound as though he were trapped and unable to leave. Was that the note the historic site wanted to strike? Surely people being held hostage at an estate was not such a common historical occurrence that the people running this place would want to lean into it.

Kip closed the diary and tucked it into the drawer of his bedside table. He'd have to look through it later, perhaps when he was permitted the role that sat far closer to Tennyson. In the meantime, he needed to go find a tool shed, which, he suspected, would not include a bandsaw or power drill. Would he be expected to make actual, legitimate repairs around the estate, or was he going to be demonstrating an approximate idea of what would have occurred? Whichever was the case, surely he didn't have to actually do it until the site opened for the season.

He pulled on the heavy wool coat he'd found in the trunk, grateful for it, and made his way through the house, aiming for the back door. He spotted a few things here and there that were indeed in need of repair. He could see to those things as a way of demonstrating nineteenth-century techniques. He didn't know what any of those techniques were, but he suspected he could guess. He suspected, in fact, that he would *have* to guess.

He stepped out into the cold ocean air. The weather would, he hoped, grow warmer as the summer went on. But he suspected it would never be truly warm. He'd often joked with Malcolm that he hadn't been warm since moving to London for university. He'd thawed out only when he'd spent time in California doing work in the States.

Now he had a job on an island that was, by Malcolm's own description, prone to storms and bad weather. This job had better bring him the kind of work he actually wanted to do, or he was going to have a very hard time thinking it was worth it.

He walked along a path edging a lawn that didn't appear to have seen a lawnmower in years probably. Somewhere on these grounds was the outbuilding with his tools. He hoped it wasn't very far, otherwise he'd be lugging equipment and wood back and forth over ground he suspected was wet more often than not. A stone wall to his right intrigued him. They'd done some filming in some historical homes, and walls without roofs out on the grounds generally enclosed gardens.

Would this isolated, sea-surrounded house have a formal garden? It *was* from a time when fancy people and fancy gardens went together. Still, it felt like a mismatched combination at Guilford. He found the iron gate leading inside and decided to take a peek.

It was, in fact, a very traditional English knot garden. Nearly all of it was overgrown and in need of attention. But a section was neatly manicured and tended. And in the midst of that section was Miss Archibald, kneeling on a small rug beside a flowerbed, a bonnet tied tight on her head, a heavy and serviceable coat in the style of the era buttoned against the wind. She wore leather working gloves, so perhaps she, too, had been assigned a less than elegant job on the island in the morning hours.

Malcolm had said the site was in need of more actors and that was why he'd been able to get Kip this position. One of those actors had to be the gardener, and Kip had to be the carpenter. It seemed "understaffed" was an understatement.

He stood there, debating whether to walk over and talk to her and try to get a few questions answered. He might have done it, too, except there was something very peaceful about watching her. She seemed very much at home in this garden, no matter that even if she were a gardener at her actual home, she would have done so in a more modern setting with more modern tools. And he suspected she hadn't taken this acting job with the intention of working with plants all summer. He was also curious about whether her limp and use of a cane was something required of her character or something real. Damp, uneven paths through unkempt lawns was a dangerous thing for someone who wasn't entirely steady on her feet. He hoped she wasn't being required to be in actual peril for a stupid summer job.

He watched her a moment longer. She really was gorgeous. He hadn't realized until seeing her in the book room the night before that he sort of had a thing for redheads. Maybe it wasn't redheads in general but this sort of soft auburn, with waving tendrils fluttering about. And she had a few freckles, which he *did* know he liked. Always had.

But he knew the rules, and he knew the expectations. And he suspected the actor playing the role of Marsh really would pummel him if he created drama on set, or on site, or . . . He needed to figure out how to refer to this place.

Kip stepped away from the gate and continued on the path, keeping an eye out for a tool shed that probably would look like some old, tiny outhouse or something. He doubted there would be a sign that said Find Super Old Carpentry Tools Here. But after a solid fifteen minutes of wandering around, seeing nothing promising, he began to wish there were a ridiculous amount of signage. In fact, it was weird that there was no signage at all. Surely tourists weren't expected to simply guess how to find their various destinations when visiting the site. They might be provided with maps or tour guides, but if there were tour guides, why had Kip not met any of them? That was exactly who he needed to talk to. They would know what was expected and what tourists would be told and what the owners would be looking for. Maybe they simply hadn't arrived yet. Maybe they also found this white-knuckle insistence on never being out of character exhausting and chose to avoid it as long as possible.

The night before, Miss Archibald—he really did need to find out what her actual name was—had told Mrs. Jagger—even if he found out what *her* actual name was, the idea of thinking of her as Mick Jagger's mom was too much fun to call her anything else—that the road connecting the island to the mainland was currently underwater. Perhaps the director of the site, the tour guides, the people with the information were in the village attached to the site. The lighthouse keeper had rowed Kip to the island in a dinghy, but it seemed no one used boats to get to and from the village when the sea road was underwater.

Just when he was about to declare his search for the Ye Olde Hut of Tools a futile endeavor, he crossed paths with a young boy, probably ten or eleven years old, whistling as he walked down a very narrow, relatively muddy footpath.

"Boy," Kip called out, uncertain why that was the word that popped out of his mouth. It got the kid's attention though. "Miss Archibald asked me to do some work about the place, but I can't find the outbuilding that has all the carpentry tools."

The boy nodded and twitched his head in a clear command to follow him. In 1805 or 1817 or whenever this was supposed to be, a boy of this age was meant to show a little more respect to an adult, but Kip was too tired of walking around aimlessly to bother being as in character as everyone else. He was sticking to his accent and dialect, and that would just have to be enough for everybody.

"Are you the one Mr. Ivers brought in from the storm last night?" the boy asked. His accent sounded a great deal like everyone else's, except Miss Archibald. And himself.

"That's me," he said. "And before you ask, I do not sound like I'm from around here because I am an American."

The boy nodded. "Everywho knows that. It's all anywho's talking about."

Everywho. Anywho. A re-creation of the way people spoke in this area at the time they were pretending to be living in?

"And how many people does that 'everywho' encompass? The island doesn't seem overly large."

"With you here now, there's eight of we on Guilford Island."

Eight. That was decidedly understaffed.

"And the baby."

Kip stopped on the path. "A baby?"

He definitely wanted to know if he was meant to also play the role of a father to an actual infant as part of this job. That would be far too much to ask. It wasn't that he wasn't good with kids. It was just that an infant wasn't a prop and oughtn't be part of something like this.

"Mr. and Mrs. Ivers' baby," the boy said. "Lives with they, don't him?"

The couple portraying the lighthouse keeper were, in fact, a couple and had their own child, who was here with them. That was a much more acceptable arrangement.

But this boy was an odd choice to be part of the cast.

"What's your name?" Kip asked.

"I'm Mick."

They had a Mick, and they had a Mrs. Jagger. That couldn't have been a coincidence. And it also helped explain why the housekeeper was so quick to deny that she was Mick's mom. That was something a new tourist might very well joke about, and the cast would have canned responses to it. If nothing else, Kip's confusion had confirmed to them the setup of that joke was going to work.

Mick led him along the curve of the path, which deposited him directly in front of a small stone building that looked absolutely perfect for a tradesman's shed from two hundred years earlier. It probably *was* a tradesman's shed two hundred years ago.

Dare he hope there was actual electricity in there? Once he could get out to the village, he would replace his phone. But he had to have somewhere to charge it.

He stepped into the shed and had a quick look around. Absolutely stupidly accurate. It was filled with the tools a person saw in a museum, not in an actual workshop. If this wasn't specifically a stop for the tourists, it was just a waste of time and effort to make the actor doing the carpentry actually do it authentically.

"You seem too Quality to be here doing work," Mick said.

"Well, needs must, as the saying goes."

"Needs must what?" Mick tossed back.

That apparently wasn't an old enough expression that he could get away with it. "Guilford needs work done. But there are only eight of us and a baby, and I seem to be the only one who knows how to do this kind of work. So, my being Quality doesn't overly matter, does it?"

Mick shrugged. "Suppose not."

"How old are you, Mick?"

The boy stood even taller, chest puffed out. "Eleven."

Too young to be working a full-time job. And child actors had limits on the time they could spend on the clock, among other restrictions. "Where are your parents?"

"Bottom of the ocean, I suppose." The boy shrugged. "Been down there ages."

It was a morbid way to reveal his character's backstory. "They drowned?"

Mick nodded. "This here area of the Channel has more drownings than any other. Far and away more. From here to the other side of Loftstone, people are always being swept off ships and piers and beaches. Down them go. No one sees they again."

It was an effective speech. The tourists would be appropriately creeped out when they were told about the history of the area.

"Truthfully, though," Kip said, "where are your parents?"

Mick's expression grew angry. "Them's dead, sir. Why would a fellow lie about a thing like that?"

Perhaps the actor really had lost his parents in an ocean accident. To make him then portray someone who had experienced the same thing was pretty heartless. And for him to be on a job like this without any kind of adult guardian was illegal.

Mick must have had someone somewhere looking out for him, but like everyone else in this place, he was completely stuck on the idea of never breaking character. Kip could respect his process even if it was ridiculously extreme.

"Who is in charge here at Guilford?" Kip asked.

Could Mick find a way to answer that question in character? He did. "Miss Archibald."

Kip knew that she was portraying the mistress of the estate and, in historical context, was, essentially, in charge.

"But who oversees her?" He felt he could ask that because he'd gotten the impression during his five seasons on *The Beau* that ladies back in the day weren't generally given free rein of anything without someone looking over their shoulder.

"Her uncle and her granddad's solicitor come and check on things now and then. Them was here only a few days ago."

Finally, Kip was getting some information. This uncle and solicitor were likely the people who ran the place but were given those "roles" in order to keep the authenticity going.

"Do we know when they're likely to return?" Kip asked.

"Miss Archibald says probably another two weeks. Them don't give none of we any warning, just arrive, look around, and decide what's being done right and what's being done wrong."

That could explain everyone never breaking character. If the people who owned this place were demanding about it being a fully immersive experience and no one ever knew when they were lurking around corners, being ridiculously method was the best approach.

Things were finally starting to make sense but in a way that was starting to give him a headache.

"Any other place on the island you've been trying to find?" Mick asked. "I know this place better than anywho."

Kip shook his head. "I need to take stock of what's in here and what to do with it. But if I have other questions . . ."

"I'm always about," he said.

"Before you go," Kip said, stopping Mick midturn. "Is there a place where the cast relaxes?"

Once again, Kip was treated to a look of such complete confusion that he began to wonder if this odd, out-of-the-way historical site managed to employ some of the most secretly talented actors in all of England. "I don't understand, sir."

"Never mind. I'll find a phone."

"A phone?" Mick shook his head when he repeated the word, as if he'd never heard it before.

Always in character.

"Never mind."

Mick went on his way. Kip leaned a shoulder against a wall, looking around at all the manual tools that, while appearing fully authentic, did not have nearly the rust or wear they ought to have after a couple of centuries. Again, unnecessarily perfect replicas.

The journal entry had indicated that he was supposed to find this place odd and confusing. That was not going to take any acting.

Chapter 7

"In this garden, I am grateful for . . ." Amelia couldn't think of a way to finish that sentence that didn't require sarcasm. Even the garden, her favorite spot on the entire island, was proving a source of frustration at the moment, on account of a particularly thorny patch of weeds. "I am grateful for very thick gloves."

She'd managed to restore only about a fifth of the garden in the month she'd been on Guilford, all but guaranteeing she'd need every day of her six months to put the entire thing to rights. She would restore it only to leave it behind.

Mick's whistling reached her before he stepped into the garden. The boy had come with the house, as it were. Mrs. Jagger and Marsh had told her that Mick had arrived on the island a couple of years earlier with no other explanation than that his parents had been swept off a ship and drowned.

The housekeeper and butler had taken him in, and he'd proved himself a joyful addition to life on Guilford. Everyone liked Mick. Amelia wished she knew the trick of that.

She was lonely on this island. She'd not truly had friends at her aunt and uncle's house, but she'd at least had company. And now, she didn't even have that any longer. She spoke with Jane now and then, but there was the unavoidable distance between a maid in a household and the mistress who employed her. Her butler and housekeeper saw to their work and kindly watched over her the way a pair of distant relatives might.

She'd held out some hope that the Iverses would prove friends, being much nearer in age to herself, but they kept to themselves. She had the impression, every time she was near the lighthouse or when she dropped into their home to offer her greetings, that they couldn't be rid of her soon enough. She told herself they weren't the spies her grandfather had predicted would surround her during this six-month imprisonment, but she couldn't entirely shake the possibility.

She looked up from pulling weeds and watched as Mick sauntered down the little path toward her. "I met Mr. Summerfield," he said. "Strange one, him."

Amelia shrugged. "He's American."

Mick nodded his agreement with the explanation. "I went and saw the Iverses' baby this morning." He picked up a rock and tossed it from one hand to the other. "Him's getting bigger."

Mick always returned from their home with tales of having played with the baby or helped Mr. Ivers at the lighthouse. Amelia hadn't managed that at all.

"Mr. Ivers thinks the road will be up from the water in another day or two. I asked he why it was that the waters come in so fast when there's a storm but dawdle on the way out."

"And what explanation did he give you?" Amelia was curious about that herself.

"Him said it's to do with the shape of the little bay and how the island traps the water. Anywhere else, him said, the road would likely uncover itself as fast as it got covered."

So it was geography conspiring against her. That somehow felt fitting.

"Him said it were likely also the reason so many ships go down here. The dip of the bay around Loftstone is shaped the same. Water gets trapped, and storms get trapped, and then people get trapped."

People get trapped. If there were a more apt description of how she felt on Guilford, she couldn't think of it.

"Don't you go talking Miss's ear off." Marsh had the ability, despite his slightly shuffling step, to arrive in a place without making noise.

"I wasn't," Mick said. "I was answering her questions."

Amelia pulled off her gardening gloves and tucked them into her gardening apron pocket. Then, using her trusty cane for balance, she got to her feet. "Mick is no bother. I appreciate that he comes to talk with me."

She gave the little boy a smile and received one in return. He wasn't a friend in the sense that someone would be were they of the same age, but he was friendly, and that was a lovely thing for a person as alone as she was.

"I think I found the paper you've been looking for, Miss Archibald," Marsh said.

Nervousness clutched at her heart. She'd told Marsh and Mrs. Jagger that she was attempting to find the papers pertaining to her requirements while on Guilford. She was certain the solicitor had left them here, but she hadn't been able to find them.

Marsh held out a folded bit of parchment to her. Grateful she had already taken her gloves off, she took it with her free hand and quickly unfolded it. Though she didn't read it in any detail, she knew it was indeed what she had been searching for.

"Well done, Marsh. Thank you."

The man dipped his head, clear pride in his posture. "You'll tell we what you discover in it?" Marsh asked.

"Yes, of course."

"And will you also tell we," Marsh pressed on, "if that Mr. Summerfield is bothering you?"

"I will. Thus far, he's not caused any difficulty, aside from the inevitable upheaval of an unexpected arrival, especially one who has arrived with nothing."

"Did him fall off a boat?" Mick asked quietly, no doubt thinking of his own parents.

"That is the impression I received." Amelia offered him a smile of understanding. "He is fortunate that Mr. Ivers found him and brought him to the island."

Mick nodded. "And I suppose us is fortunate him knows how to build and repair things. Him will be helpful at Guilford."

Marsh didn't seem to understand what was being referenced.

Amelia took pity on him. "I discovered in conversation with Mr. Summerfield this morning that our American visitor has some carpentry skills."

Marsh was clearly surprised. "Him has the mark of Quality about he."

Amelia nodded. "The only explanation I can think of is that things must be different in that respect in America. A person can be a gentleman and yet still have the skills of a tradesman. He didn't seem embarrassed by the ability, so it must not be something they are taught to be ashamed of."

"And him said him would be willing to work about the place?" Marsh didn't manage to hide his doubt.

Amelia nodded.

"Him asked me to show he where the work cottage is," Mick said. "When I left he there, him was looking over the tools and asking after others I'd not heard the names of before. But, then, I weren't never apprenticed to a carpenter."

Mr. Summerfield was already setting to work? That felt like a very good sign. A whisper of hope bubbled, something that had happened with little enough frequency in the last month that Amelia almost didn't recognize it.

"Us'll leave you to your work and to your papers." Marsh set a hand on the scruff of Mick's neck and turned him about to face the exit to the garden. He gave the boy a tiny nudge, and the two of them made their way past the gate.

Amelia had intended to keep working for a while, but the unread paper in her hand proved too pressing. She took the garden's paved walkway to the gardening shed. Clearing the path and making it safe for her to navigate with her sometimes-precarious balance had been her first task in the garden when she'd arrived weeks earlier.

She pulled off her gardening apron and straw bonnet and placed both, along with her gloves, in the gardening shed, then she closed the door and made her way back out of the garden entirely, her cane offering a needed bit of stability. Away from the distraction of weeds and flowers and shrubbery, the ocean was uncomfortably loud. Fortunately, she had another ready distraction in her hand.

She took a deep breath, reminding herself that the house sat high enough on the island that should a storm whip up immediately, the sea wouldn't reach her where she was. She unfolded the parchment once again. She held it in her left hand, used her cane with her right, and carefully traversed the familiar path back to the house as she read.

To prove herself able to look after an inheritance, one which might lead to the purchase of an estate of her own, I am requiring her to look after this *estate for six months.*

She remembered that part. She had to prove her aptitude and intelligence and trustworthiness. She dropped her focus lower on the paper, to where the requirements for her had been summarized.

> *My solicitor as well as my son, Woodrow Stirling, will make regular unannounced inspections of the estate, to make certain it is being cared for, its needs are being met, and Miss Archibald has not left.*
>
> *Should Miss Archibald meet these requirements, at the end of her six-month sojourn on Guilford Island, she will be granted the entirety of her inheritance and the freedom to live her life in the way she chooses with the generous windfall she has been provided.*
>
> *Should she fail, the entirety of her inheritance will be reverted back to the Stirling estate.*

Caring for the estate and remaining on the island were both required for her to receive her inheritance. Both. So she did have to convince her uncle and the solicitor that she was undoing the neglect of decades.

She slid her eyes once more over the words. At the bottom of the last page, in the style of a footnote, was more writing.

> *For purposes of this binding contract, remaining on the island is understood to mean that at all times, Miss Archibald will maintain physical contact with the island itself. Swimming in the sea, venturing out on a boat, stepping onto the sea road, and any other activity that results in her not being in physical contact with Guilford Island will be considered leaving the island and will result in a forfeiture of her inheritance.*

Did Grandfather truly think he had to specify that she wasn't permitted to undertake any sea bathing? While Amelia could see herself growing desperate enough to attempt a flight down the road when it was not buried under the ocean, she would never intentionally head out into the surf. Even doing so on a boat sounded utterly horrifying.

A second footnote sat beneath the first.

As the purpose of this exercise is to prove whether or not Miss Amelia Archibald can, with capability, oversee the fortune that awaits her, an accounting must be made of how she executes the responsibilities she is given at Guilford. A report is to be made at the end of the six months, detailing what was accomplished, what was not, and what might have been done differently. Declarations of unfitness must be supported with evidence so as to meet the legal requirements of denying Miss Archibald her inheritance.

There was the answer to the question that had plagued her. She couldn't be denied her inheritance simply because someone said she had done a poor job. There had to be evidence—proof.

At some point she had stopped walking and was simply staring at the paper in her hand. Her mind had begun spinning so hard that her feet no longer knew what they were meant to do. Just as well. Walking while distracted was a good way to end up on her face.

She didn't think her uncle or the solicitor were intent on finding evidence of ineptitude. Her uncle often treated her with indifference and dismissal, and he was notoriously stubborn, single-minded when he had decided on a course of action. But he'd never truly been cruel or unfair. It would be a significant change in him if he were suddenly to become that sort of person. But should she fail at this test, he would receive a tremendous amount of money and the ability to see her married to someone who might allow him to keep the dowry meant to be hers, or to share it with him.

Money changed people. It was one of the truths most in Society learned quickly.

Regardless of whether Uncle Stirling was hoping to see her fail, she needed to make sure that she didn't. She needed to do a good enough job that there simply wasn't the necessary evidence.

Amelia folded the parchment once more and tucked it up into the sleeve of her coat. Wind off the sea clutched at her, but she stood stalwart against it.

She had the funds to put Guilford to rights, but she would never have sufficient staff. Jane, who had grown up there, told her that not everyone in the village at the other end of the sea road was willing to come to Guilford.

Amelia was beginning at a disadvantage, something her grandfather had no doubt planned on, but he could not have planned on Mr. Summerfield. The usually heartless ocean had brought her the potential for salvation. But it had done so in the form of a stranger she didn't understand and didn't fully trust.

Mick had said he was already setting to work. If that was true, there was a chance this could work.

The sight of him that morning, bare-chested, muscled, tattooed, of all things, flashed quickly through her mind. She pushed it out just as quickly. She hadn't the luxury of indulging even in a moment of girlish swooning. Her entire future hung in the balance.

For twenty years, all she'd been able to hope for was survival and tranquility, and both had depended on staying quiet, staying out of the way, never taking any risks. For the first and likely last time in her life, she now had a chance for something more. But reaching for it meant being bold and risky and aiming for something that felt impossible.

All her hopes were tied up in this place that struck such fear into her and in this mysterious stranger the ocean had brought to her doorstep.

Chapter 8

Amelia couldn't bring herself to spend even one more minute looking at her list of tasks needing her attention. But neither could she sit in the silence of the house, listening to the storm that had arrived without warning. Mr. Summerfield had taken his evening meal in his room, and she was alone in the drawing room. To her frustration, his absence disappointed her.

She remained entirely certain he was hiding something. And nearly everything about him was unnervingly mysterious. Yet she'd missed him as she'd eaten alone in the dining room. Missed a gentleman she'd spoken with only three times.

The isolation was beginning to addle her, she sometimes feared.

Mr. Summerfield was likely still mildly upended and mildly uncomfortable, not to mention still exhausted after his battle with the sea the night before. And it was not the done thing for a single gentleman and a single lady to spend time together alone, in England at least. She wasn't sure of the expectations in America.

Still, the oddness of their situation required some adaptation. He could certainly have passed the evening in the drawing room with her. The door would have remained open, allowing for the possibility of Marsh, Mrs. Jagger, or Jane to step inside. Mick didn't always spend time up at the house, but he was known to wander in and out.

Still, the tattooed American needn't have spent the entire night alone in his room while she was alone in the drawing room.

She leaned on her walking stick as she plunked a few notes on the pianoforte. She was not an accomplished musician, but she could play a few songs. It was how she had entertained herself through much of the last month. When the book room grew too monotonous or the sea grew too loud, she sat at the instrument and did what she could to distract herself, filling those evenings with silent declarations of "Tonight, I am grateful that Susanna's music tutor spoke loudly enough for me to overhear and learn a few things."

She'd found, within a few days of her arrival at Guilford, printed music in a cabinet nearby and had been slowly teaching herself to play a few things in addition to the pieces she had already memorized.

She had started and restarted the same sonata four times when Mr. Summerfield's odd accent interrupted. "I didn't realize you played."

She looked over her shoulder at him. "I do not play well."

"Did you put it on your CV and now you're stuck with that as part of your character?"

Amelia didn't have the first idea what he meant by that.

He wandered toward her, seemingly pleased to be there, so she didn't press the matter.

"I have looked around," he said, "and I'm beginning to understand just how intense this place is."

Intense was an odd way of describing Guilford, yet she thought she knew what he meant. There was an unrelenting nature to the island. A person felt closed in and trapped.

Mr. Summerfield motioned for her to sit on the stool, which she did. Then he pulled a chair over and sat beside her. So much about him was unexpected.

With one finger he plunked out a tune. She wasn't at all familiar with it. It had a delightful bounce to it and an interesting combination of intervals. Her accidental education in music was too limited to identify a musical style or era from which it might have emerged.

"You have had some musical instruction?" she asked.

"Just enough to tell people it's a skill of mine and not get accused of lying." He continued on with his tune, one that was proving somewhat repetitive.

"Don't tell my cousin that you have any ability at the pianoforte; she'll make you play every time she and her friends wish to dance."

"I can't imagine people dancing to 'Heart and Soul.'"

"'Heart and Soul'? Is that what this tune is called?"

He seemed to expect her to have known that.

"I fear my exposure to music and culture and such is rather limited," she said. "The life of a poor relation is not often rich in any sense of the word."

"A poor relation." He nodded. "I'm familiar with that archetype."

"Archetype?"

"That word has to be old enough."

Mr. Summerfield had the uncanny ability to confuse her.

"A type of person," he said.

Ah. "Poor relations are often lumped together, always assumed to be mousy or weak or unwilling to stand up for ourselves. We are very seldom given credit for the monumental effort required to resist punching people in the nose when they say things like that."

"For the sake of my nose, I will point out that I was only trying to say that I know what the term 'poor relation' refers to, though we don't really use the term in America. I hadn't meant to imply that those who find themselves in your life situation have no claim on individuality." He watched her out of the corner of his eyes. While there was the tiniest hint of teasing in his expression, she could see that he also legitimately was not certain if she was going to belt him.

Most people would absolutely never believe she had it in her. *She* wasn't sure she did.

"I have been a poor relation nearly all my life," she said. "If I am successful during my remaining time at Guilford, I do not have to return to that role. Despite not preferring a life of dependent poverty, I'm grateful to have been taken in by my uncle and aunt. I would have been in difficult straits otherwise."

He nodded as he plunked out another tune. "Being a carpenter in the mornings and a very lonely gentleman of leisure in the afternoons and evenings wasn't quite how I envisioned spending my immediate future."

She rose awkwardly from her stool and paced, her cane punctuating her movements. "I worry that I offended you by suggesting you take on that role. I don't know how things are done in America or what it is that you are accustomed to and are willing to do, but Guilford needs a great many repairs. And if they are not made to the exacting standards of those who will ultimately decide if the next few months are a failure, then everything will come to a very abrupt end."

She likely wasn't explaining things in enough detail for him to make sense of it all, but opening up entirely to a stranger felt far too vulnerable.

"This, then, is a crucial summer season," he said.

"I cannot even begin to express how crucial. With you now here, even for a short time, there is a chance of salvaging the situation. Yet I am certain you can ascertain that I am not entirely comfortable with you here. I don't consider myself an entirely untrusting person, but I *am* cautious with people I don't know, especially before I know if they are trustworthy."

"I'm not a saint, I'll confess that."

She nodded. "I saw the tattoo."

"Always in character." The underlying laughter in his voice brought her eyes to him.

For a moment, she braced herself to see mocking derision or a man who would prove to be more of a rake than a potential help. She was in a vulnerable situation. But what she saw was legitimate, friendly amusement. She hadn't offended him, nor had she upset him. It was a surprisingly good beginning, even if she didn't know what he meant by, "Always in character."

"Do you know how to play anything else?" she asked him.

"Beyond a carpenter or a gentleman of leisure?"

She motioned to the pianoforte. "I mean, do you play any other tunes?"

"Ah." His eyes were particularly beguiling when he grinned. "If I have sheet music, I can manage uncomplicated tunes."

Sheet music must have been the Americanism for printed music. She took up those few that she had found and brought them over to the instrument, retaking her seat there. "A few of these have proven simple enough for me to begin learning them. A couple are very complicated."

He looked through them. His light-brown brow tugged low, and his mouth tipped in a bit of a frown. Heavens, he was handsome. She could hardly countenance how very perfect his teeth were. Most everyone's teeth had some imperfection to them. But not his.

"This notation style is very unfamiliar," he said. "It's, no doubt, very accurate."

"Is music written differently in America?" she asked.

"Eventually," he muttered.

"Eventually?" she repeated, confused.

"This *is* different from what I'm used to," he said. "It may take a few of my 'gentleman of leisure' evenings to learn how to read it well enough to play it." He set the music atop the pianoforte. "Once I know a tad more about the hours I'm expected to work and when people will actually be here, I will sort out whether that seems a good way to spend an evening."

"Has this been a terribly unpleasant way to spend *this* evening?" She had thought their conversation had been congenial; talking with him had helped ease some of her anxieties. And listening to his admittedly inexpert tune had proven enjoyable.

Her question proved a bad idea, as it turned his smile on her, which only added to its potency. "Not terribly unpleasant at all."

"For me either. And I've heard a tune I didn't know before."

"We have the entirety of the summer season for me to teach it to you."

Her breath caught. "You would consider staying the entire time? Working here and helping for the next few months?"

He shrugged. "It is my best option at the moment."

That was a relief in so many ways. "When my uncle and the solicitor return, they'll need to see that improvements have been made and that things are functioning as they ought. Your efforts in that area would help ever so much."

"I am here to take on whatever role makes the most sense."

"You can play some music, and you can obviously swim. You are a carpenter and a gentleman of leisure. Have you any other skills?"

"Is this an audition or a friendly conversation?"

"It must be a friendly conversation, as I haven't the least idea what an 'audition' is," she said.

"Everyone here is far too method," he said with a laugh. While she wasn't certain what he'd meant by that, his laugh brought hers bubbling to the surface. He stood up from his chair and stepped slightly away from the pianoforte. "I think it would behoove me to let you know that I am an exceptional dancer."

"Are you? Do people dance in America?"

"Do we dance in America?" His scoffing expression was so overly done, it only broadened her smile. "You tell me, Miss Amelia Archibald." And he proceeded to twist and flail about in the oddest assortment of movements that didn't look at all like dancing. Had she seen him doing this from a distance, she would have assumed he had a bee in his trousers.

He stopped abruptly and burst out in the most joyous sounding laughter. "I can tell by your expression that you are far from impressed."

Amelia assumed a theatrically earnest look. "I am still waiting for the part where you demonstrate your dancing skills."

That made him laugh harder. She'd never met anyone quite like him. They hardly knew each other, yet he already felt more like a friend than people she'd known her entire life. Fate seldom showed her kindness, but it seemed poised to do so at last.

The room suddenly shook with thunder. Amelia closed her eyes and breathed through the rumble.

"Do you not like thunderstorms?" Mr. Summerfield asked.

"I don't like *the ocean*," she said, "and storms make it very angry."

"You don't like the ocean, and yet you've accepted a position on an island?"

"It was not my idea."

"That seems to be the most common way of finding oneself at Guilford."

Though the wind continued to howl outside, she was able to open her eyes again and breathe. The waves would be loud that night, and she wasn't entirely sure she would sleep. But for the moment, she was somewhat calm.

"Are there specific things you need me to work on during my carpentry hours?" he asked.

"I have a list."

With another one of those smiles that sent her heart fluttering, he said, "I don't even have to guess at my assignment? How refreshing."

"There may be some things I have not sorted or discovered yet."

"And when does everyone else arrive?"

"I'm not entirely certain." She shifted on the stool. Thoughts of her uncle and the solicitor returning made her too anxious to sit still. "It could be within the week. It could be a fortnight."

"There's not a set date?" That clearly surprised him.

She would eventually have to fill him in on more of the details of the situation. But for the moment, she was so grateful that he was willing to help that she didn't want to risk undermining that.

"No one will come to Guilford until the sea road is above water again," she said. "And it takes time for it to dry out sufficiently for travel."

"After which, people can come and go again."

Come and go. *And go.* If only she were permitted to do so.

Chapter 9

Kip couldn't remember the last time he'd spent a night plunking out tunes on a piano and just talking. His days were usually filled with scrolling on his phone or streaming something online. But his phone was probably somewhere at the bottom of the ocean, and there were no computers or televisions anywhere on Guilford. There were also no outlets, no lightbulbs, no cameras. There wasn't even electricity. And to his horror, no plumbing.

He'd finally gotten desperate the day before and gone on a search to discover how it was that he was meant to take care of business. What he'd found was an outhouse. And he'd discovered it because he'd spied Mick and, later, Marsh stepping out of it, having made use of the "facilities." Not the sort of bare-bones campground bathroom with a flush toilet in an otherwise empty room. It was an honest-to-goodness, no-toilet-paper, no-sink, wooden-bench-over-a-hole-in-the-ground outhouse.

If he hadn't lost his phone in the world's biggest dunk tank, Kip would have sent Malcolm a series of devastating GIFs over that discovery. And if not for the fact that such an authentic setting would actually make him more convincing when Osbourne eventually visited, Kip would have quit right there on the bench.

Amelia—it felt too strange *thinking* of her as "Miss Archibald," even if he'd be required to speak of and to her in the formality of the nineteenth-century—had indicated that the place was struggling. But that wasn't much of a mystery.

What tourist would want to spend an entire day on an island where their only option for facilities was a literal outhouse? And many historical and cultural sites around the UK had tea shops attached so visitors could linger over a bite to eat. Guilford House was so dedicated to history that the kitchens for the house itself were historic. And the food he'd had thus far had kind of felt too authentic as well. He assumed the village was more updated, and people came out to the island for brief jaunts and tours rather than spending an entire day there. Once the sea road was accessible again, he intended to go see if he could switch roles and do something in the village instead. Surely Osbourne could be just as impressed with him in a location with plumbing.

Still, he'd enjoyed himself the night before, which had helped him feel more patient with the situation. It had also made him worry about Amelia. She'd spoken of herself in terms of being trapped in this job. Her career had likely not gone as she'd hoped; he hadn't heard of her, and he knew a lot of people in the industry in the UK. Maybe her aspirations weren't in acting but in history. Still, to take a position on an island when she was afraid of water seemed unnecessarily torturous.

Maybe she could be reassigned to the village as well.

She'd provided him with a list of things that needed repairing around the place. It was exactly the sort of carpentry he would have expected a man of olden times to work on: furniture that was unsteady, broken balusters, split stair treads. Nowhere on the list was anything like "wire the house for electricity" or "install a toilet." He wasn't an electrician or a plumber, so he would have struggled with that, but he felt like it should have at least been thought of.

He nailed the list to a wall in the tool shed, then made his way toward the lighthouse. He needed to return Mr. Ivers's clothes. If there had been such a thing as a washing machine on this site, he would have cleaned the clothes before bringing them back. As it was, all he could really do was fold them and hope they didn't stink.

Mr. Ivers had said that he lived near the lighthouse—well, he'd nodded when Kip had asked him if he lived near the lighthouse. So Kip was looking for a house somewhere close by. And if the Iverses did indeed have a child, which Mick probably wasn't wrong about, surely that house would have the most basic of amenities. Children's Services would have had something to say otherwise. With that possibility dangling in front of him, Kip was determined to go form something of a friendship with the man he had only two days before assumed was a serial killer.

He watched the water lapping against the rocky shore below as he made his way along an island path. His eyes wandered now and then out to the horizon and the Channel beyond. He even sometimes spun about to look behind him at the distant shore of the mainland. It was a shame Amelia was afraid of the ocean. This place was beautiful. He could understand why someone had built a home here. At the time, things like the ability to run electrical wire or set up internet access hadn't needed to be taken into account.

As he drew closer to the far side of the island, he spotted Mick scrambling over some rocks in the midst of some sort of adventure. Why was it Children's Services hadn't taken him into care yet? He was orphaned; Kip was absolutely certain the boy hadn't invented that as part of his character's history. He lived on this island in the company of adults who clearly didn't rein him in or really look after him. Kip didn't think it was neglect or indifference; it seemed to simply be the arrangement of things. And even if Mick were employed to portray the island's resident orphaned scamp, there were laws to protect him from being overworked or put in dangerous circumstances. It was worrying... and weird.

A rise in the path revealed a humble house not too far distant from the lighthouse. Smoke rose from a stone chimney. It was precisely the sort of opening shot that would have been used in a drama about life on the rugged shores of England in centuries gone by. Kip could practically hear any number of the directors who had undertaken various episodes of *The Beau* expounding on how perfect it was. Perhaps it was the view that kept people coming back to Guilford, even without any of the amenities. If Kip could negotiate a new character for himself, one who occasionally visited the island but didn't have to actually live there, he might be able to survive the summer.

He made his way to the door of the little cottage and gave a quick knock. If his previous encounters with Mr. Ivers were any indication, he would need to do all the talking. And it would be a short visit. But hopefully long enough to spot an electrical outlet or beg for a chance to use their bathroom. He would never again look at a toilet without tremendous gratitude.

The door was opened, but it wasn't Mr. Ivers who stood on the other side. It was a woman, likely about Kip's same age, with a small child on her hip. Mrs. Ivers, no doubt. Not knowing if she, too, was a super fan of the never-be-out-of-character approach that the rest of this place took, Kip chose to stick with the gentleman-of-the-manner role he had played for so long.

He took off the tricorn hat he'd been wearing since finding it in the trunk and tucked it against his chest. With his other hand, he held Mr. Ivers's clothing. "Pardon the interruption to your day,

Mrs. Ivers, but I've come to return the clothing your husband so generously lent me upon my arrival."

A look of understanding flashed over her face. He did think he'd guessed her age right, but she had the look of someone who'd experienced a lot in those thirty-something years. Her head twitched him inside, and he gladly accepted. He took a quick gander at the wall near the door. No light switch. Another quick look around showed a few lanterns and unlit candles. The windows were uncurtained, allowing sunlight in, the only source of light in the place. It was not promising for his search for civilization.

"Where would you like me to place the clothing?" he asked.

Again, she motioned with her head, this time toward a small bureau. "In there'll do."

Here, at least, was something he didn't have to worry about not doing historically accurate enough. He crossed to the chest, pulled open the top drawer, and set the items inside along with the other items of clothing in there.

He turned back around in time to see Mr. Ivers step in. He offered his wife a smile, which detracted from the potential-mass-murderer vibe he had given off before.

"Sir's brought back your clothes," Mrs. Ivers said. "Him's younger than you said."

"I don't think him actually is," Mr. Ivers answered. "I only think him's not aged as much as most do."

"Could be."

It felt like the early-nineteenth-century equivalent of wondering who someone's plastic surgeon was. If he knew how to say it in the vocabulary of the era they were pretending it was, he would have wondered aloud which tabloids they'd been reading.

Mr. Ivers took hold of his little child, then turned to face Kip.

"You have a rowboat," Kip said. "Do you ever use it to get to the village when the road's underwater?"

"I do," he said.

"Any chance I could convince you to take me along if you're heading there before the road is usable?" He offered a friendly smile, unsure if Mr. Ivers wondered about *Kip*'s tendency to murder massive numbers of people. His smile had smoothed over a lot of things over the years.

It didn't work this time.

"Taking you'd be too dangerous," Mr. Ivers said.

"Why would it be dangerous?"

"Because I suspect you haven't sorted it out yet. And until you do, the fewer people you see, the better."

"Figured what out yet?"

The Ivers exchanged heavy glances, the type people used when they both knew something, were fully aware the people around them didn't, and suspected that was going to be a significant problem.

"I've sorted out that Guilford is a strange place," Kip said. "The trunk of clothes I was given offered a few clues as to what I am meant to be doing here. Am I missing something else?"

The real question was, *How much* was he missing? He simply wasn't being told enough to take on his role with any degree of expertise.

"How different is what you've seen on Guilford to what you saw before coming here?" Mrs. Ivers asked. "Is it jarringly different or only little things?"

"Jarringly," Kip acknowledged. "But it's supposed to be." Of course, what he'd expected was not quite as drastic as what he'd found. Still, the lack of modernization might have been part of the appeal to some people.

Mr. Ivers eyed him sternly. "The truth is staring you in the face, Kipling Summerfield. It's right there looking at you. But this truth's a hard thing to see."

"You could just tell me what it is rather than speaking in riddles," Kip suggested. "I've been handed more than enough of those since coming."

Mrs. Ivers shook her head. "There's really only one truth you need just now, Mr. Summerfield. Once you sort it, all the rest will make sense."

"Terrible sense," Mr. Ivers added. A "supporting character ominously foreshadowing something" speech delivered in only two words. The man might not be a serial killer, but he was proving himself an impressive actor.

Another knock sounded at the door. The Iverses exchanged yet another glance, this time one of surprise and confusion as opposed to "this guy we're talking to is a moron."

"Who do you suppose that is?" Mrs. Ivers asked.

"This is Guilford," her husband answered. "Half the options are inside already."

"How many people are on Guilford during open days?" Kip asked Mrs. Ivers as her husband stepped over to the door.

"Can't say that I understand what you're asking," she said. Either she, too, was a tremendously good actress, or she legitimately couldn't make sense of the very simple question.

An actor learned to recognize when other people were acting, in part because they were constantly trying to do better and learn from those who proved great. This was something else.

"The truth is staring you in the face, Kipling Summerfield," Mr. Ivers had said.

The truth of *what*?

Amelia stood on the other side of the Iverses' now-open door. She carried a small basket and wore an uncertain smile.

"I cut some herbs in the garden today," she said. "I thought you might be able to use some." Her explanation was offered almost in the form of a question. And he knew the look in her eyes: it was the "Please like me" look he himself had often worn when going to auditions or wandering into a group of fellow actors. It was the look of someone who hoped to make a friend, or at least a good impression, but had reason to believe she probably wouldn't.

Mr. Ivers gave a simple, silent nod. The man was not one to usually be friendly or talkative, that much was clear. Mrs. Ivers's smile was quick and fleeting as she accepted the offering and slipped into a corner where a small table held jars and pots of what appeared to be other herbs. It was only then that Kip realized this place didn't appear to have a kitchen. It was one big, open room, with a single door leading off. That door was ajar enough for him to see a tiny bedroom on the other side, barely large enough to hold the bed inside.

This was the entirety of their house. No sink. No stove. A quick glance at the baseboards and around the walls revealed no electricity. Again, he didn't see a bathroom. They were legitimately living the lives of a poor couple in perhaps *not even* 1800. And they had a tiny child here with them. Why was that being permitted? Who would even choose this situation?

"The truth is staring you in the face, Kipling Summerfield."

He shook that off.

"I have a long list of repairs at the house." He dipped his head to all of them. "Good day."

They offered very quickly muttered words of farewell. Neither of the Iverses had been gushing with friendliness before Amelia's arrival, but what little welcome had been there seemed long gone now. Maybe when he was alone at the lighthouse, he was to play the role of local carpenter and laborer, which eased some of the class restrictions that were so stringent at the time—*thanks, historical accuracy*. But when Amelia was there, he would be playing the part of gentleman visiting the manor and would be treated accordingly.

This place was going to give him whiplash.

He stepped back outside and plopped his hat on his head once more. It fit snug enough that even with the stiff breeze, it was unlikely to be torn off his head. He flipped the collar of his wool coat up. It offered something of a buffer against that same cold breeze.

He'd not gone more than a step when Amelia's voice called out to him. "I'll walk back with you, Mr. Summerfield."

He stopped and waited for her to catch up. She moved slowly and with some difficulty, but there was also confidence in her use of the cane. Was it acting? He was all but certain it wasn't.

"The Iverses can be very standoffish," she said with a tone of apology. "I don't know if they were very welcoming to you."

"We spoke before you came, and while they were perhaps not the most vociferous of people"—he'd learned the word *vociferous* on *The Beau*—"I didn't feel ignored."

That brought her hauntingly beautiful brown eyes to him with a look of both hurt and confusion. "Truly? They spoke openly with you? They were friendly?"

"In their own way."

She walked alongside him, her basket swinging in the hand that did not hold her cane. Her eyes were set on the path ahead, though he suspected she wasn't really looking at anything in particular. "They're usually very suspicious of people who aren't from the area. I'm still attempting to convince them that I needn't be treated with such wariness. You seem to have managed it in less than two days."

"That, Miss Archibald, is because I am an incredibly affable fellow." He used a feigned tone of arrogance that had won him a few hearts when Tennyson Lamont had employed it.

Her smile blossomed, one of the better reviews he'd had of a performance. "You're also a very amusing fellow. I don't know if you realize that."

"My friend Malcolm says I'm sometimes more obnoxious than amusing."

"He must not be much of a friend if he calls you obnoxious. Unless, of course, you truly are an offensive and objectionable person."

Note to self: Obnoxious was, apparently, a stronger word two hundred years earlier, and Amelia wasn't opposed to calling him out on his word choices.

"The word is clearly used differently here."

"Then he was not being unkind?" She seemed pleased at the possibility.

"I cannot imagine Malcolm being unkind to anyone."

"At the moment, I would say the same about you, Kipling Summerfield."

He knew he didn't hide his surprise at that declaration. He did consider himself pretty easy to get along with, but he hadn't known her for even two whole days yet. How had he made a good impression already?

"You are in a less-than-ideal situation after a horrible ordeal in the ocean." She shuddered as she spoke the last word. "Despite all that, I've never seen nor heard of you being unkind to anyone here."

"Had you expected me to be?"

"A lot of people are."

He studied her a moment, his heart unexpectedly going out to her. "Are these people unkind to you in particular?"

A fleeting and heartbreakingly sad smile tipped her mouth. "More often than I'd prefer."

A particularly large wave crashed against the shore below them. Her eyes darted toward the sea, and he saw her stiffen. Perhaps a buffer from the view would help. Subtly, so he didn't embarrass her, he managed to get on the other side of her, so he was between her and the ocean.

"If the Iverses aren't very accommodating of people not from here, what do they do when all the visitors arrive?" he asked.

Being the grumpy lighthouse keepers might simply be part of the act. But the place was already not overly inviting. Maybe that was something else that needed to change if they were to save the place from bankruptcy.

"We don't get visitors other than my uncle and my late grandfather's solicitor. And I'm the only one they come to check on."

He hadn't meant the owners and managers of the place, which was what they'd established *uncle* and *solicitor* were code for.

"I meant all the visitors to the historical site," he said.

Once again, she looked at him with complete confusion. People kept doing that. For some reason, it bothered him more that *she* kept doing it.

"There's nothing on Guilford but the estate and the lighthouse," she said. "There's no . . . historical site."

There was a point at which a person took keeping in character too far. No one was telling him what he was meant to do or what was expected of him. He couldn't even find out when the site was going to open for the season or what each day would look like. And he suspected that if he even tried to ask why in the world there was no electricity or plumbing or how he could go about replacing his phone, they would all just look at him with that same blank expression and tell him they didn't know what he meant.

The path he and Amelia were walking split into the main one leading up toward the house and the smaller one leading toward his work shed. "I will see you this afternoon, when I'm permitted to be in my second role of the day."

"You sound upset," she said.

The declaration contained a hint of worry, and guilt tugged at him. He didn't think she'd been acting when she'd said people were often unkind to her. He didn't want to give her reason to worry that he was going to join those ranks just because he was slightly exhausted. "I'm not angry."

But she still looked wary.

"I am a tad frustrated," he said. "I just wish there were someone on this island who would talk to me authentically without playing a part."

Chapter 10

Kip had once been voted one of the industry's nicest actors. But after another dinner of strange and unfamiliar food, which he once again chose to eat in his room, and another frustrating trip to the oh-so-luxurious outhouse, he was ready to have an on-set meltdown for the ages.

He didn't grow frustrated easily. Even when he was annoyed or anxious, he worked through it quickly and moved on. But Guilford Island was starting to get on his nerves.

If he still had a phone—and electricity—he would send some very colorful descriptions of the situation Malcolm had arranged for him. Then Malcolm would probably rent a helicopter and come get him. It might be entertaining to watch the method-acting crowd attempt to interact with a helicopter while in character.

He didn't want to go to the drawing room and be "Kipling Summerfield, gentleman of antique leisure." He didn't fully trust himself not to be frustrated, and Amelia seemed particularly in need of patience and humor at the moment.

He lit a candle on the small round table by the window in his bedchamber and plopped down in the chair next to it with the journal that had been in his costume trunk. That, at least, was meant to give him some idea of who he was supposed to be while at Guilford.

He flipped past the first entry he'd already read, the one about the people being strange and the writer thinking there might be others in a similar situation. It was too on the nose, but he could forgive the poor writing since it was the only reason he had any idea what was going on.

The second entry was dated the day after the first one, 350 or so years ago. The re-enacting was supposed to be taking place a century after the journal was dated. The set designer had a good eye for detail, but the journal's slightly worn appearance wasn't quite right. It should look older. Still, the designer had also done a very believable job of writing in old-timey script.

They'd opted, in *The Beau*, for an only slightly outdated style so it would be easier to read. But this was Guilford Island. Authenticity was more important than anything else.

Kip had to work at deciphering it, but what else was he going to do with his time?

> 13 *May* 1692
>
> *My initial feelings of confusion, I assumed, were the result of discombobulation after having spent as long as I did in the water. My physical disorientation, I felt safe in assuming, had also caused a mental disorientation that had lasted longer. But I have been here a week, and I am more confused than ever.*

This character, who was meant to be informing Kip's, had also been fished from the water. But that hadn't been planned. There was no way the director of this historical site could have guessed that would happen. It was more than strange; it was unnerving.

The questions I ask of the resident family are met with confusion. I do not think it is a matter of them not knowing the answer but rather not even understanding why I would ask the question.

Also unnervingly familiar.

When I speak to them of very ordinary and common things, they respond with more bafflement still. They cannot possibly be ignorant of the very simple things I have mentioned, and yet that is precisely how they respond.

Could it be that I am the victim of a very complex plot? I can think of nothing I have done to deserve such treatment. What could be accomplished by undertaking such treatment of a hapless traveler?

The people in this place are pleasant despite this odd behavior. The island itself is beautiful. Still, I find myself in a position of wishing to offer a warning to anyone else the cruel tides might bring to this place of mystery and confusion.

Something is very wrong on Guilford Island.

So he was *supposed* to feel confused and frustrated? Why couldn't he have just been given a character sheet? He could at least have been given some tourist talking points and a list of open days and hours. Maybe whoever concocted this approach had assumed Kip would arrive with a working phone and could just pull up the webpage and check those things.

17 May 1692

I am choosing to record on this day a most unsettling conversation I had with a member of the resident family.

ECHOES OF THE SEA

I asked the youngest gentleman of the family, who had shown himself to be of a kind disposition and entirely in command of his faculties, what the date was. I felt certain, despite my experiences in the sea, that I knew the date, or would be, at the very least, within a day or two of accurate. I had asked in the hope of correcting my entries in this diary, should they be incorrect, but his answer has upended me.

He tells me it is the 21st of August—in the year 1773. He said it without hesitation, without affect. Indeed, his answer was given as though he were hardly even thinking, precisely as expected from a person being asked such a mundane question.

While I am not entirely certain of the day, I know the month to be May. Of greatest upheaval to my mind, however, is that I know the year to be 1692. I know it.

I know.

Wait, time travel? Was this historical site actually some sort of fantasy-enactment amusement park? That could actually be really fun.

But no. The amount of attention given to strict historical authenticity wouldn't make sense. Having no bathroom facilities wasn't a big plus for a sci-fi park.

Kip set the diary on the table beside him, thinking. A person who hadn't time traveled but thought he had . . . Was he supposed to be playing someone who was a few donuts short of a dozen? Maybe he was supposed to have sustained brain damage from nearly drowning in the sea.

But the owners of the place couldn't have guessed he would be tossed into the ocean by a freak storm.

None of it made sense. Not a single bit of it.

Yet the entries matched so closely what he was experiencing that he couldn't dismiss them. The other people there were pretending to be confused by the things he said when none of it was actually confusing. And then they pretended to be even more confused by the fact that *he* was confused by their confusion. Just like the journal described.

Guilford didn't make sense as a fantasy role-play excursion.

So what was it, really?

The door to his room flew open without warning. The sudden rush of air blew out his candle, but there was still dim light from the fire. He hadn't yet gotten the knack of igniting it with flint and steel, so he spent a lot of time in the evenings hoping it didn't go out. Again, the adherence to historical accuracy was way over the top.

Mick came bounding over to him. First, Jane the morning before, followed shortly by Amelia, and now Mick. He really needed to start locking his door.

The boy held out a wooden contraption of some sort, one easily held in one hand. "My toy is broken. You can fix it."

"I'm only a carpenter in the mornings."

Mick eyed him with that same look of confusion everyone here had perfected. How could he not understand the reference, even if he didn't recognize that it was kind of a funny line? Mick must have known the dual parts that Kip had been assigned.

"That was a jest, Mick," Kip said. He was pretty sure *jest* was a more historical word to say than *joke*. But what did he know? He was as confused as the rest of the cast was pretending to be.

He eyed the "toy" as Mick handed it over to him. It wasn't something he was familiar with. Though there had been child characters on *The Beau*, he hadn't paid much attention to any toys they had played with in scenes. There were some moving parts that he suspected were meant to be flapped back and forth. One of those parts was hanging loose.

"I saw a bird," Mick said. "But it wasn't a gull. I usually just see gulls. I don't know what kind of bird it was."

"Did you try googling it?" Kip asked while he studied the toy.

"Did I *what*?"

Kip rolled his eyes. Always in character, even the kids.

"The Iverses' baby is trying to say 'Mick.'" The boy rolled right into a new topic. "All him says now is 'mum' and 'da.'"

"Maybe we can teach the baby to say 'Kip.' That's an easy name." The hanging part of the toy did seem to be the part that wasn't working.

"Is that your name?" Mick asked. "Kip?"

He nodded. "Short for Kipling."

Again, Mick jumped topics. "Miss looked sad tonight. I don't like when her looks sad."

That pulled Kip's attention away from the misbehaving toy and back to Mick once more. "Did Miss Archibald say why she's sad?"

He hardly knew her, and she was participating in this make-Kip-think-he's-losing-his-mind strategy, but she hadn't been acting when she'd confessed to being afraid of the ocean and feeling trapped in this job and having a long history of being mistreated.

"Her didn't say. Probably her's lonely. It's only Mrs. Jagger, Mr. Marsh, and Jane here at the house with she."

"Miss Archibald and Jane are the same age. They could be friends."

Mick looked at him like he was entirely off his rocker. "A maid and the mistress of the house?"

Were they observing the social hierarchy of the nineteenth century to the point that the person selected to play the role of mistress was relegated to isolation? The separate lives of servants and those who employed them was touched on in *The Beau*, but there was friendliness between those characters. And the actors themselves were friends.

"Jane says you have a drawing on your arm and on your chest, and it is not the sort of drawing that can be washed away. I told she a person didn't have drawings like that on their skin, but her said I was too little to know. I think her was telling tales. Why would her have ever seen your arm and chest?"

"Because I have not yet learned to lock my door."

The little boy sucked in a breath. "You *do* have a drawing that won't wash away?"

"I'm sure you've heard of tattoos." He eyed Mick, truly growing more confused at the boy's unwillingness to break character. Children on set often slipped up *during takes*.

Mick shook his head. "What's that?"

"I will not be the facilitator of your education." Kip held the toy up. "There's a pin missing from this hinge here; that's why it's not holding together. Have you seen a long, narrow piece of wood or metal, probably shaped like a cylinder?"

"What's a cylinder?"

The boy was eleven years old. He absolutely would have learned that in school by now. Which brought up another question.

"I didn't think school had broken for the summer holidays yet," Kip said. An eleven-year-old actor who was working instead of being at school was supposed to be getting schooling through an on-set tutor. Was the historical site flouting that law too? "What's the date?"

"The Iverses' baby had his birthday a week ago. That'd make today the sixteenth of May."

That couldn't be right. It was the beginning of April. Maybe it was May 16 in this fantasy world they were all creating, but why change the baby's birthday?

Kip needed to get Mick to step out of character for a minute. "How long have you worked at Guilford? Is this your first summer?"

"I told you yesterday I've been here years and years."

"And do you always begin your summers here this early?"

"Summer starts when nature wants summer to start. I'm here either way."

"You're here year-round?" That didn't make sense. The site wasn't open all year.

"Where else would I go?" Mick shook his head. "You're strange, Mr. Kip."

I'm strange? "What's the year?"

"You don't know what year it is?"

"I do," Kip said. "I'm wondering what year *you* are going to say it is."

"1803."

The site was re-creating life in 1803; that was helpful information. "What year is it really though?"

"1803."

"I mean in reality. In real life."

"1803." Mick's confusion was giving way to what almost looked like worry, exactly like it would if the year *were* 1803 and someone didn't believe it.

Kip would have to suggest Malcolm recommend Mick to casting directors. The kid's acting was incredible. Of course, he'd have to warn them the boy was unnervingly method.

"Meet me at my work cottage in the morning, and I'll see if I have something to replace the missing pin." He handed the toy back to Mick. "If not, I'll have to make something to replace it."

Mick looked partially disappointed but not entirely discouraged. "Yigh, Mr. Kip." It wasn't a word Kip knew, but context told him Mick had agreed to the plan.

As Mick made his way to the door once more, Kip called out to him, "Where is it you live, Mick?"

"In an attic room," he said.

"They make you sleep in the attic?"

Mick chuckled. "Not the attic with all the old, dusty things, Mr. Kip. An attic room, where the servants would be if there were enough of they."

"And you're up there all alone? Who's looking after you?"

"I look after myself." There was an implied "duh" in that. On that cheeky remark, Mick continued out of the room.

A place with no electricity. A young family raising an infant in a house that wouldn't pass even a basic safety inspection. An eleven-year-old boy who didn't seem to have any schooling, who ran wild on an island with no safety precautions, and who lived alone in a house with no one to look after him.

1803.

It was authentic to that time. Too authentic.

"The truth is staring you in the face, Kipling Summerfield. It's right there looking at you. But this truth's a hard thing to see."

His eyes slid to the journal still lying on the table. The character who had written it had insisted he'd found himself in a different year. He'd written, using old-fashioned words and handwriting, that he had time traveled. Even if that was supposed to be the storyline enacted this summer at the historical site, sticking to it in a way that endangered children didn't make sense. Something else was going on at Guilford.

"*Something is very wrong on Guilford Island.*" More of the journal writer's words flooded back through his mind.

1803.

Nope.

But there was absolutely nothing modern in this place, including people's worldview. It was almost as if they were actually in 1803.

Nope. Nope. Nope.

He snatched up the journal and tossed it into the drawer of the bedside table, then shoved the drawer closed.

Nope.

This place was weird and confusing, and he wouldn't be sad when the summer was over. But it was just a stupid job, something he and Malcolm would laugh about later.

"*The truth is staring you in the face.*"

Nope.

Absolutely not.

Chapter 11

In the twenty years Amelia had lived in her aunt and uncle's home, she'd very seldom truly had her feelings hurt. Looking back, she felt it was as much a testament to the fact that they were more indifferent than cruel as it was to her resilience. She'd never been one to dwell overly long or overly much on slights or insults. She didn't dismiss people's misbehavior or refuse to acknowledge that people could be hurtful. She simply hadn't the disposition for dwelling on such things. But that history made it all the more baffling that her heart still ached the next morning when she thought of the long hours she'd spent in the drawing room, waiting for Mr. Summerfield to join her there the evening before.

The evening they'd spent at the pianoforte had, she thought, been pleasant. They'd had a friendly conversation walking back from the lighthouse. She'd thought he had developed some degree of a fondness for her and would have looked forward, just as she had, to spending time together.

She'd waited for hours, but he'd never come to the drawing room. And she'd been very alone, as she so often was.

As she made her way to the walled garden this morning after breakfast, she leaned not only on her cane but on her tried-and-true method for regaining her equilibrium after life set her figuratively off balance.

"This morning, I am grateful for . . ." The sound of waves crashing made it difficult to think. The frustrating realization that her heart was broken only added to that struggle. "I am grateful that Kipling Summerfield is kind even if he isn't . . . interested."

She refused to ponder her choice of the word *interested*. It was far more comfortable to focus on the garden.

With so much else to do, tending the gardens seemed, on the surface, like a wasted effort. But she'd discovered that improving the grounds of Guilford helped the house itself seem in less disrepair. When viewing the house from the area of the garden that she had tamed and tended and fixed, it looked more impressive. The next time her uncle and the solicitor came to check, she would make certain they were able to see the house from the right angle in the garden.

It would help; she knew it would.

And her next task in the garden was trimming a misshapen and overgrown boxwood. It was something of a tall ask, literally and figuratively. She didn't feel entirely equal to it, but it had to be done.

In her gardening shed, she tied on her apron. She put on her wide straw hat and tied it in place with the sturdy ribbon attached to it, then tucked the gloves into her apron pocket. Amelia took the old but serviceable hedge shears from their nail on the wall and tucked them into the large pocket of her apron as well. The more difficult part was going to be transporting the ladder.

It wasn't truly heavy, but its length and width made it awkward. And she couldn't carry it with just one hand, which meant she couldn't use her cane. She could walk without her cane, though doing so was precarious and necessarily slow. But what choice was there? She alone looked after the garden, and the *entirety* of the estate had to be put to rights.

She began the painstaking journey from the shed along the garden paths. An extra moment's care accompanied every step of her right foot; she needed to make certain her balance wasn't off or that the damp pathway wasn't dangerously slick. She also needed to be very careful not to get entangled in the overgrown shrubs and plants and even more careful not to do damage to the area of the garden she had worked so hard on already.

By the time she reached the boxwood, she was already tired. Guilford, she sometimes suspected, was actively trying to crush her. But life had tried that often enough that she knew herself able to rise to the occasion.

"Today, I'm grateful to know I'm not easily defeated."

The boxwood was at least two feet taller than she was. She was actually a very ordinary and common height for a woman, but people were forever describing her as small, likely owing to the fact that she was "wispy," as her aunt so often put it, and quiet, as a poor relation was generally required to be.

She turned the ladder upright and leaned the top into the boxwood shrub. She had to move it a few times before she found a position that seemed likely to hold. She even nudged it a smidge so that it was wedged between a couple of branches. That would do well enough for her to see to her task. The day was misty, which meant the ladder was already wet. And there was a breeze, which simply blew more moisture onto the rungs.

It was more than mildly dangerous. But she couldn't simply wait around for the weather to improve or an army of helpers to unexpectedly arrive. No one was willing to come to Guilford, and without people to do the work, the work couldn't get done, and if the work didn't get done, she could be labeled a failure, incapable of seeing to the inheritance that would be taken from her.

She had just under five months remaining in which to work a miracle. And miracles, in her experience, were fickle things.

It was enough to make a person want to quit before she'd even begun. That, she knew with perfect, horrible clarity, was what her grandfather had counted on. He had set her up to fail.

And that made her ever more determined to try. This was her one chance, and it was supposed to be no chance at all. Even if she did fail in the end, she would do so having accomplished more than any of them would have ever believed she could.

She took a fortifying breath, then stepped onto the lowermost rung with her left foot. The next step would be the telling one, it requiring her to depend on her less reliable right foot. She set it on the rung beside her left. Carefully, she raised her left once more. Her balance held long enough for her to step onto the next rung.

Following her newly established approach, she made her way a few rungs up, stopping at the first place she needed to begin trimming. She pulled the hedge shears from her apron pocket and set to work. She pushed repeatedly from her mind the knowledge that, behind her, was a garden with near-endless work needing to be done. Of course, in front of her was a house with even more needing to be done.

She continued carefully up the ladder, stopping to trim the shrub as she went. A few times, the wind picked up, and she had to pause and hold tight to the ladder and the shrub she was trimming. But she kept at it.

Her inheritance would let her purchase a home of her own, and she would find one not surrounded by the sea. She would not be left trying to stay ahead of nature and the relentless destruction that time inevitably wreaked on a property that wasn't maintained. And she wouldn't be so alone. She could find a home in a neighborhood, with other families who would welcome her and be her friends, where she could walk to the other homes nearby and pass an afternoon in friendly conversation. She wouldn't be dependent on her aunt and uncle, required to adhere to their schedule and their tasks for her. And she would never again have to bow to the dictates of her late grandfather.

A sudden, sharp whip of wind moved the entire shrub and the ladder with it. She grabbed hold of the sturdiest branch she could find and held fast. Her unreliable foot didn't have the sure purchase she needed, and she was high enough on the ladder that she was now trimming the top of the shrub. That would be a long way to fall.

Amelia held her breath, kept her white-knuckle grip, and waited for the wind to die down. But it didn't. If anything, it seemed ever more determined to toss her to the ground below. A quick glance at the sky revealed that it had turned ominous. She had been told time and again that this area of the Channel, the section stretching from the shoreline around Guilford all the way to the far side of Loftstone Island, was the most prone to sudden and violent storms than any inlet along the southern coast. Some ascribed the tendency to ancient curses and unexplained magic. Others insisted it was to do with the geography. In that moment, she didn't care what was causing it; she simply wanted it to stop.

And almost as suddenly as the thought occurred to her, the ladder grew very steady once more. She looked down and saw Mr. Summerfield holding the base of the ladder.

"What the blazes are you doing?" he demanded.

She was so grateful not to be left clinging to a questionably steady shrub that she would have forgiven him an even sharper tone than he was using. "I'm trimming the shrub," she said.

"On such a windy day?" he asked incredulously.

"Every day on Guilford is a windy day." Indeed, if she had to wait for ideal weather to get work done, she would be a failure without question.

"Then at least make certain you're undertaking this wind-challenged task with someone else nearby to help make certain you don't fall to your death."

"I don't know that I would actually die," she said. "I might break an arm or something."

"I would like to request that we not discover what that 'something' might be." He didn't seem like he meant to abandon her there. If anything, his grip on the ladder appeared to tighten.

"I don't have very much left to trim. If you'll hold the ladder steady, I think I could finish quickly."

"I will hold on tight if you promise to as well."

"A good arrangement."

With him there, she felt safe resuming her work. She snipped quickly but carefully. She leaned more on her left foot than her right, not wishing to press her luck beyond bearing.

"I hope whoever assigned you this role realizes this is a health and safety nightmare."

That was a very succinct way of putting it. Her health and her safety were most certainly on the line, and not just in the matter of shrubbery trimming.

Satisfied that she'd done enough, Amelia began descending. Her right foot slipped a degree, but the ladder was so steady that she was able to quickly regain her footing.

"Please, be careful," Mr. Summerfield said.

"Contrary to the impression my uncooperative right foot is giving, I am being exceptionally careful." She reached the bottom of the ladder. His position, holding it in place, meant she arrived on the ground with his arms very nearly around her. Amelia looked at him, meaning to thank him but finding herself too mesmerized by his dark eyes to say anything or step away.

"I will understand if you'd rather not answer," he said, "but may I ask why it is your right foot is so uncooperative?"

"I was born with a twisted foot," she said.

"Can nothing be done for it?"

She shook her head. "The cane helps my balance. And my shoes have to be made with some adjustments. Other than that, I make do."

A surprised confusion tugged at his features. "Make do? I would think it could be fixed, at least to a degree."

"How could it possibly be fixed?" One didn't simply *un*twist bones.

That seemed to just confuse him more. "It can't? At all?"

"No, but I'm used to it. It complicates things, but it doesn't stop me from doing most of the things I set my mind to."

"Like climb ladders in storms because . . . why not?" A corner of his mouth tugged upward. He wasn't going to berate or belittle her. How refreshing.

"Someone has to climb ladders." She shrugged. "It might as well be me."

He stepped back from the ladder, allowing her to step away as well. "Once the road is accessible again, how many additional people will be coming out to Guilford?"

She shook her head. "No one in the village wants to come."

He took up the ladder and walked alongside her as they made their way back to the gardening shed. She might not have been carrying the ladder, but she was still without her cane, so their progress was very slow. He didn't seem frustrated though.

"I can't really blame the villagers for preferring to be in the village," she said. "I would prefer to be there myself."

He looked over at her as they approached the shed. "When the road is uncovered, we can go to the village and see if that can be arranged."

"I have to stay on Guilford Island; that cannot be changed."

Mr. Summerfield leaned the ladder up against the tallest wall of the shed. "Surely you cannot be legally held here against your will."

"The terms of the arrangement I agreed to *are* legally binding. I have a solicitor's confirmation of that."

"You agreed to this?"

She knew that tone. He felt she'd been foolish, perhaps even weak. Far too many people, at least those whose safety and existence didn't depend on being unobtrusive, looked at that as proof that poor relations were naturally weaker or not trying hard enough.

"I have not simply shrugged and said, 'Whatever someone else chooses, that's what I will accept.'" She leaned against the worktable. Her cane was doing the same. "This is how I can gain my independence. This is how I can finally claim my future. I understand the trade-off, and if I can manage it, my current misery will be worth enduring in the end."

"Worth it even if you die trimming a shrub?" He shook his head. "Imagine that etched into your grave marker."

Relief washed over her immediately. He wasn't going to continue arguing that she had been foolish or weak-minded. He was already teasing her again, which she couldn't remember anyone really doing.

With the hint of a smile, she said, "I can see it already: 'Here lies Amelia Archibald, who died of shrubbery-related causes on 17th May 1803.'" She shook her head. "That would be both tragic and embarrassing."

His response wasn't a laugh. He eyed her contemplatively. Why was he never what she expected?

"You didn't come to the drawing room last night," she said hesitantly. "I'd hoped you might play that tune again."

"I still can hardly believe you haven't heard 'Heart and Soul.'"

"Music seems to be very different where you come from from what we're accustomed to here."

His attention then diverted to the papers she had nailed to the wall. It was a list of the things needing to be seen to on the grounds of Guilford, and she'd not managed to mark off hardly any of them yet. Beside the list was a hand-drawn calendar she had made, marking the entirety of the time she would be spending at Guilford. Each time she was out here, she marked off the days that had passed: forty-one so far.

Mr. Summerfield tapped her list of items. "This is far too much for you to accomplish alone."

"What choice do I have? The Iverses run the lighthouse, and that is all that can be asked of them. Marsh and Mrs. Jagger keep the house running. Jane is both the upstairs maid and the cook. Mick is just a child, though he helps where he can. And you have agreed to help with repairs around the house, which is really all I can ask of you. There's no one left but me."

"And you truly can't convince anyone in the village to relocate out here?" He turned back to face her, obviously frustrated on her behalf. That was not an experience she was familiar with.

"Some might be willing to come up the road for a very brief time," she acknowledged, "but they are not keen on being stuck here."

"That isn't an entirely unreasonable concern, I suppose."

"I certainly can't argue with the fact that being stuck on Guilford Island is not a pleasant experience. There are legends about Guilford that add to their nervousness."

He faced her with a look of curiosity. "What are these legends that keep them away? I don't know much of the story of this place."

"All anyone will say is, 'Time behaves strangely on these waters.' They seem to believe there's a dangerous magic in it."

"A friend of mine said that used to be believed hundreds of years ago," Mr. Summerfield said. "The people in the village can't possibly refuse to help you because of something no one believes in anymore."

"I don't know that I believe in magic," she said, "but there *is* something odd about Guilford Island. I want to believe it is nothing more than my dislike of the sea, but I know there is something more to it. Storms form here so quickly. And the one we had the night you arrived was very strange. The air felt different. It crackled in a way I haven't experienced before. It was . . . unnerving."

"And you aren't 'allowed' to leave this island that unnerves you so much?"

She was reluctant to simply explain to him that she'd been dropped here by a grandfather who disliked her and was at the mercy of an uncle who had some motivation to see her fail. Mr. Summerfield treated her as someone capable, and she didn't want him to stop believing that. "I only have to remain for five more months in this house that is falling apart and this island where the sea feels as though it's crashing in on me." She emptied her lungs in a quick exhalation. "I have to set the place to rights in that time, then I can leave and never look back."

Mr. Summerfield's forehead creased with concern. "No one should be able to force you to be miserable, Amelia."

Amelia. He said it as though he didn't even realize he'd used her given name. She didn't want to correct him. She hoped he would do it again. And in the privacy of her own thoughts, she suspected she would begin thinking of him as Kipling.

"I've always been at the mercy of someone's whims," she said. "That has sometimes meant being unhappy. But if I can manage this, I'll never have to be a poor relation again. I'll never have to be the one who bows to the dictates of people who dislike me."

"I'm sure we can get you a new role," he said. "Renegotiate so you don't have to stay on this island. When I next go to the village, I'll see if I can't sort something out."

"It really can't be done," she said. "I promise you it can't. Besides, once you leave, you won't come back. No one does."

"Because of the superstitions?"

"Because of me. I'm a very easy person to walk away from, Kipling Summerfield."

He reached out and took her hands. She had certainly not been expecting that. The way her heart fluttered and pounded and leaped and spun all at once caught her off guard as well. She found it a smidge difficult just to breathe.

"Firstly, you are not in any way a forgettable person. Secondly, I, too, have a very long history of people walking out on me, which makes me very reluctant to be the sort of person who abandons someone else."

"I don't want you to feel you have to stay out of a sense of guilt or pity." That would be horrible.

"I assure you, my motivation would be neither of those things." His voice had dropped a degree and grown softer, deeper. The air around them had turned warm, which was a strange thing inside this perpetually dim shed on an island where the wind never stopped blowing.

"Why would you want to stay here?" Her voice emerged as little more than a whisper.

"Because I'm discovering I like spending time with you."

His gaze held hers. She simply melted inside. There was a warmth to him, an invitation to trust and to lean on him, the unspoken promise that she could believe what he was saying. And though it likely was an unforgivable bit of foolishness, in that moment, she believed it.

Chapter 12

Kip had "fallen in love" with a girl he'd acted alongside in their high school production of *The Importance of Being Earnest*. He'd discovered in talking with others in the profession that a lot of people crushed hard on costars during their teenage years. As they grew up and understood acting better, hearts didn't grow confused as easily.

So why in the world did he feel this tug toward Amelia?

He'd known her only a few days, and the insistence among this group to stay entirely in character meant he wasn't exactly sure what was her and what was the part she was playing. Falling for someone's character was a mistake a teenager made, not a grown man who knew better.

And yet there was so much sincerity in her that he'd begun to believe he was actually seeing the real Amelia Archibald simply reframed to fit the narrative of this time and place.

And when he'd held her hand in the garden shed, her reaction had not been feigned. He knew what it looked like when someone was playing the role of smitten lady. The last few months he had been with Giselle, he'd seen it in her face more and more often. Amelia hadn't been pretending. His simple touch had at first surprised her, then softened her. And the way he had reacted to her brief touch the night before hadn't been fake either. She intrigued him more than he could have predicted, which confused him.

But it was not nearly as confusing as her easy rattling off of the date: 17th May 1803. Exactly one day after the date Mick had given him the night before that. She hadn't even needed a moment to think about it. Not just a different year but also a different month and date. But she'd just tossed it out casually and easily.

She'd said the folktales in the area insisted that time behaved weird on the ocean here.

1803.

Except Amelia really did seem genuine, even when adhering so stubbornly to her character. Kip couldn't make a lot of sense out of it.

And he'd been sincere when he'd told her he liked spending time with her. He really did. And Guilford Island had him confused enough that he really needed more information, even if he had to keep tiptoeing around it. So instead of eating his dinner in his bedroom like he'd been doing, he changed into the pirate-like fancier clothes he wore in the evening and joined Amelia in the dining room.

The dining room was a lot like the ones they'd used on *The Beau*, just smaller and with much less fancy table settings, the first sign Kip had seen that even a fleeting thought had been given to how ridiculous it was to adhere to unnecessary accuracy when there were no tourists around.

"Thank you again for holding the ladder this morning," Amelia said between bites of boiled potato. "It was good to finish trimming the boxwood, but I am grateful not to have broken any bones in the process."

"Do you resent having to work in the garden?" He'd wondered about that. It seemed like a precarious assignment for someone who wasn't totally sure on her feet.

"I love being in the garden. I always love being in gardens." Her smile was soft and sincere.

So she had a green thumb. That wasn't surprising, really. "Do you have a favorite plant?"

"In which category?"

Kip laughed lightly. "You really do love gardens."

"With all my heart," she said earnestly. "Even here, where the ocean is too loud for me to ever fully forget it's there, I love being outside in the garden."

Kip took a sip of what he'd guessed the last few days was probably watered-down wine. He had no idea why that was what this place chose to serve with dinner. Straight-up wine would be unnecessarily expensive. So why not just water?

Historical accuracy, probably.

"I can't say I know all the plant categories," Kip said, "but I'll try a few. What is your favorite . . . flower?"

"Larkspur." She didn't pause even a moment to think about it.

He had no idea what that flower even looked like, but the joy in her eyes at simply saying the name made him smile. "Do you have a favorite tree?"

She nodded. "Beech trees. There is a large, old beech tree at the house where I grew up, and it has a very low branch that dips downward and creates the perfect place to sit and read a book."

"Something I suspect you did often?"

She sighed nostalgically. "As often as I could manage. I love that tree. And the garden it is in is very peaceful."

"There was an oak tree at my house when I was growing up," he said. "I climbed it all summer long when I was little, imagining

I was Robin Hood in Sherwood Forest making daring escapes from the Sheriff of Nottingham."

Amelia's laugh was not in any way mocking or dismissive. She sounded genuinely entertained by his remembered adventures. "That must have been wonderfully diverting."

"Some of my favorite memories."

"I once tried climbing to a higher branch in the beech tree," she said. "I couldn't manage it, but I always thought it would be quite a lark sitting in the top branches of a tree."

He still found it odd that her foot couldn't be surgically fixed, or at least improved. But she'd said it couldn't be, and she would know better than he.

"Do you have a favorite carpentry project?" she asked.

He'd not really given that any thought. Carpentry was a skill he'd developed so he wouldn't starve during the starving-actor phase of his career. He didn't hate it, but it wasn't a passion of his by any stretch of the imagination.

"I once fixed a broken drawer on an armoire that belonged to my best friend Malcolm's granny. It was her grandfather's, and she was devastated that it was broken. She actually cried when I finished repairing it." That had been one of his proudest moments. "It meant a lot to Malcom to see his granny so happy. And seeing him happy meant a lot to me. That's definitely on my list of favorite projects."

"Then it isn't the work that speaks to you most; it's the opportunity to show kindness."

He smiled at her. "You make me sound like a saint."

"Are you a saint?" There was a great deal of mischief in the question.

"Malcolm probably is," Kip said. "I'm not sure why he keeps me around."

"To repair his armoires, most likely."

The very serious answer pulled a laugh from him.

"There is actually one in the east sitting room that needs repairing," Amelia said. "Perhaps you could fix it as well."

"Impossible." He sighed dramatically. "I don't know where the east sitting room is."

"I'll show you." Amelia stood.

He stood as well. "Lead the way, *mon capitaine*."

"*Parlez-vous français?*" She looked excited at the possibility.

"Sadly, no, other than a word or two." That had been a slight difficulty during *The Beau*. Apparently, during the Regency Era, the British upper class usually learned French as children. Americans who grew up lower middle class . . . not so much.

He walked beside her out of the dining room.

"You haven't been to the east sitting room," she said. "What other parts of the house have you not seen yet?"

"It might be easier to tell you which parts I have seen: The drawing room. The dining room, as of tonight. The book room. My bedchamber. A few corridors. And the attic. Loved the attic. I highly recommend it."

He was quickly growing to like the sound of her light laughter. It was something real in this place that seemed so fake-real. Fake-real. He shook his head at that phrase. It weirdly made no sense and total sense all at the same time.

1803. He pushed that from his mind. They were all just very in character; he shouldn't let the weird date they'd settled on bother him as much as it did.

He and Amelia passed a table with a vase of flowers in the corridor.

"Are these from your garden?" he asked.

"It's not my garden."

"Oh, I think it is."

That brought a grateful smile to her face. "I cut these flowers earlier today."

He paused and eyed them. "Are any of these larkspur?"

"Do you not know what larkspur is?"

Kip pressed a hand dramatically to his heart. "You have discovered my greatest character flaw: I have no idea what larkspur is other than a flower that you are particularly fond of."

"The garden here doesn't have any larkspur, at least not that I've found. It might be hiding in the sections I haven't cleared yet."

He pulled a small pink blossom from the vase. Then he turned to her and presented it with a flourishing bow. "A flower for m'lady."

"Are all Americans as humorous as you are?" she asked as she accepted the flower.

"Sadly, no. But it does mean I have the privilege of being the country's designated jester."

Amelia kept the flower in her hand as they walked on. "How did a jester come to be friends with a saint?"

"Extremely good luck on my part."

She offered him another of her soft, kind smiles. "I suspect he would say that he was lucky to have become your friend."

"He would," Kip acknowledged. "He is a saint, after all."

"I would like to meet him some day." Nothing in the declaration sounded like a fangirl excited to meet the Malcolm Winthrop. Either she was as unaware of Malcolm's celebrity status as she was of Kip's, or she didn't put as much importance on that sort of thing as a lot of people in their business did. It was refreshing, actually.

Amelia motioned to a lit lantern on a table beside an open doorway. "I haven't a free hand. Would you carry the lantern inside?"

He took it up and followed her into the dark room. The lantern was the only source of light, but it did a decent job. He could see well enough to know the room wasn't very large, about the size of a kid's bedroom in the older suburban neighborhood he'd grown up in. It didn't have much furniture: two chairs, a very small table, and an armoire.

"Is this the troublemaker?" He crossed toward it.

She nodded. "One of many pieces of furniture needing attention." She turned toward him. It must have been too sudden or too drastic of a turn. Her cane slipped, and she stumbled.

Kip reached out with his free arm and caught her around the waist, keeping her on her feet. "Careful."

"I am always careful," she insisted. "That, however, isn't always enough."

"But you have to live here, where the ground outside is uneven and wet and treacherous?"

"For another five months."

"That feels very unfair."

"Life isn't often fair." She adjusted her footing and her cane, then stepped back. He dropped his arm away, but he wished he didn't have to.

Her gaze shifted to the window. Worry pulled at her brow, and her posture stiffened.

"It's too dark to see the ocean right now," Kip reminded her. "You're spared that until morning."

"But I can still hear it. The sound of waves is constant."

"Some people find that tranquil," Kip said.

"I can't imagine feeling even the tiniest whisper of peace when I am anywhere near it."

She needed to get off Guilford Island. Kip had promised her he wouldn't abandon her. And going to the village to argue for both of them to get transferred wasn't abandonment. She would understand that, surely.

Deciding to negotiate a change of jobs after only a couple of days wasn't the enormous betrayal she had made it out to be. Had she grown attached to him that quickly too? Or maybe it was just that someone with a degree of fame situated in her part of the site meant it would get more visitors.

No. He legitimately believed the people on this island he'd encountered didn't know who he was. It was both humbling and relieving. And confusing.

Amelia motioned to the armoire. "The left door hangs down when it's opened."

Kip set the lantern on the small table, then opened the armoire doors. The left one shifted forward and down. A quick inspection revealed a missing hinge pin.

"I think I've stumbled on an epidemic." He eyed the rest of the door, checking for any other problems. "Mick brought me a broken toy that was missing a hinge pin. This door is also missing a hinge pin."

"Is that something you can replace?" She moved closer and eyed it.

"I'll see if there's anything in the outbuilding that will work. If not, I'll make something."

"Thank you." She set her hand on his arm. His pulse responded with an oddly pleasant sort of hiccup. "Thank you for all that you've done and are doing. I would be sunk without you."

"I suspect you are more unsinkable than you think," he said. "It is a trait I have always admired in people. And even envied."

"Do you not consider yourself unsinkable?"

He turned to face her. She dropped her hand away, which was a shame.

"I have had a very difficult year," he said. "I'm beginning to suspect that I'm 'unsinkable' in the same way the *Titanic* was."

"What is 'the *Titanic*'?" She smiled, but like she was curious, not joking. Genuinely curious. About the *Titanic*!

"The *Titanic*," he repeated. "You know, the ship. That sank."

Her brow tugged sharply. "But you said this *Titanic* was unsinkable."

"Everyone said it was, but—" He studied her but didn't see any signs of humor or teasing.

1803.

She was sticking to character. A friendly moment together, one that had felt so real to him, and she was still in character.

"Never mind," he said, trying to manage a casual smile.

Her attention shifted again to the window, her mouth turning down in a frown. They could hear the waves, but he didn't think they were overly loud.

"You really are afraid of the ocean?"

She nodded, paler and overly still. That part of her "story" was true. He suspected the beech tree where she'd read books was real, as was her love of gardens. And he did think that she enjoyed his company. So why weave in things that weren't real?

"What year were you born?" he asked her.

"1778." Again, she hadn't hesitated or calculated. She seemed unsure of his reason for asking but not at all unsure of her answer.

She claimed her birth year was 1778. She and Mick had both said the year now was 1803. And neither had needed to think for even the length of a single breath. Both had made the declaration after what would have been normal business hours. And both had said it to him when only he had been around.

"Am I older than you thought?" she asked. "Twenty-five is considered rather ancient for an unmarried lady. Some gentlemen object to spending time with spinsters."

How was it that she could sound and look so sincerely concerned that her fake birth year made her a candidate for fake spinsterhood in this fake version of reality when she had to have known that wasn't why he was pressing her about the year?

"I don't entirely know what to make of you, Amelia Archibald. You are sincere but confusing."

An easy smile lit her eyes. "And you, Kipling Summerfield, are also confusing."

Despite his frustration, the corners of his mouth tipped upward. "No compliment first? Something along the lines of, 'You are handsome and funny and excellent company but confusing.' Flattery goes a long way."

"You said yesterday that you like spending time with me."

"I do." And that surprised him even more than it had in the moment he'd said it.

"I like spending time with you," she said. "That is a rare but very real compliment from me. Most people make me far too nervous."

"I don't make you nervous?"

She shook her head. "There's kindness in your eyes, and I appreciate that."

They wandered around the house a moment longer, with Amelia pointing out a few things he might consider of interest. And through it all, he very much felt he was seeing the real Amelia but through the lens of a historical character.

Confusing, as he'd said. And yet he felt an undeniable pull to her. What he didn't truly understand was why.

Chapter 13

Kip's thoughts were still on the supposed year throughout his work the next morning. Two people had insisted it was 1803 in a house that didn't violate that illusion at all.

He felt like an idiot even considering it, but the idea that everyone here legitimately believed it was the year 1803 wouldn't leave his thoughts.

He was a fan of fantasy films and shows. He had thought about the idea of time travel, but it had always been a science-fiction thing. He wasn't truly considering it now as part of reality. He couldn't be; it was too ridiculous.

Having finished his morning of home repairs, he changed into his gentleman-about-the-house clothes, which were shockingly similar to his man-fixing-the-broken-banister clothes. Then he went back to the book room. He'd not really taken a good look around when he'd first visited it. He had been somewhat overwhelmed at the time, having only just been plunged into the icy ocean.

Doing more of an inspection now, he discovered it was a lot like the rest of this place. Everything looked appropriate to a house of the late 1700s, early 1800s. Except, again, none of it looked over 200 years old. Had they gone to the trouble of removing all the books, even the historical ones, and re-creating the collection to look kind of new, like everything was actually happening two hundred years ago?

The degree of overkill at Guilford was still baffling.

He walked along the bookshelf, eyeing the spines. But most of them didn't have titles printed on them the way modern books did. He pulled a few out and flipped them open. The titles were the old-fashioned kind, long and complicated. The authors were people he'd never heard of, and the publication dates were all in Roman numerals. His fourth-grade teacher would be appalled if she knew how hard he was having to think to remember how to decipher the numbers. But he figured it out.

Every book he looked at was published in the 1790s or earlier. But they weren't actually antique books. He finally came across some that looked as old as they should have been if they had actually been from the late eighteenth century. These, the Roman numerals declared, had come from the 1600s, in which case, they should have been far more worn and delicate than they were. All reproductions?

No, that couldn't be right. It was a type of detail that didn't make any sense. He didn't imagine the visitors to this site were invited to simply sit in the book room for days at a time and read through the collection of antique recreations.

He found a book entitled *A History of Guilford Village and the Surrounding Environs*. That actually seemed useful. And though it insisted it had been printed in the late 1780s, there was every chance that it was actually brand-new and was there to help the people who worked on this site know what it was they were presenting. Naturally, it was hidden somewhere unlikely to be found.

So much about this place didn't make any sense.

Except Amelia. She felt real and peaceful and genuine in a way nothing else did here, in a way no one in his life but Malcolm and Jen had in years.

How did he square that with her always being in character?

Kip skimmed through the book. Neolithic settlements of the area . . . Losses in the Battle of Hastings . . . He needed to find the bit about 1803, apparently, since that was when he was meant to be. But before he got to that portion, his eyes caught a heading halfway down a page, nearly a third of the way into the book.

"Odd Arrivals by Sea."

Kip's arrival by sea had been very odd.

> Since before we've had a written record, the inhabitants of this area have spoken of the oddities of the sea.

"Time behaves strangely on these waters."

Amelia had said that was what the local villagers insisted.

> People pulled from the water speak of strange things and strange happenings. Many claim to have arrived not from distant places but from distant times. This local legend has been used to explain the oddities of a great many people, and it is assumed, this is a case of a search for proof creating the proof itself. Still, the legend holds fast. When a person is found to be lacking in judgment or mental acumen, it is not uncommon for the local population to question whether or not this person is one of the legendary odd arrivals.

Was this what Kip was encountering? Because he had had the misfortune of being swept into and then plucked from the water, they were going to resurrect this ancient legend as a way of adding authenticity to the experience for visitors? Thus far, no one had even brought up the possibility of his being from a different time or had demanded to know why he was confused or unaware of things. The closest they'd come to that was Jane's and Amelia's odd reactions to his tattoo. If they were women from 1803, he supposed they would have found it shocking.

Kip continued flipping through the pages of the book and came across another section that stopped him.

SUDDEN STORMS THAT GROW

It has been posited that there is no area of the southern coast more prone to dangerous and violent storms than that stretching from the coast beyond Guilford to the far side of Loftstone Island. Those of a scientific bent have hypothesized that it is the shape of the bay and the placement of its islands that traps storms, much the way the narrow neck between Guilford Island and the shore traps sea surges. This, they believe, causes the storms to sit and brew and grow in strength. Though the phenomenon of green lightning striking the water has not been explained, it is considered, by many locals, to be part of the odd phenomenon of the visitors over the water.

On neighboring Loftstone Island, these are called the Tides of Time, storms that bring people from other times into the one in which they are found. Guilford Village and its residents do not have a name for this occurrence. Nonetheless, it, too, boasts its own legends of strange travelers and green lightning, tales that are woven into the echoes of the sea.

Green lightning. Kip had seen green lightning when he'd been in the water. That could not have been planted or faked. There was no way the people running this place could have predicted it would happen and set this storyline in action. Unless they kept all these things around and had this backup plan on the off chance that someone arrived in just the right way.

"Begging your pardon, Mr. Summerfield."

Kip turned to look at Marsh, standing in the doorway of the book room.

"Thank you," Marsh said, "for repairing Mick's toy. I know Miss has given you a great deal of work to do. Us is appreciative that you took time to help he in that way."

"I'm glad I could do it and that I had the tools I needed."

Marsh dipped his head.

"How long have you lived here?" Kip asked. "Not necessarily on Guilford Island but in this general vicinity."

"All my life. I grew up farther inland than Guilford Village."

More inland might not help, but Kip hoped it was near enough. "This book"—he held it up—"talks of a lot of legends in the area. I'm wondering how many are widely known and widely believed."

Mr. Marsh's expression was solemn. "Like most places, us has plenty of legends."

"What about the one Loftstone Island calls the Tides of Time?"

Mr. Marsh grew stiffer, which was an accomplishment. He had the starchy butler role down to a science. "Time behaves strangely on these waters."

"Miss Archibald said she has been told that as well," Kip said, "but she has not been offered an explanation as to what that means."

Still looking uncomfortable but pressing forward, the butler said, "It is believed that when the green lightning hits the water, it opens a door."

"A door?"

Marsh nodded. "A door between places in time that aren't meant to be connected. People, legend says, are pushed through it against their will."

The legend, then, was about time travel, exactly the sort of odd phenomenon Kip was beginning to consider in some small way.

"Do you believe the legend?" Kip asked.

"Most everywho here about does." The man turned and left.

Time travel. Either that was Kip's storyline being revealed to him in an unnecessarily complicated way, or they were trying to make him think it was true.

From the drawing room below, he heard the sounds of Amelia playing a tune. She had to be in on this conspiracy, whatever it was exactly. Until he sorted that out, he needed to approach everyone here with caution.

Chapter 14

Amelia found Kipling every bit as perplexing as she had on his very first day at Guilford. But she also liked him quite a lot. And she believed him when he said he wouldn't abandon her. That was an unusual but rather wonderful promise for her. She might finally have an ally.

"Today, I am grateful for that," she said.

She was getting ready to go outside and begin work in her garden for the day when Mrs. Jagger came running up the corridor, calling out, "He's come! He's come!"

Amelia stopped her and, in as calm a voice as she could, asked, "Who has come, Mrs. Jagger?"

"Mr. Stirling, Miss. He's come back!"

Her uncle—curse it all.

"It's not been that long since he was last here," Amelia said. "I hope he doesn't expect things to be significantly improved in such a short amount of time."

"Who can say what him expects?" Mrs. Jagger set her shoulders, though she still looked worried. "Us'll make the best showing for weselves that us can."

"I will invite them to take a walk through the garden. It *has* noticeably improved just since they were last here." And if they were particularly difficult, she might accidentally take them through a patch of stinging nettle she hadn't yet cut back. There was no revenge quite like a gardener's revenge.

Mrs. Jagger nodded. "Marsh will have they ushered inside and do so impeccably."

Amelia didn't know what she would have done if the servants hadn't remained at Guilford.

She made her way to the drawing room, and standing in front of the small mirror hanging on a wall to one side of the door, she checked her reflection. She needed to make as good an impression as she could, and that meant not looking haphazardly put together.

Her uncle had always thought her red hair something of a tragedy, but she didn't think he held it against her. He had, however, shown undeniable embarrassment at her ever-present limp. Gentlemen who carried walking sticks they didn't actually depend upon were considered quite sophisticated. Ladies with a twisted foot who often desperately needed their walking stick weren't given that same glowing compliment.

Still, her appearance was tidy. And while she wouldn't ever be declared an unparalleled beauty, she felt she had the air of one who was in charge of her situation and was managing it reasonably well. That was precisely the impression she needed to give.

At the sound of footsteps approaching, she took a deep breath and then another. She leaned on her cane, turned, and faced the door.

Marsh stepped inside and, in the ringing tones of a very proper butler, said, "Mr. Stirling and Mr. Winthrop to see you, Miss Archibald." He then stepped aside and disappeared.

Mr. Winthrop? She didn't know any Mr. Winthrop.

Her uncle stepped through the doorway, looking a touch more friendly than the last time she'd seen him. It wasn't that he had been particularly unfriendly; his mood simply seemed to have improved. Beside him was a man likely about his own age, just on the other side of fifty. His hair was a mixture of light, almost golden, brown and a few wisps of gray. He was tall, appeared to be one who undertook regular exercise, and was dressed as a gentleman of means and sophistication. He executed a flawless bow, which she returned with a curtsy.

Her uncle immediately began the formal introductions. "Amelia, this is Mr. Winthrop. He has an estate in the vicinity. I was pleased to make his acquaintance quite recently."

Quite recently. Something in that declaration made her nervous.

"Winthrop, this is my niece, Miss Amelia Archibald."

They both expressed themselves pleased to meet the other. And where Amelia felt certain she wasn't entirely hiding her confusion, Mr. Winthrop didn't appear to be even attempting to hide his assessment of her.

"Your uncle didn't tell me you were—" His eyes dropped to her cane for the length of a breath. His mouth twisted, and his brow creased deeply.

Amelia had heard a great many descriptors acknowledging her limp and her difficulty walking. Not all those descriptors were polite. Few were flattering. What would this newly met stranger choose?

In the end, he didn't choose anything. Mr. Winthrop just turned back toward Uncle Stirling and didn't say anything further.

After an uncomfortable moment, Uncle Stirling looked at Amelia and smiled stiffly. "I suspect you have been hard at work since I was last here, Amelia."

"I have been," she said. "In fact, you would be most pleased to see the progress that has been made in the garden at the back of the house."

"Your uncle did mention you are fond of gardens," Mr. Winthrop said.

"I am."

The smile he gave her was clearly meant to indicate that he felt she would be or ought to be impressed with his memory. Why her being impressed mattered to him at all, she couldn't say. By her uncle's own description, they were not friends of long standing, and Amelia was a poor relation who, while not mistreated, was of no real importance.

Still, the two gentlemen walked with her toward the back of the house. The clunk of her cane filled the silence among them. At the door in the back, they were given their outer coats to put on, as the weather was still cold.

"I have not had the opportunity to visit Guilford, though it is much spoken of in this area of the country," Mr. Winthrop said. "'The Little Sister of Mont-Saint-Michel.' Watching the sea pull back from the road these past twenty-four hours has been fascinating."

"Have you been in the village?" she asked her uncle as the three of them walked along the path toward the garden. She did her best to ignore the sound of waves crashing against the island.

"We have. We thought to come out and visit sooner, but the sea was being uncooperative."

He had returned to the area before today. *Odd.* Still, he seemed in a good mood, which increased the odds that he would approve of what he saw.

She pushed open the iron gate of the garden, and they followed her inside. She was exceptionally grateful that she had started her improvements in the section most visible from the gate. It meant one's first impression was a very pleasing one.

"You have made some progress," Uncle said, looking around. "I don't know that the rest of it can be completed in the remaining four and a half months, but you've clearly worked hard."

It was a compliment but one steeped in far too much doubt for her peace of mind.

"The house is also seeing improvements," she said. "Furniture has been restored. Broken balusters and banisters are being repaired."

Uncle's mouth tightened in a look of perplexity. "I didn't realize you had that skill, Amelia."

"I have hired a carpenter who is making excellent progress."

Uncle's brow drew low. "I was under the impression that local people don't generally like coming out to Guilford."

Amelia motioned ever so subtly toward Mr. Winthrop. "Clearly, not all local people are unwilling to do so."

"I am, perhaps, braver than most," the gentleman said. "They fear that water manipulates time. But I find that to be a great deal of nonsense and choose not to allow it to upset me."

"Multiple people have spoken to me of that," she said. "'Time behaves strangely—'"

"—on these waters," he finished. "I think it is far more likely that *people* behave strangely here, and the locals wish for an explanation as to why."

Amelia didn't think so. She would not have heard tales of the strange happenings on the water from so many people and read it in one of the books in the book room if there weren't something to it beyond local stubbornness. Time behaved strangely. Storms brewed suddenly. The locals gave Guilford and the water around it a wide berth. It was more than grumblings. But what exactly it was, she didn't know.

"I'd very much like to go see the Guilford lighthouse," Mr. Winthrop said. "The day is a clear one. We might be able to spy the dual lights at Loftstone."

"Let's trudge over that way," Uncle said. "Ivers and his wife aren't the most genial of people, but they won't refuse to allow you to look around."

Maybe that was part of the reason Mr. and Mrs. Ivers were standoffish with her—because her uncle was a bit arrogant with them.

They all began walking from the garden, but she spotted Kipling a ways off in the direction of his work cottage. The two men didn't seem to notice him there, which was for the best. She wouldn't have to answer too many questions.

"While you two make your trek down to the lighthouse, I am going to check on the progress of one of the projects we have here." She didn't leave them any opportunity to argue with her but turned on her cane and began making her way down the footpath. They didn't follow. She moved as swiftly as her unsteadiness and the unevenness of the path allowed. She caught up with Kipling just outside the door to his work cottage.

"Mick says there are people on the island," Kipling said without preamble. "How many have come?"

He'd mentioned before that he expected a great many people to visit the island. She wasn't certain what had given him that impression.

"It is my uncle and a . . . a new friend of his."

"Oh, I've been hoping to talk to your uncle. He oversees all this, I believe you said?"

She shook her head as they walked along the path leading back to the house. "He has control over me, but he doesn't run Guilford. I do that."

"The management of all this is very strange. I'm having a difficult time sorting it out."

"That your confusion stems not from the fact that a woman is in charge of something but rather that you aren't certain who answers to whom is the strangest thing about it."

"The *strangest* thing about this place?" He chuckled lightly. He had a captivating smile. "That is a label that would be difficult to assign with any hope of accuracy."

"There is something additionally strange," she said. "While my uncle and his friend are here, I think you need to be very circumspect. I told them we had a carpenter who was working here, and I suspect they thought very little of that. But if they knew you actually were a gentleman of leisure who lived here and once even spent an evening in my company, they would be scandalized to the point that my entire future would be in danger."

"I realize that's the way things were in the past, but to hold to that now—"

"There is nothing 'in the past' about this. A young, unwed lady sharing a house with an eligible, young, unwed gentleman is simply not done, not without ruining them both."

He held his hands up and blinked a few times. "Wait. You're serious?"

"The rules about this might be lax in America, but they are not at all here." She actually found it shocking that there would be that much of a difference between their two countries. "The slightest show of failure, and my uncle could take everything from me. I cannot risk giving him reason to do so."

He held the door on the back terrace open for her, and she stepped through it. The tip of her cane had grown wet outside, and it slipped on the polished wood floor. Kipling's arm wrapped around her and helped keep her steady while she regained her footing, just as he'd done in the sitting room several nights earlier. She wanted to ask him not to let go, to suggest he could keep his arm around her, walk with her, hold her . . . It was very unlike her to be so bold.

"What is it your uncle is threatening to take from you?" Kipling asked, having dropped his arm away already.

"My grandfather left me an inheritance. His will said it was enough that I could live in some ease, without having to continue being a poor relation in my uncle's home. But because my grandfather was a vindictive and unkind man, he's requiring me to prove that I can be a good steward of it by showing myself a good steward of Guilford for the half year I am required to be here."

Though he seemed to understand her, he still had the look of someone sorting through a mystery.

"If my uncle declares that I didn't do a good job or if I outright fail, the inheritance I have been promised will be given to him, and I will be required to marry whomever he chooses for me."

"What?" He didn't sound shocked; he sounded utterly baffled.

"There were laws passed in recent years that allow ladies to object to matches chosen for them," she acknowledged, "but they can't truly be enforced. The ways in which ladies can be coerced or forced into marriages are multitudinous. Contracts such as this supersede even laws when it comes to the realities of life."

He stopped in the middle of the corridor. "In this day and age, you cannot be forced to marry someone."

"A lady's ability to choose her future is no more within her grasp in *1803* than it was in *1703*."

He shook his head slowly, his brow pulling tighter and tighter.

She reached out and set a hand on his, similar to how he had to her in the gardening shed. And just as it had then, the light touch brought a surge of warmth and awareness but also a degree of peace and calm. "I know this is less than ideal. I don't want you to think that I'm ashamed of your being here. It isn't at all the reason I'm asking you to play least in sight. Your company is far preferable to my uncle or his . . . friend. But Uncle never stays more than one night. I simply need you to take your meal in your room tonight. You've done so most of the time you've been here, so I assume it won't be a terrible thing for you."

"But I suspect it *will* be a terrible thing for you. Whenever you speak of your uncle, you do so in terms of anxiety and worry. And this friend of his seems to make you even more uncomfortable."

He had sorted that even though she had hardly said more than a word about Mr. Winthrop.

His brows suddenly shot up. "I've just realized. If they have arrived, that must mean the sea road is uncovered."

Amelia's heart dropped. "It is. Provided we don't have a full moon anytime soon, it should remain entirely above water until the next storm."

"We could go into the village. You could get away from the sea while we attempt to convince people to come out and help look after the place."

"I'm not allowed to leave," she reminded him.

"I realize you're supposed to make your home here, implement changes and improvements. But I—"

"I'm *literally* not allowed to leave. If I take even a single step away from Guilford Island, I will be in violation of the terms of my grandfather's will."

"*I'm* not subject to those terms," he said firmly. "I'm going to take the sea road up to the village."

"Stirring up a hornet's nest will only make this worse. I don't know who in the village might be reporting to my uncle and be willing to tell him things that would make him look down on me."

"You think the village is crawling with spies?" he asked dryly.

She squared her shoulders and looked him in the eye. "My grandfather's will said there would be people willing to tell my uncle if I violated the terms of the agreement."

That seemed to give Kipling a degree of pause.

"Please be careful when you're in the village," she said. "Not just for my sake. They are a superstitious lot. If they find reason to think you too much of an oddity, I don't know what they would do."

"I know how to be unobtrusive," he said.

She gave him a jokingly withering look, which made him laugh. Heavens, she liked the sound of his laugh and the way his eyes danced with amusement.

"I'll finish my work this morning, then I'm going to go see what I can find on the other end of the sea road."

And her enjoyment of only a moment earlier all but evaporated. He was leaving. He'd said he wouldn't, and she supposed this wasn't really violating that promise. Guilford Village wasn't so very far away. And he hadn't said he *wasn't* coming back.

But what did he have to come back to? Living half his days like a carpenter? Mick dogging his heels? The Iverses being *almost* friendly to him?

Her?

With such unappealing enticements, what hope was there, really, that, upon leaving Guilford, he would ever look back?

Chapter 15

Guilford didn't have a car, obviously. It also didn't have a horse and carriage. Or a bike. Or scooter. Or roller skates. And Kip discovered the sea road was long. Walking it took probably half an hour. The ocean lapped against the edges of the damp road, reminding him that it hadn't been uncovered for long.

He wasn't afraid of the sea the way Amelia was, but even he was nervous. By the time he reached the shore, he wasn't certain he had the guts to make the walk back. Why in the world did the owners of the historical site think they had to keep things this precarious simply because it used to be that way? No one visiting the place would feel like their experience was ruined because they weren't threatened with drowning.

Guilford Village looked like any number of small English villages that Kip had driven through or visited or filmed in. Except the streets weren't paved, and there were no streetlights or cars or SPARs. There was always a SPAR.

"Historical accuracy," no doubt. But had there been modernization that had been ripped out when the place had been turned into a historic destination? That probably hadn't gone over well with the locals.

Which brought to mind other questions: How many here were locals who lived in the area, and how many were simply hired to enact the roles of those displaced citizens? A combination of the two would likely be a powder keg.

Time for a charm offensive. They needed help up at Guilford House, which meant convincing someone to switch roles. If that someone would make the switch permanently, that would get Amelia off the island and away from the sea. She could also be removed from the creepy-friend-of-her-uncle part of the story that they were just starting, which was obviously making her legitimately uncomfortable.

He saw a few people as he walked along the high street. Some stood in the doorways of their shops, dressed *precisely* as they would have been more than two hundred years earlier. Two girls, probably in their early teens, hurried across the street up ahead. Neither had a phone in their hand, which was a strange thing. He could hear a conversation outside a shop door as he passed; the topic was Napoleon. *Napoleon.* Not a single tourist was there yet, but they were still completely in character. And living without electricity, probably without plumbing, definitely without a SPAR or a Co-Op.

There was, however, a pub. He'd gained a great appreciation during his years in the UK for the magic of dropping into a pub when a person had a problem to solve. That problem didn't always get fixed, but he always left feeling marginally better about the world in general.

He stepped inside, pulling off his tricorn hat. Removing his hat had become a habit during *The Beau*. The place didn't look seedy, like some of the locations they'd created for the show. A nice, local haunt was a far better option for a place tourists were supposed to enjoy visiting.

Kip counted eight people sitting about the place, gabbing and nursing pints. No one looked sketchy. No one looked like they'd ever even heard of the comfort of putting on an old T-shirt and well-worn jeans.

A man built on a scale roughly that of a rhinoceros whacked a tea towel over his shoulder. "Welcome to the Rusted Anchor, stranger. What brings you to Guilford Village?"

As greetings went, it was rather brilliant. Tourists would eat that up. Maybe they thought Kip was a visitor rather than a colleague. It would be so much easier to just tell them, but the people working at this place were stubborn about never breaking character. "I've been working up at the house on Guilford Island," he said.

That brought everyone's eyes to him instantly. Dramatic.

An old man in the corner, his silver hair unkempt and boasting a couple days' worth of scruff on his face, eyed him closely. "You've a strange sound to your speech. Where're you from?"

Again with insulting his accent. What was it with the people here?

"America," he answered, still using the accent they were intent on finding unimpressive.

Understanding dawned on all their faces, and a few even ah-hed. Not very subtle acting for a bunch of people who embraced group mockery of a brilliantly managed British accent.

"Don't know how you came to be employed up there," the tea-toweled rhinoceros said, "but us'd advise against it. The sea's an unhappy mistress in these parts. Her can't be hidden from on Guilford."

"I keep hearing about the sea around here, that the people don't like it or don't trust it. But no one will tell me the whole of it."

The entire pub turned to look at the old man. Of course they did. The wizened elder of the village. If they'd gone this cliché on *The Beau*, they would have been canceled after only a few episodes.

The Gandalf wannabe rose and slowly walked toward him. "Everywho hereabouts knows of the Tides of Time, as them's called over at Loftstone. Us've been brought up on tales of its merciless pull. When the storms rage, the water swirls about the islands set in the bays of this stretch of the coast—swirls and whips and forms a spinning target that sinks ships and drowns doomed souls."

A geographical explanation for the legends everyone kept hinting at felt odd delivered in this over-the-top style. But everything about this place was unnecessarily dramatic.

"Should the lightning turn green and should it reach the water, the tragedy is doubled."

Green lightning. Again. It had been mentioned in the book he'd read. And he'd seen green lightning during his dunk in the sea. "I read in a book that the green lightning opens a door."

The man's eyes pulled wide. His voice turned even more dramatic somehow. "A door through time."

Time travel really was the plot line, then. "Why be so dedicated to the history aspect of this place if it's going to be a fantasy park?"

Utter confusion touched every face. This was getting ridiculous. Sticking to the plot and never breaking character even when it caused chaos was the kind of method-acting madness that frustrated an entire production. Kip had never been that disruptive, yet he'd been the one tossed off a show he'd been a very crucial part of.

Stay in character no matter how stupid this is. You need this job. "Miss Archibald is working tirelessly to put the house to rights so her uncle doesn't take away her inheritance and make her live in poverty or misery." It already felt too melodramatic, so he didn't add in the bit about forcing her to marry a probably lecherous man old enough to be her father. And all that was mixed in with time travel, apparently. A soap opera would struggle to sell this storyline. "Is there a reason, beyond nervousness about the Tides of Time, that the people of this village are so indifferent to the misery of a lady who is in such a dire situation not of her making or choosing?"

They had the acting instincts to look somewhat guilt-riddled.

"Her uncle sat in here for the better part of two days," a young man said, rising from his chair. "Him didn't seem entirely terrible of a person, but there was something in his eyes I didn't like."

The rhino nodded his agreement. So did the rest of the pub.

"And that man what was with he made a person's skin crawl," the old man added.

"That man is likely the person her uncle intends to make her marry should she fail to set Guilford to rights." Kip watched that sink in. For all their frustrating stubbornness, they were good actors. Just the right emotions flickered over their faces.

The young man, who now stood beside re-creation-Merlin, asked, "How much is needing to be done up to the manor?"

"Quite a lot. The place isn't crumbling, but it needs repairs. I'm only one person and not nearly enough help to see to it all in the little time Miss Archibald has to satisfy her obligations."

The young man exchanged a look with his aged companion. Nothing was said, but plenty passed between them. A debate, he'd guess. Were they allowed to change their characters' locations or occupations? Amelia certainly seemed to think their assignments were iron-clad.

"I'll work a spell up at the house," the young man said.

That earned him wide-eyed stares from around the room.

The old man shrugged. "Him's a rare one for going a-hoop. Us'll not talk he out of doing what him wishes."

And *Kip* was the one constantly being called out for his "odd" way of speaking?

"Watch yourself, nipper," the old man said as his younger counterpart walked toward the door. "The Tides of Time aren't merciful."

"Them also hasn't any power out of the water," was the tossed-back response. "I'll keep dry." He motioned Kip out of the pub with a quick flick of his chin.

Apparently, this was their new side quest. Kip inwardly shrugged. Very little would surprise him about this job anymore.

Outside on the unpaved street, he popped his hat back on. "I'm hoping you have a name and a carriage. The sea road made for a long walk."

"I've a pony and cart."

Kip nodded. "That'll do."

"And I'm called Smudge, if *that*'ll do."

"Smudge? I'm assuming that isn't your actual given name."

Smudge grinned as they walked up the street. "I'd a fondness for the mud as a small child. So 'Smudge' I've been ever since. What're you called?"

"Kip, though my given name is Kipling, and Miss Archibald calls me Mr. Summerfield."

He was eyed with an evaluatory expression. "You seem Quality enough for she to call you that. But you're doing tradesmen's work, which'd make me think I ought to call you Kip. But that don't seem fitting."

"Being called Kip would be a nice change," he said. "I'm not accustomed to the formality."

"Things're done differently where you're from, I suspect."

"Yes, America is quite different."

They reached a mews—authenticity taken to the point that Kip could smell it long before he saw it—and Smudge quickly had a pony hitched to a rickety cart. No modern shock-absorbers to ruin the effect.

"How old are you?" Kip asked as Smudge drove the cart back toward the Channel.

"Twenty-seven, though I don't look it."

"No, you don't." Kip would have guessed twenty, if that.

The wheels rolled off the mainland and onto the narrow sea road. The ebb and flow of water was somehow less overwhelming in the cart. The vehicle offered no actual protection, and he ought to have felt just as uneasy. But somehow, he didn't.

"If you're willing to come help at Guilford," Kip said, "then you mustn't believe the tales about the Tides of Time and the green lightning and all that."

"Oh, I more than believe it. I *know* it to be true." Without showing the least hesitancy nor sounding the least rehearsed, Smudge pressed on. "My grandmother was a traveler on those tides. Her was brought here to this inlet as a young woman, said her had been some hundred fifty years ahead of where her was dropped."

Okay. A time-travel-family backstory. That was unexpected.

"Spoke of things now and then that I couldn't believe. But her didn't want to accidentally change things to come, so her kept mostly mum about it." A bit of sea spray misted over them. "Grandmother weren't the most clever of women—I'm not saying her was lackwitted or any such thing; her was intelligent and had her faculties intact right to the end—but imagining fanciful things wasn't who her was. Her couldn't have invented the tales her told me. Couldn't have."

"What tales did she tell you?"

Smudge shook his head. "I'll not risk changing those things that'll happen in times to come. Her warned me not to."

"Then tell me how she came to be on the Tides of Time." That seemed a safe enough way to sort out what Kip was meant to have experienced.

"Her said her had been out on the Channel in a boat. A storm whipped up without enough warning for returning to shore. A wave washed she into the water."

That sounded familiar.

"Her kept sheself above water as best her could. And in the midst of it all, the green lightning struck. Her said it reached clear to the water and lit it for just a moment."

Kip hadn't been paying enough attention to know if that had happened during his accidental swim. He knew there had been a green lightning strike, but he didn't know any other details.

"And when that moment was over, the boat her had been on was gone, the time of day was different, and the sea was a touch calmer. But it weren't until her returned to the village that her knew something had happened. Gone were the trappings her was accustomed to seeing, modern things her said us'd struggle to believe."

Struggle to believe didn't begin to describe it.

"How long ago did your grandmother arrive?"

"Be'est at least forty years now."

"And 'now' would be the year . . . ?" He let that dangle, hoping he didn't get the answer he expected he would.

"1803."

1803. A consistent year.

Those answers could have been coordinated. But no one could engineer storms on the sea. And no one could change the color of the lightning. He hadn't told anyone what he'd seen, so they couldn't have adjusted their story afterward to match his experience.

Historical sites could be *un*modernized. But too much of what he'd experienced at Guilford couldn't be manufactured. Something was decidedly wrong here. And, though he felt like an idiot even considering the outlandish explanation, he was beginning to think he might know what that "something" was.

Chapter 16

Amelia wasn't entirely certain if Mr. Winthrop thought Guilford was part of her inheritance, but the way he inspected it, with an assessing gaze rather than an appreciative one, led her to suspect that was exactly what he believed. He had undertaken a rather meticulous tour of the public rooms of the house after having returned from what was likely an equally painstaking tour of the island, and she was more than ready for him to leave. She knew, however, that her uncle intended to remain overnight, which meant Mr. Winthrop would as well.

This was her home for the time being, and she was within her rights to ask them to leave, but she knew that would be seen as the mark of a poor hostess. Her uncle might very well declare that a show of ineptitude. She didn't dare risk it.

She stood near her desk in the book room, watching as Mr. Winthrop eyed the spines of the various books. He had been making a very slow circuit of the room. Was he counting to see just how many books were there? None was particularly valuable, but there was likely some worth to the collection as a whole.

Uncle stood nearby and had already lost interest in the collection. Amelia took advantage of the opportunity and motioned to the chair at the desk. "The broken spindle in the back of the chair has been repaired," she said. "You, I am certain, took note of the repairs made to the banister on the main staircase. The armoire in the sitting room has been repaired as well. Progress is being made around the estate."

He eyed the chair, though whether he was doing so to appease her or because he was actually interested, she didn't know. It was disconcerting how their current arrangement left her so confused about a man she'd felt, up until now, she had more or less understood. He didn't feel as trustworthy as he always had before.

Amelia didn't care to be one who jumped to conclusions about people. But she knew *instinctively* that Mr. Winthrop, while perhaps not actually dangerous, was not the sort of person who ought to be trusted overly much.

"You made good progress on the garden as well." Uncle seemed reluctant to admit as much. His innate stubbornness was likely making it difficult to adjust his expectations.

"I have kept a very detailed accounting of all the work that has been accomplished and all that is currently being undertaken." She had not known him to be truly dishonest, but she still intended to make it difficult for him to misrepresent the truth at Guilford.

"I am certain you're being very thorough," he said.

She smiled benignly. "I thought it a wise thing to approach such a significant undertaking with an equally significant plan. This way, I'm unlikely to miss something that should be done or forget something that was accomplished." At the last minute, she'd decided to use the word *forget* instead of saying "not be given credit for." She didn't want to set his back up.

"That is a good approach," he acknowledged. The tiniest bit of worry entered his expression. Though she didn't know for certain if he had already decided he meant to declare her a failure either way, she knew in that moment, he was at least considering it, and her detailed accounting was undermining his plan.

In this moment, I am grateful for my love of lists.

"This is a fine collection, Miss Archibald." Mr. Winthrop sidled up near her, his smile both insincere and unnerving.

"I have not had the time to peruse it properly myself, but what I have seen is very nice, indeed."

His smile expanded. "A lady ought not spend all her time reading, after all."

"Perhaps not *all* of it," was all she could think to say. The fact that she had agreed with him in any way seemed to meet with his approval.

He inched closer. She attempted to inch back but couldn't get her cane moved in a way that would facilitate it.

"I noticed a pianoforte in the drawing room," he said. "Do you play?"

"A little," she said.

Thoughts of Kipling sitting at the instrument, playing his unfamiliar American tune, flitted through her mind. Would he do so again? Would he actually teach her how to play the tune he'd played that evening?

Mr. Winthrop set a hand atop hers, holding her cane. She couldn't pull her hand free without losing the steadying assistance of her much-needed walking stick. "I can see by your smile that you have a fondness for music. How fortuitous. I like music myself."

"I am fond of music." She wrapped her fingers more tightly around her cane, then attempted to slip free of his hold. "But I am also no virtuoso."

"Humility is an admirable trait in a lady," he said.

She managed to free her hand. "I have found in my nearly twenty-six years that unwanted arrogance is not particularly admirable in anyone."

Amelia watched him for his reaction to the mention of her age. It was precisely what she had thought it would be: He seemed both surprised and a little displeased. Though he was decidedly more than twice her age, he had given the impression of being the sort of gentleman who wished for a wife who was even younger than she. In revealing that, he had given her a means of dealing with him.

Quiet ladies were so often dismissed as weak and ineffectual. People would be surprised if they knew how many of those "quiet, helpless, useless" ladies were actually brilliantly navigating sticky situations in ways so subtle no one knew what they were up to.

"Of course," she continued, "when a lady reaches my age, she has learned a thing or two about when to deflect a compliment and when to acknowledge that it is not the truth. There's also a lesson to be learned about having discovered which accomplishments are worth pursuing and maintaining and which do not offer enough benefit to continue on with."

It was an innocuous statement, one he couldn't really argue with, but it also did the trick of showing him that she had opinions and thoughts of her own. It would give him pause, and that was what she needed. She didn't dare give offense, but hesitation was well worth engendering.

His pause didn't last nearly long enough though. He stepped closer once more. She shifted enough to keep her cane hand at an inconvenient distance from him, reducing the chances that he would manage to trap her.

"Your uncle tells me you like working in the garden, but you aren't overly tanned, as so many ladies allow themselves to become. Indeed, you have a very pleasing complexion."

She knew that was meant to be a compliment, and she was meant to be very flattered by it, but all it did was make her skin crawl. "I do make certain to wear a bonnet when I am outdoors. Though I understand the harshness of the wind off the sea can undermine a complexion, even with the use of a bonnet."

Let him ponder that for a while. A lady who was older than he preferred, had thoughts of her own, and would soon enough be grizzled and aged by the sea was not exactly what he was hoping for, she would wager.

His encroachment on her had led her to back up to the window. Through it, she spotted a pony cart making its way along the side of the house. With her eyes straining just a mite, she could make out the two occupants. One was a man she didn't know, and the other was Kipling. She'd seen him leave for the village and had told herself he would come back, even though she'd struggled to believe it. But he had returned.

"You must excuse me," she said. "Two of our workers have returned, and I need to consult with them as to what else remains to be done."

Though she was not one who could walk swiftly away from anyone, she turned as quickly as she could. That would allow her to simply ignore any spoken objections. Fortunately, Mr. Winthrop didn't make any. With her cane echoing down the corridor, the stairs, and the exterior steps, he wouldn't exactly struggle to follow her if he chose to.

Amelia took the path leading past the garden and back toward the stables. She attempted to take in a deep breath of relief, but she found her heart was pounding a little too hard for it. Kipling had come back. He'd had the chance to escape the island and leave her behind, but he hadn't.

And he'd brought someone with him, someone from the village. How had he managed that?

She paused at the large entrance to the stable, watching as the men saw to the cart. The man Kipling had brought back with him was doing the bulk of the work. Kipling didn't appear to entirely know what to do.

He smiled when he saw her, which flipped her heart over again.

She smiled in return. "You came back."

"I told you I would."

She stepped closer to him, feeling better just having him nearby. "I have never been very important to anyone. I have every reason to believe that will continue to be true."

"Perhaps I will, in time, sort out what it is I need to do to give you 'every reason to believe' *me*."

It wasn't launched as a complaint but almost as a glimmer of hope. And that did her heart even more good.

"This is Smudge." Kipling motioned to the man beside him. "He's come up from the village and says he'll do some work around the place."

From the village? Come to work? Kipling had managed a miracle.

"Thank you both. There is so very much to do, and my uncle is being very hardnosed about it all."

"I am correct, then, in assuming your visitors have not been as pleasant as one would hope?"

"My uncle's being critical," she said. "Mr. Winthrop is being too . . . familiar, I suppose. Assessing. I don't know how to characterize it, but he makes me uneasy."

"His name is Winthrop?" That appeared to be a significant discovery for Kipling.

"Yes."

"Do you happen to know his given name?"

Amelia shook her head. She hadn't the first idea.

"Is he about my age, thick, golden hair, blue eyes, probably too handsome for his own good?"

A laugh burst from Amelia. "Not at all. At least twice my age, thinning brown hair. I don't know what color his eyes are, only that I do not like them."

"Have any other Winthrops been in the area?" Kipling pressed. "*Malcolm* Winthrop, by chance?"

"Your friend Malcolm—the saint—his surname is Winthrop?"

Kipling nodded.

"Maybe the Mr. Winthrop who is here at the moment is related to him." That seemed unlikely though. Kipling, after all, was from America, which made it likely that his friend was as well. And a gentleman whom Kipling had described as a saint didn't seem enough like the Mr. Winthrop she'd been enduring all day for her to assume the two were family, even distantly.

"I supposed they could be." Kipling looked uneasy, almost bothered. "I have some work I didn't get done this morning. I'll go out to my work shed and see what I can accomplish before the day grows too late. Smudge can sort out whatever it is he can do around here."

With a quick dip of his head in place of a bow, Kipling turned around, put his hands in the pockets of his coat, and walked off. Something in his stooped posture spoke not of defeat but of a heavy mind.

"I am a quick study at most things," Smudge said. "Tell me what's needing done around here, and chances are, I can manage it."

"Thank you for coming," she said. "Most people in the village stay away from here."

"The power of the water is a fearful thing."

"So, why were *you* willing to come here?"

He twitched his head in the direction Kipling had gone. "Him's a long way from home."

"America *is* far from here."

But Smudge shook his head. "Him's traveled much farther than that but doesn't know it yet."

Chapter 17

Kip was more than capable of linking together an impressive chain of profanities. He was tempted to do exactly that as he walked toward the old-timey tool shed, but he suspected it would be even more shocking to anyone nearby than his tattoos were.

"A door through time."

Time travel was the realm of fantasy. To even be thinking about it in terms of reality was ridiculous. But it was the only thing that made everything he'd seen and experienced add up.

A tourist attraction with no facilities.

A low-paid summer job attracting the best actors in existence.

A young couple with an infant in a house that would never pass even a casual safety inspection.

Panic at the sight of Kip's tattoos.

Mick's wandering the island unsupervised.

No one knowing who Kip was, let alone Malcolm Winthrop.

Amelia strictly bound by the terms of a will that, in modern day, would never be enforceable.

It wouldn't make sense in the "now" that he knew. But in 1803? Yeah, probably.

He stood in the middle of the stone work shed, not really seeing his surroundings. 1803. It was impossible. But it also sort of felt . . . true.

A shadow blocked most of the light from the open doorway behind him.

"Did you sort it out yet?" Smudge asked.

Kip tried to roll the tension out of his shoulders. "Sort what out?"

Smudge stepped inside. He stopped next to the workbench and leaned against it, watching Kip. He didn't say anything, didn't answer the question. He looked very much as though he could stand there all day and wait.

He had told Kip he believed in the Tides of Time. He'd said he knew someone who had traveled over them. Of all the people Kip might share his suspicions with, Smudge seemed a good option. He'd known him for only an hour. But, then, there was no one nearby he had known for very long.

In the end, Kip lost his nerve. "Did you get an assignment from Miss Archibald?"

"Her said, for now, I'm to help you."

"What skills do you have?" Kip asked.

Smudge shrugged. "I can do most anything."

Hesitantly, Kip asked, "Plumbing?"

Smudge shook his head. "Can't say I've heard of that."

"Electrical wiring?"

"Not that either."

Without quite as much hesitation, but with a bit of panic he couldn't entirely hide, Kip pressed on. "Phone? Internet? Touch-entry keypad?"

A look Kip could only describe as empathy crossed Smudge's expression. "How far have you traveled, Kipling Summerfield?"

ECHOES OF THE SEA

Kip ran a hand over his forehead and rubbed at a temple. He was starting to get a headache. Did 1803 even have aspirin? Probably not. "I don't know."

"Time behaves strangely on these waters." Smudge knew. He knew.

"Can you prove to me it's 1803?" Kip asked.

"If all you've seen hasn't proven it to you, I suspect you might be too thick for sorting it out."

"It's not a matter of being stupid," Kip said. "It just doesn't make any sense. I think I would have noticed if I'd gone through time. Surely something would have said, 'News flash. It's two hundred years ago.'"

"That you didn't notice isn't a flattering reflection on your intellect."

It wasn't that he hadn't noticed. There'd just been an explanation. A historical site would be restored to what it would have been like in history, though perhaps without quite as much over-the-top effort. And a place that was meant to have historical reenactors would have people who seemed to be from a different time.

But some things were *too different* for a reenactment. His British accent wasn't actually terrible, but it would seem off to people from over two hundred years ago. The British accent had changed in that time. RP English hadn't even been a thing in 1803. He had learned that from dialect coaches. And absolutely no one reacted with terror to the sight of a tattoo anymore. But Amelia and Jane had honestly looked horrified.

"I am in deep waters." Kip turned enough to lean back against the workbench as well, standing next to Smudge. "Now what am I supposed to do?" he muttered, though he didn't know if he was actually asking the question or just expressing his hopelessness.

Smudge answered anyway. "My grandmother said her cried for a couple of weeks."

"Crying isn't really my thing."

Smudge looked at him out of the corner of his eye. "You are gonna have to learn to speak more like a person of now."

"Like a Miss-Archibald person of now, or like an everyone-in-the-village person of now? Because those are two very different things."

Smudge offered a small smile. "You'd likely do better mimicking she."

That was probably true.

"If I really am in 1803, how do I get back to *my* time?"

Smudge shook his head. "Don't know that you can. The tides can't be controlled or manipulated. Even if you managed to get back in the water when the right type of storm was raging, there's no telling when the tides would take you."

Kip might end up in a time he understood even less than this one. "Then I'm trapped here. I'm trapped *now*."

Smudge stood up straight once more and turned to look at him. "May I make a suggestion?"

"Please do."

Smudge held his gaze, confident as anything. It was something those portraying servants or people of the working class were generally not scripted to do in *The Beau*. Mick had said that Amelia couldn't be friends with Jane because servants weren't friends with those who employed them. But Smudge was something different.

"Keep on as you have been," Smudge said. "You're finding a place in this corner of this time. Us is isolated enough here that you're unlikely to find yourself in a great deal of trouble over things you get wrong. Once you've sorted out how to manage in this unfamiliar time, you can decide *where* you mean to go, even if you can't control *when*."

"Are you going to tell the village? They obviously know about the tides."

"Maybe not just yet," Smudge said. "Them knows, and most aren't overly suspicious of people claiming to have come here that way. But them'd have a heap of questions, and until you have a heap of answers, it might be simpler to keep mum."

"What about Miss Archibald? Do I tell her?"

Smudge's expression turned into that of a person who couldn't decide what to say or what to think on a matter.

Ought Kip to tell Amelia? Would she even believe him?

Chapter 18

Amelia had made her way to the outbuilding where Kipling kept his tools so she could ask if Smudge would look after the horses tonight. She'd arrived just in time to hear the most befuddling discussion between the two men.

Kipling thought himself to have journeyed across time.

"There is nothing in the legend that says a person can return to his own time?" Kipling asked Smudge. "If the tides shoved me over two hundred years backward, why couldn't they toss me those two hundred years forward again?"

"Them could, but only by coincidence. It can't be forced or arranged."

"You cannot honestly believe any of this," Amelia said, stepping fully into the outbuilding.

It was testament to how deep in conversation the two men were that they both jumped at the sound of her voice. She might have found it amusing if what they'd been discussing weren't so delusional.

"What did you overhear?" Kipling asked.

"That you believe you have arrived here from two hundred years in the future."

He held his hands up as he shrugged. "Very few things have made sense from the moment Ivers pulled me from the water. Believe me, this was not the explanation I was expecting, and I am well aware that it feels improbable."

"Im*possible*," she corrected. "People do not jump across multiple centuries."

"I agree," Kipling said, "and yet I seem to have done precisely that."

She shook her head. "This is absurd."

"It isn't though," Smudge said. "Us've known about the Tides of Time for generations."

The pull of a local legend could be strong for those who had grown up hearing it. But Kipling was not from this area of the world. He would not have a lifetime of tales clouding his judgment. Why, then, was he trying to convince her that he believed all this? Not merely *believed* it but had *experienced* it.

"Is this a jest?" she asked him.

"No. I am, to my own shock, in earnest. I am stuck here." And he smiled. A laughing sort of smile.

Laughing.

"'Stuck here,' just as I told you *I* am." She swallowed down a surge of emotion. "You are mocking me."

"Not at all." He stepped closer.

She stepped back. "Why are you doing this?"

"Amelia—"

"I have not ever treated you unkindly. Why are you returning that with cruelty?"

"Miss." Smudge bent into her line of sight. "I'm overstepping myself, but I think it needs doing. You should listen to he. What him's been through'll make you at least wonder."

She leaned more heavily on her cane, eying Kipling. "Why should I entertain any of this?"

"Because I didn't let you fall off a ladder to your possible death?"

"Broken arm, at the worst," she countered.

"An *un*broken arm in exchange for hearing me out?"

She glanced at Smudge.

He nodded earnestly.

Kipling watched her with pleading eyes.

"I can hardly believe I am allowing this." She motioned for him to make his explanation.

"You say I speak oddly. You mentioned how strange the clothes I arrived in were. I have a tattoo, which is unheard of. I asked Smudge about plumbing, electricity, internet, phones. He hadn't heard of any of those things, and I suspect neither have you."

"I haven't."

"But I have." He looked and sounded entirely sincere, which only added to her confusion. "You told me about the will you are subject to and how your uncle can force you to marry someone of his choosing."

"And you were absolutely certain that the law didn't permit that." She *had* found that odd.

"The tune I played for you," he said. "I was so confused that you didn't recognize it."

"You were absolutely incredulous." She shook her head. "But you are American, and that—Are you actually American?" She ought to know which parts of his story were true.

"I am," he said.

"Your odd way of speaking. Is that how Americans sound two hundred years from now?"

"No."

"Is it how the English speak?"

The answer to the question seemed to elude him for a moment. "I'm not entirely certain how to answer that. I've been told that when I speak with an English accent, it sounds authentic. But I suspect no American can affect an English manner of speaking without some errors in the doing of it. And just as is true now, there isn't just one English accent or dialect."

"And is your name actually Kipling Summerfield? Because, forgive me for saying so, it sounds very much like the sort of name a person would give himself in order to sound as if he were born to a higher station than he was."

His smile tiptoed back. "Forgive *me* for saying so, but I could say the same about Amelia Archibald."

She had never thought her name particularly elegant or impressive. Perhaps its alliterative nature gave him that impression. "You still didn't answer my question."

"It is my actual name."

She refused to ponder too deeply why that was a relief. "Why were you in this part of the world if you are from America?"

"I have lived in England for more than a decade," he said.

"An England that won't exist for two hundred years?"

He held his hands out, palms up. "I know it sounds absurd, and I can't explain it. But to me, 1803 was over two hundred years ago. And this being the year everyone keeps telling me it is actually explains so much of what I've seen since coming here."

It actually did make a strange and mind-boggling sort of sense. That didn't mean she was ready to believe the theory. "It is absolutely absurd."

"And?" Smudge pressed.

"And still somehow strangely rational."

"Then him's convinced you?" Smudge asked.

"No," she was quick to say. "But I am willing to accept that he isn't trying to make me look like a fool and isn't one himself."

Kipling nodded. "I'll accept that."

"You *were* pulled out of the water by Mr. Ivers? That part wasn't fabricated?"

"I was swept off a small pier in a sudden storm. Green lightning struck the water. Next thing I knew, Mr. Ivers was pulling me out of the water, and I was here . . . I was *now*."

"A person has to be in the water for the tides to pull he," Smudge said.

Traveling through time. Was she actually considering the possibility? She was but couldn't truly explain why.

"What do you intend to do now?" Kipling asked.

"Stay out of the water," Amelia said dryly.

His eyes sparkled as his smile broadened. "I have adopted the same philosophy."

"Mind you," she said by way of warning, "I have not adopted your same ready acceptance of this . . . fable. But I'm willing to accept that you accept it without believing you are entirely touched in the head."

"But maybe *a smidge* mad?" He didn't look offended, which was reassuring.

"My uncle is, I am certain, looking for any reason to declare me inept, to say that I ought not be trusted with the inheritance that awaits me. Should he discover that I have given house room to a man who thinks he has come from two hundred years in the future, he would most certainly point to that as proof of how unreliable my judgment is."

Smudge leaned back against the worktable once more. "The village would believe him had come from the future, but it'd still make he an oddity and a thing to be gabbed about. It might get whispered to your uncle."

They were in a bind, to be sure. She didn't particularly want Kipling to have to endure the indignity of being stared at like an animal in a menagerie, no matter that she wasn't convinced that he wasn't at least marginally dotty. But equally, as she'd surmised days ago, she couldn't simply toss him out when he had nowhere to go. He'd likely be locked up in an asylum if he wandered about telling people he was from the future.

"You'd best continue on as you have been, pretending you're simply from America and that is why you don't understand anything or make any sense."

He looked to be fighting a laugh. She liked that about him, that he found humor even in difficult moments.

"I need you to keep helping me here," she said. "Without you and without the help you brought in from the village"—she motioned to Smudge—"I have no hope of securing my future."

"I will help in any way I'm able," he promised.

"Does that include teaching me that tune on the pianoforte? You did say you would."

His expression softened. Genuine fondness entered his eyes. "I would love to, Amelia."

"Where would you like me to drop myself?" Smudge asked, reminding her that he was there.

"Where would you be most comfortable?" It likely would not be in the house, but she didn't know what else she had to offer.

"I like being around horses. Most stables have a room for the hands."

"I actually intend to ask if you would look after the animals stabled at the moment."

Smudge offered a bow, then sauntered out of the building, whistling to himself and, generally, not seeming the least overset by all they had discussed.

"Do you need me to find a place to stay other than the blue bedchamber?" Kipling asked. "Mick said there are servants' rooms up on the attic level. Or Smudge might let me bunk with him."

She likely would be wisest to have him stay somewhere else, but thoughts of that distance made her nervous. More than nervous, it made her feel lonely. How was it that in such a short time, this man she was discovering she knew so little about had managed to become essential to her? "Mr. Winthrop makes me uneasy." She switched her cane to her other hand, better situated for pacing. "I don't think he would do anything underhanded or untoward, but"—she turned and faced Kipling directly once more, finding herself standing closer to him than she'd expected—"I would feel safer if I knew you were in the house."

He didn't mock or belittle her concerns, neither did he puff up like a peacock. He took her hand and held it in a gentle and reassuring grip. "I'll do what I can to keep an eye on everything, though I assume I need to do so while continuing to keep myself hidden."

"Yes. A tradesman wouldn't be living in the house, so your presence there, if we introduced you as the carpenter, would be considered ineptitude on my part. But a gentleman staying in the home of an unmarried lady—that would be a scandal, which would be worse."

"And a man who thinks he's a time traveler would be worse still?"

She nodded. "Infinitely worse."

"I can pretend I was simply out for a leisurely swim when Mr. Ivers plucked me from the water and leave out just how far I actually . . . swam."

She smiled and held more tightly to his hand. "I'm grateful he found you. Too many people are lost in this stretch of the sea."

"I am mildly lost, I confess. And I suspect once I'm better able to wrap my mind around my situation, I'm going to be horrified."

"Because you have come here from a different time?"

He raised her hand almost to his lips. "You don't believe it yet."

"Can you blame me?"

"No." He lightly kissed her fingers.

Feeling simultaneously bold and bashful, she asked, "May I, when there aren't others around to object to it, call you Kipling?"

"That would please me immensely. And with the same caveat, may I call you Amelia?"

She hazarded a glance at him, and the warmth in his gaze brought a blush to her cheeks. "I would like that."

As she made her way slowly and carefully to the house, she had to admit to herself an unexpected truth: She was beginning to fall in love with a man who just might be partially mad.

Chapter 19

*T*wo hundred years.

Kipling believed the story he'd told her, a story she couldn't entirely dismiss despite its being impossible. She couldn't deny his sincerity or that he was distressed about his circumstances. Regardless of whether those "circumstances" really were being centuries out of his own time, he wasn't entirely happy on Guilford with her.

And yet, Kipling held her hand and spoke kindly to her. He was cheerful and eagerly helped where he could. He'd left the island *and come back*. He made her smile and laugh. With him, she felt more confident and competent. She felt safe and cared about.

Two hundred years.

She didn't know how to reconcile that.

"How discouraged you must be, Miss Archibald, that this estate is not part of your inheritance." Mr. Winthrop's voice broke into her thoughts.

Her uncle and his new friend hadn't needed her input through most of their dinner conversation. Not being Mr. Winthrop's focus for the first part of the meal had been a welcome reprieve.

"I have never had any wish to lay claim to Guilford," she said.

His smile leaned too close to patronizing. "Your modesty does you credit."

He made her so deeply uncomfortable. If only there'd been a way to include Kipling in the evening meal. He might have managed to dampen Mr. Winthrop's disagreeable attentions. And she would have enjoyed having Kipling there for his own sake.

"Guilford is part of the Stirling estate entailment," Uncle said to his friend. "My niece's inheritance is quite substantial, I assure you." He wore the look of one on the verge of panic. His fish was wriggling on its hook. "There is more than enough for purchasing an elegant estate and seeing it run and kept up properly."

"An elegant estate"—Mr. Winthrop leaned forward, gazing intently at her from across the table—"and an equally elegant and beautiful lady. What a remarkable combination."

How was it that a compliment could make a person feel so entirely belittled?

"Rest assured, Winthrop," Uncle said, "even half her inheritance is more than sufficient for making improvements to an already elegant estate."

That brought a flash of remembered understanding to Mr. Winthrop's face. And on the heels of that reminder came an expression of increased intrigue. Indeed, his gaze on her grew warmer, more intense.

A tiptoe of misgiving crawled over her skin. There was no doubt any longer of her Uncle's intention where his mercenary friend was concerned.

"*Even half her inheritance . . .*" That was what a future husband would receive if she were declared a failure at Guilford. Mr. Winthrop already had plans for using her dowry for his own benefit. She suspected her best hope in being forced to wed Mr.

Winthrop would be that he would get her money and forget all about her.

But she likely wasn't that lucky.

She simply couldn't fail at Guilford. She would record every single thing she accomplished. Perhaps Smudge would talk with the people in the village to see if they would take her part. They didn't have to make the journey to the estate, but if they would at least support her in making her case to her uncle, she might manage to weather this storm.

The time came for her to withdraw so the gentlemen could enjoy their port. It was the perfect escape.

She rose, as did they. "I fear I am exceptionally weary this evening." It wasn't untrue, although her weariness was more mental and emotional than physical. "I will bid you both farewell in the morning when you depart."

Afraid they might seize upon the topic to declare themselves content to remain beyond the morning, she curtsied and, cane firmly in hand, made the swiftest retreat she could manage while still maintaining a semblance of elegance. She didn't stop until she reached the corridor leading to her bedchamber, where she fully intended to unabashedly hide. Even Mr. Winthrop, with his uncomfortable gaze, wouldn't breach that threshold.

Or would he? Amelia hated that she didn't know for certain.

Her rush toward her bedchamber came to a sudden halt. There was a footman standing against the corridor wall not terribly far from her door. He was dressed in full livery, which only made the sight doubly surprising. They didn't have any footmen. And she didn't think the estate had livery for any hypothetical footman to wear.

She approached slowly, unsure what she intended to do. Insisting he explain himself would only work if he actually chose to do so. The same was true of demanding that he leave. He didn't work for her, so what motivation would he have to comply?

But as she drew close, he winked. *Winked.* And she knew him in an instant.

"Kipling, what are you doing here? And what are you wearing?"

"The remarkable Marsh knew where the livery for the Guilford footmen was stored belowstairs. He kitted me out."

Amelia wasn't familiar with that phrase. She assumed it meant Marsh had given Kipling the livery to wear.

"But why are you dressed as a footman?"

"A footman posted in the corridor prevents a lot of mischief, at least according to *The Beau.*"

"When did you speak with Mr. Brummell?" she asked.

"Brummell?" His confusion quite suddenly turned to understanding. "Beau Brummell. He lives now, doesn't he? A real flesh-and-blood person." He shook his head in amazement. "Beau Brummell. Man."

He lives now.

Two hundred years.

"I still don't understand why you are dressed as a footman," she said, "and are standing in the corridor."

"Because Mr. Winthrop makes you uncomfortable. I think he even frightens you to a degree." Kipling gave a quick, firm nod. "If I am here tonight, he will be far more likely to behave."

He was protecting her—and at cost to himself. "You intend to stand up all night?"

"Once the potential mischief maker is in his own room long enough to have fallen asleep, I'll sit in a chair and doze a bit."

"You will be exhausted come morning."

His eyes softened on her. "But you will be safe. And you will sleep better if you aren't afraid."

Good heavens. She didn't think she'd ever known anyone quite like him. "I am beginning to suspect you are a remarkable person, Kipling Summerfield."

"Feel free to tell that to—" His brow pulled. His mouth twisted tight. Whatever he'd originally meant to say, he finished his sentence with a quiet "hmm." And whatever thought was pulling that "hmm" from him appeared to be a heavy and even difficult one.

Sensing he needed a moment to himself, she took a step toward her bedchamber door. "Thank you, Kipling. I will feel better tonight knowing there is someone watching for mischief."

"I am glad to help." His thoughts clearly remained elsewhere.

Amelia slipped into her room. Having not had a lady's maid of her own at her uncle's house, her wardrobe consisted entirely of clothes she could, with a great deal of twisting and bending, change in and out of on her own. She was able to prepare for bed quickly, without having to wait for anyone to come help her.

Warm in her nightdress, a wrapper on over it, and donning thick-knit stockings, she tiptoed back to the door. She hesitated a moment. It really was rather bold of her to be even considering gabbing with a gentleman, one dressed as a footman, while in her nightclothes.

And yet she found she couldn't entirely stop herself.

She opened the door a crack and peeked out, keeping most of herself in her room. He looked over at her. And he smiled. Amelia suspected that smile would always melt her heart.

"I'm still here," he said with a laugh.

"I wasn't doubting your dedication." She hoped he could hear how sincere she was. "I wanted to ask . . . I still don't know how certain I am of your . . . travels. But I know that you do believe it. And that leaves me wondering how you are faring with all you have . . . learned today. With what has happened to you."

His expression clouded once more.

"But only if you wish to talk about it," she quickly amended. "I'm not attempting to pry. I only wanted to offer a listening ear if you wished for one."

"You wish to listen to me opine about something you are relatively sure isn't true or possible?"

"I am certain that you are a person deserving of being listened to and worthy of being believed. Accepting impossible things takes time, so I hope you will be patient."

He glanced down the corridor toward the turn that led to the grand stairs, the direction her visitors would eventually be coming. Amelia leaned back into her room, but didn't close the door. She stood very still and waited. And listened.

"If I weren't the one personally experiencing these 'impossible things,' I think I wouldn't believe it. But it's true, Amelia. It's mind-bogglingly true. The reality of it is crashing down on me, creating wave after wave of realizations that I am not entirely prepared for."

Amelia pressed her back against the wall beside the door, feeling somehow closer to him, knowing his back was pressed to the other side of that same wall.

"There are people I will never see again." Pain punctuated the words. "And while it is truly daunting to know that I will never again see *anyone* I know, it is the moments when specific people enter my thoughts that I am overwhelmed by it all."

"Your family?" she guessed.

"I will miss my family." There was a caveat coming. "But there is a great deal of difficulty there. That makes it harder in some ways. The rift between us will never be healed."

"I am sorry, Kipling."

"If you grew up in your uncle's home, you must have lost your parents as well."

She didn't know if he was changing the subject because he didn't want to talk about his family or if it was a helpful way of coming to terms with his loss. Either way, she felt herself equal to the task of talking about the parents she still deeply grieved. "My parents died when I was five years old. My grandfather was supposed to take me in, but he didn't want me. So I was sent to my uncle and aunt's house, and I've lived with them ever since."

"How could your grandfather possibly not want you? I can't imagine you were a particularly rotten child, seeing as you're a particularly lovely person."

If not for the wall obstructing his view, her ever deepening blush would have immediately given away her tenderness for him.

"Grandfather was often unkind, and I think, to an extent, he enjoyed that about himself. While there is a degree of pain in having a close relative who wanted nothing to do with me, I think if I had been forced to live with him, it would have been far worse. My aunt and uncle, at least, weren't cruel. And my cousin wasn't either. I was lonely, but I wasn't unhappy."

"This is the same uncle who you suspect is now trying to marry you off to someone who would make you unhappy?" He sounded doubtful, and rightly so.

"I've been struggling to make sense of that myself." It weighed on her, in fact. "I think the money has proved too alluring, and he is allowing it to change him, which is a shame."

"The money? You mean *your* money?"

"If I fail at my task here at Guilford, half of my inheritance will be his. The other half will be my dowry to go to whomever he chooses as my husband. I suspect he is hoping to make some kind of arrangement with Mr. Winthrop in which a portion of that dowry will stay with my uncle. I don't know that for certain, but I can't shake the suspicion."

A moment passed without a response. She closed her eyes, hoping Kipling hadn't walked away or that their conversation was abruptly ending.

"We have to make certain your uncle isn't able to do that."

She pressed one hand to her heart, holding back a sigh she wasn't ready for him to hear. He not only wasn't abandoning her, but he also meant to keep helping. And he cared what happened to her. This stranger she still understood so little about and still struggled to believe had come to Guilford from so very far away had quickly found a place in her heart. She cared about him and wanted him to care about her. And it seemed as though he did.

"I believe I hear the voices of your uncle and Mr. Winthrop," Kipling said. "They'll likely reach the corridor in another moment. I'll stay at my post. You get some rest."

"Thank you, Kipling," she said.

"You're welcome."

She heard his steps move away. He would stay close enough to her room to make certain she was safe but far enough away not to draw too much attention.

He was remarkable, and she suspected he didn't know it.

Kip was stationed in his place, and Amelia had closed her door by the time Mr. Stirling and Mr. Winthrop appeared in the corridor. They both took note of him at almost exactly the same time, and they both looked thoroughly confused. Kip remembered from *The Beau* that footmen at their posts kept very still, their eyes focused ahead, pretending they were unaware of everyone and everything.

"I didn't realize your niece employed any footmen," Mr. Winthrop said, sounding thoroughly displeased at the idea.

"He must be newly hired."

"How did she manage that? She's not to leave the island." Mr. Winthrop sounded almost excited. "Does that mean she did leave? Have you caught her out already?"

They were drawing nearer but not lowering their voices. Did people in this time truly think their servants couldn't hear things? He'd always thought it had been done on *The Beau* to simplify scripts and to make the upper-class characters seem fancier or stuffier. Apparently, it was a real thing.

"Someone else here must have made the arrangements," Mr. Stirling said.

"There isn't a carriage of any kind," Mr. Winthrop countered. "The housekeeper and butler are too ancient to walk across the sea road."

"There's a maid who works here who could have made the journey," Mr. Stirling said. "Or the Iverses at the lighthouse."

Mr. Winthrop and Mr. Stirling didn't spare Kip so much as a glance as they passed him. Their brief look upon reaching the corridor was to be all the scrutiny he'd receive. Hopefully, the brevity of that, combined with the white-powdered wig and livery, would make him difficult to recognize should their paths cross again.

"She said there was a local man doing carpentry," Mr. Winthrop said. "A man from the village could certainly manage to bring others from the village across the sea road to work. If she's made inroads there, we're sunk."

"Don't lose hope," Mr. Stirling said. They were making their way farther down the corridor, and their voices were growing softer. "She has to stay on this island for four and a half more months. I don't think she'll be able to do it."

"However long she manages to endure being here, this estate will be in better condition than it was before," Mr. Winthrop said. "It already is, from what you've said."

Mr. Stirling nodded. "Let us both hope she doesn't manage to bring it into *excellent* condition, or I'll have a very difficult time arguing that she has failed."

They separated, and each went into his bedchamber.

Kip stayed precisely where he was, not letting his servant's demeanor slip at all in case either of them very suddenly poked his head out. Kip hoped Amelia hadn't been listening. While she already suspected what he had just heard, there was something awful about hearing it stated so bluntly.

Her grandfather had rejected her out of hand. She'd lived with an indifferent uncle who was beginning to follow in her grandfather's footsteps. She didn't deserve the mistreatment she had so often been subjected to. It was unfair the way families could hurt each other. He knew that all too well.

Chapter 20

Kip was exhausted. Sleeping in a chair in a corridor wasn't the most restful arrangement. And jolting awake at every sound in case Mr. Winthrop was on the prowl hadn't helped. He'd mused at one point that it was good practice for if he were cast in a role that required a believable jumpscare. But his heart had dropped in the next instant. There would be no more roles. There would be no regaining the career he'd lost. Everything he'd ever known was gone.

He admitted to himself that he wasn't in a great mood as he walked out to the work shed the next morning. He was tired, frustrated, and entirely out of his element.

Film and movies didn't exist in 1803. There was the theater. Season three of *The Beau* had included a plot line in which one of the main characters had decided to "tread the boards." But that had taken place in London, where the theaters had been. Kip didn't know that he could keep up this I-belong-in-this-century facade in such a complex city.

What chance was there that he could make a convincing gentleman by borrowing from his portrayal of Tennyson Lamont? That role had all been scripted. He was managing to improvise well enough in this tiny corner of England, but he'd need a lot of coaching and practice to pull it off long-term. He was probably more suited to a carpenter in the working class.

Of course, Amelia was a lady of the upper classes, no matter that she'd been a poor relation. A carpenter and a lady didn't move in the same circles in this era. If he leaned into that role, he'd never see her again after they left Guilford.

Getting ahead of yourself, Kip.

They weren't together, and they didn't know each other very well yet. Making huge life decisions based on what she would think and whether or not they could be together—even just as friends—was an incredibly odd thing to be doing.

In the midst of these spiraling thoughts, the sound of Smudge's whistle reached the work shed. Whistling didn't usually bother Kip, but it grated on him in that moment. He kept his eyes on his list of tasks to be accomplished and kept his mouth shut so he wouldn't say anything he would regret. Smudge had become a quick friend. He'd given Kip answers to impossible questions and was someone he could talk to about it all. Kip wouldn't be a jerk to him.

"Miss Archibald's visitors left this morning," Smudge said. "Mick had a few choice words to say about both men. The boy don't mince words."

"I had a chance to listen in on them last night," Kip said. "They don't deserve to have words minced."

Smudge looked concerned. "Them's making trouble for Miss Archibald?"

"I believe they intend to 'prove' she didn't do a good job managing Guilford."

"I'm here to help you do whatever it is her needs you to do. What task do you have for me?"

"This is what I'm trying to get done." Kip tapped the list he'd nailed to the wall. "You let me know if there's any of it you can do."

"Can't read a lick," Smudge said, "so you'll have to tell me what's on it."

They went over it one item at a time. Smudge said he was able to do a lot of things listed, so with the both of them working, they might get through the list in the next few weeks. And if Smudge would stay on, that would give them the freedom to work on other projects Amelia might need done.

"I've been curious," Smudge said as they made their way back to the house, tools in hand. "How is it you went as long as you did without knowing you weren't in your own time?"

"I would guess most people don't assume they've traveled through time just because things seem a little odd."

"But I think it'd be more than just 'a little' odd. You can't tell me not much has changed in two hundred years. You was tossing out words I'd never heard before and seemed to think I ought to know them without even a thought."

"Oh, more has changed than I could possibly explain."

Smudge didn't know what plumbing was. Trying to explain things like space shuttles and the internet was likely pointless.

Smudge gave him a side eye as they stepped through a door at the back of the house. "You just looked around at this place that ain't got any of them things and thought, 'Seems normal to me'?" There was just enough of a laugh in his voice for Kip to know that he was enjoying the ridiculousness of this all.

In an unexpected way, it helped Kip feel better about it too. A *very little*.

"In my own time," he said, "the place I was about to go to before the ocean decided to take me for a ride was intentionally supposed to mirror life two hundred years before my time. It was supposed to be the exact kind of odd that I found here. I just thought the people running the place had gone to the extreme."

"And is that a regular sort of thing in two hundred years? Pretending like all the changes that happened haven't happened?"

Kip gave that some thought. He supposed it was true. Some of the most popular movies and television shows were set in the distant past, or a fantasy version of it. Historical-themed destinations were pretty common. Museums were erected to keep the past alive and known. "I guess it is a regular sort of thing."

"What is it us has in this time that people are missing so much?"

Another good question. This time had diseases that were unheard of in the future. None of the modern conveniences. No modern medicine to help treat things that killed people in the 1800s but were merely a blip on the radar in Kip's time. Travel was so much easier. Communication was so much more convenient. What was it people missed?

"It's an escape, I guess," Kip said. "We spend bits of time pretending it's long ago, but don't have to actually live it every day."

"It's more like a game than a goal," Smudge said.

"Sometimes, yeah."

They made their way to Amelia's book room. A few of the shelves in there were either rickety or broken, and they were going to see those fixed. They'd have that room sorted, as there wasn't much that needed to be done.

"And in the future, do all Americans sound like you?"

Kip actually laughed. "Miss Archibald asked me the same thing. No Americans sound like me. I've lived quite a while in England, and my occupation required me to sound as though I were from here."

"It's strange on the ears, I'll tell you." Smudge actually winced.

Kip shook his head even as he grinned. "Your manner of talking is strange on my ears."

"Our way of talking don't exist anymore?" That seemed to hang heavy on his mind.

"It actually probably does," Kip said. "I just never visited this area of England."

Relief flitted over his face.

Kip would have to be careful what he said to people. It wasn't just a matter of worrying about setting in motion something that would change the future but also not inadvertently causing people sorrow over things that couldn't be avoided or things they would never see happen. He could only imagine how it would feel to tell the people of this area about the devastation that would come in World War I and World War II.

That thought made him stop for a moment. 1803. *The Beau* took place later than this, when the war with Napoleon was in full swing. That was in the future. If Kip decided to make himself a person of the lower classes or found he had no choice but to do so, he might very well find himself conscripted into the army, fighting in a war he knew was going to be long and bloody and in many ways horrific. And the war of 1812 lay in the future as well, when America, which everyone would know he was from because, apparently, his accent was so atrocious, would go from being a tense former colony to an enemy again.

This was getting complicated.

They were in the midst of their work when Amelia stepped into the room. He expected her to look relieved and lighter in spirit now that her uncle and his unwanted guest were gone. But she didn't. While a very large part of him wanted to drop what he was doing and assure her that everything would be fine and that she didn't need to worry, he was too tired and overwhelmed to do much more than glance over at her and hope that she wasn't about to announce yet another complication he'd have to sort out.

"My uncle says he'll return soon," she said. "He didn't say how soon, but I suspect he doesn't want to give me very much time between disruptions to make headway."

That lined up with everything Kip had heard from him. "Is he bringing his friend back with him?" The question emerged grumpy.

The change in tone clearly caught her attention. She looked at him with more uncertainty than before. "I don't know. I suspect he will."

"It might make sense to try to hire an actual footman," Kip said. "We can station that fellow outside your door so I can get some sleep."

She nodded. "I did think of that, actually. Smudge, perhaps you would be willing to return to the village in the next few days to see if anyone else would come up here to work. I can pay them. I've been given sufficient funds for that. I simply can't go beg them myself. And I can't change the fact that this island is surrounded by these fearful waters."

"The people are hesitant, but I think them can be convinced." Smudge kept working as he talked.

Marsh and Mrs. Jagger always stopped whatever they were doing when he or Amelia addressed them. Was that actually how it was supposed to be done? Servants and tradesmen had casual and friendly conversations with members of the upper classes on *The Beau*, but he knew not everything on the show had been accurate. Problem was, he didn't know which parts of it were inaccurate, and the stuff they'd had on the show was all he had to lean on to navigate this time period.

"It's a shame you can't come to meet the villagers," Smudge added. "That'd help a heap."

"I truly can't," she said. "But not because I don't want to."

Smudge nodded, though whether he knew the details of her situation or not, Kip couldn't say.

"I'll bring Mick with me," Smudge said. "Him's been down to the village enough. Everywho's fond of the boy. Them'll think well of you, hearing from Mick how you're fond of he and have looked after he."

"I know what it is to be an orphan," she said without emotion or self-pity.

She'd touched very briefly on the loss of her parents the night before. Kip had wanted to ask her how they'd died but hadn't yet felt himself in a position to press.

Amelia turned to Kip. In tones too pleading for his peace of mind, she asked him, "May I speak with you for just a moment in the corridor?"

Why did she seem so sure that he would say no or be upset at the request?

He nodded his agreement and, setting his tools down for the time being, walked with her out into the corridor.

"Thank you for all you did last night," she said. "I can't imagine you rested well."

He shook his head. "As fitful as my sleep was sitting up in the corridor, I think it would have been far worse in my own room, worrying that Mr. Winthrop was causing you grief."

Her expression turned pensive. "He worries me," she whispered. "And now, so does my uncle. He never used to, but he is proving himself greedy."

"He and his friend spoke in the corridor last night," Kip said. "They are hoping to see you fail; they said so."

She released a tight breath, one heavy with distress.

"We'll thwart them," Kip said. Firmly.

Amelia's shoulders relaxed somewhat. "I should allow you to return to your work. I need to see to my own. I have come to the conclusion that should I manage to keep my inheritance—" She gave a tiny shake of her head. "*When* I secure my inheritance," she amended, "I will find myself a home that doesn't need nearly as much work as this one. I'd far rather spend my days beautifying a garden than restoring a house."

"Sounds to me like you need to go spend some time in your garden. Smudge and I'll keep at our work in here. You go resecure your peace."

A hint of a blush touched her cheeks. "I think you are the first person I have ever known who has understood that about me so quickly."

It was, truth be told, a proud moment for him. To be understood and seen was a powerful thing. He liked knowing he had managed that for her.

"What is it that gives you a measure of peace?" Amelia asked him. "I suspect it isn't gardens."

"I can't say I've ever felt that way about gardens. However, I don't dislike them."

She smiled softly. It was difficult to think logically when she did that. Did she have any idea how hauntingly beautiful she was? He suspected she didn't.

"I will discover what it is that brings you peace and a feeling of belonging," she said. "I'm going to discover what your garden is."

He watched her walk away, both sad to see her go and delighted at the possibility that she intended to study him. But along with that came the realization that if she was able to sort out what would bring him peace and contentment, she would manage to do something he himself never had.

Chapter 21

A storm broke over Guilford that night. Amelia stood at one of the drawing room windows, trying to breathe while telling herself she was safe even if she didn't feel safe at all.

"The ocean is angry tonight." Kipling spoke from directly beside her. Though she hadn't heard him approach, he didn't startle her the way almost anyone else would have. He was a peaceful person. Perhaps that was why she was struggling to discover what his "garden" was. Maybe he didn't need something like that to bring him peace; he brought it with him. "I have been told many times that storms are more common in this area of the Channel. I don't think I appreciated how true that actually is."

A strike of lightning was followed very quickly by a furious clap of thunder. She wrapped her arms around herself, watching the nearly black night through the window. It didn't comfort or reassure her. Why, then, didn't she simply walk away, turn her back?

Because one ought never to turn her back on something as dangerous as the sea.

"You had seemed to be less unnerved by it these past couple of days," Kipling said.

"I've had a few moments in which I almost forgot it was there. Even the sound of it seemed to have quieted."

Another flash of lightning and a rumble from the clouds made her shudder. And then, without warning, Kip wrapped his arms around her from behind, holding her in a warm and protective embrace. She likely should have been shocked. Society certainly would have insisted on her feeling it. But instead, she leaned against him and set her arms atop his.

"Do people often embrace like this in your time?" she asked.

"Your question makes me think that such things are *not* done often in *this* time."

She shook her head.

"Clearly, I am not doing a very good job of adhering to current protocol."

"You will eventually have to learn the trick of it," she said. "But maybe not right this moment."

When he spoke again he'd leaned close enough that his breath tickled her ear. "I'm rather enjoying the arrangement myself." He didn't say it in an overly flirtatious way, but it still made her heart flutter.

She'd known him for such a relatively short amount of time, but she'd come to like him deeply. Her heart had formed an attachment to him that she couldn't have predicted. Perhaps it was that they understood each other in such a profound way: both displaced, both trapped, both finding their footing in an unfamiliar situation. But she knew it was more than that as well. He was something unique and remarkable.

In this moment, I am grateful for that.

The pounding of the surf grew softer as the flutter of her pulse grew more intense. And the way his chest rose and fell with each breath pushed from her thoughts the reminder of the unavoidable incursion of the sea on the road. She wasn't allowed to take that road, but there was something comforting in knowing it was there. When the storms raged and it disappeared, she felt even more closed in.

"Feel free to tell me to mind my own business," he said, "but I've been curious ever since our conversation in the corridor a couple of nights ago."

She wasn't sure what he would ask about but felt certain she'd be happy to talk to him about anything.

"You lost your parents when you were very young," he said. "I suspect I might be guessing correctly how they died."

She closed her eyes against the reminder and held more tightly to his arms. She never talked about their deaths with anyone, not even her aunt and uncle. But most people who heard of her crushing fear of the ocean could piece together the reality of it.

"They were taken by the sea, weren't they?"

"Yes," she answered quietly. "Not in this stretch of it. We were in the North Sea, and there was a storm. We thought we'd passed the worst of it, but the ship had sustained damage, and no one realized it soon enough. The ship sank."

"*We?* You were on the ship as well?"

Again, she nodded, but this time, she couldn't bring herself to say anything. Very few people had survived that shipwreck. Her father had placed her and her mother in the only rowboat available but had not managed to get in it himself before a wave on the still-rough waters had pulled him under. Mother had been injured, though Amelia had been too young to remember precisely what that injury was. By the time their rowboat was found, her mother was close to death, and her father was gone forever. Within a day, Amelia was an orphan.

"I'm sorry you endured that," Kipling said.

"But I lived," she countered. "What right do I have, really, to feel sorry for myself when so many others—more than just my parents—died in the water that day? I should feel grateful, but I struggle with it."

She'd not told anyone that before. She hadn't dared.

"In my day, there is a name for that feeling, and there are people who'd know how to help with it."

She turned slightly, enough to look up at him, but not so much that he'd have to drop his arms away. She didn't want to lose that connection when she felt so fragile. "There is a name for the weight that has sat on my heart for twenty years?"

He nodded. It wasn't pity in his face but understanding. "They call it 'survivor's guilt,' the weight and the grief and the, as it says, guilt of being the only person, or one of the few people, who survives an ordeal that others don't. That's a difficult thing for the mind and the heart to make peace with. It eats away at a person."

To her horror, tears stung at the back of her eyes. He was describing so perfectly what she had felt for so long. She usually pushed it down, pretending it wasn't there because it didn't make sense. Guilt at not being dead? Guilt over something she didn't cause and couldn't have prevented? She'd always felt so foolish.

He tucked her ever tighter against him, hugging her truly and properly. She closed her eyes and wrapped her arms around him as well.

A vicious burst of thunder rattled the windows.

"It wasn't green lightning, was it?" In her own question, she found the answer to why she had tortured herself that night by watching the storm. Green lightning. She was beginning to believe the tales—more than *beginning*.

"No green flashes," he said. "For the time being, I'm the only burden the Tides of Time intend to bring you."

Though she could hear the laughter in his voice, his declaration still pained her. She looked up at him. "You aren't a burden, Kipling Summerfield. I promise you aren't."

"That is because I have been on my best behavior."

"Are you usually prone to mischief?"

When he laughed in response, she did as well.

"I am exceptionally good at mischief," he said. "At the moment, though, I'm choosing to focus on another talent of mine."

"What talent is that?" she asked, knowing she would be delighted at whatever answer he gave.

"My ability to give remarkable hugs."

She did like that answer. She leaned into his embrace once more. The storm continued, and the thunder still made her jump, but she felt safer.

"I've been pondering the declaration you made regarding the house you hope to someday purchase for yourself," he said. "I think you should add another item to your list beyond its being a place that doesn't need a great deal of repairs."

"What should I add?" It was not at all the done thing to have a conversation with a gentleman one was not married to while standing in his embrace, alone, in an entirely empty room. Even with the door open, they were pushing the bounds of propriety. And yet she didn't care.

"I think you should find an estate far away from the ocean," he said.

She smiled broadly. He hadn't made the remark in tones of mockery but a lighthearted teasing rooted in truth. "An excellent plan," she said.

"Chatsworth is landlocked," he said. "Perhaps you ought to see if the family's willing to sell."

She laughed. Chatsworth was enormous, beyond grand and elegant. It was the sort of home that made the royal family wish for the ability to seize properties with equanimity as they'd once been permitted to do.

"I have heard of Chatsworth," she said.

"I have been to Chatsworth," he said. "It is overwhelmingly impressive."

"Then it is still standing in two hundred years?" Wasn't that a remarkable thing?

"It is, and is a popular place for people to visit."

"It's open to the public?" People of their class who happen to be in the area could sometimes receive a tour of fine homes if their timing was good. But the general public certainly didn't.

"Things are quite different two centuries from now." His hand was slowly rubbing her back, and she found it both soothing and thrilling. "Smudge warned me I'm supposed to be careful what I say about things to come, because it is believed that the things a traveler over the tides does in the past could change things in the future. I suspect I'm permitted to say that it's very different."

She hadn't really thought of that. If he revealed things that changed what people did or said or chose now, it might alter things yet to come. How very precarious.

"Even if I were to discover that *this* house was one open for public tours in years to come, I don't think it would change the way I'm approaching my work here." At least she didn't think it would.

There was an added stillness to him. Was he trying to decide if he ought to tell her something? Perhaps Guilford *was* one of those homes available to be toured and enjoyed by a great many people. If it were still used in two centuries' time, that must mean she had managed to restore it. Or that someone had.

And quick as that, she understood the perilousness of learning things yet to come. Because she suspected what he wasn't telling her was precisely what she had guessed at: She now knew that, one way or another, Guilford would be put to rights. And if she didn't manage to do it, her uncle likely would, using at least some of her inheritance. And it added a franticness to the situation that she didn't think was entirely helpful.

She took a deep breath, hoping some of the tension would leave her shoulders and that the knot in her stomach would untie.

"One consequence of incredibly effective hugs," he said, "is I can tell that you've grown very suddenly tense. I've said too much, haven't I?"

She wanted to deny it entirely, but she didn't feel comfortable being untruthful with him. "I'm pondering the ways in which knowing things about the future could change that future. It's a smidge overwhelming."

"Well, I can tell you, Amelia, that being in this time when I'm not at all used to it is *exceptionally* overwhelming."

She looked up at him again, and he looked back in that very instant. He had such beautiful eyes.

"I can help you know how to live in 1803," she said. "I think Smudge will help too."

Kipling nodded. "At the moment, I'm too unaware of what I don't know to even ask questions." His smile grew once more, adding a measure of merriment to his already expressive eyes. "Though I am in full receipt of the information that this arrangement"—he managed with a single lift of a brow to indicate their current embrace—"is not at all the usual thing in 1803."

"Not even a little bit."

While his smile was disappointed, there was no finality to it. "Then I will require myself to behave for the rest of the evening."

But before he stepped away, he bent and placed the lightest and briefest of kisses on her forehead, the tiniest whisper of his lips.

That she managed to stay on her feet was more of a miracle than she knew how to express.

He was dressed in out-of-date clothes and moved with a gait that didn't quite feel right but somehow fit him perfectly. He was not from this time or this place and would likely never entirely fit. But the Tides of Time had not brought her a burden at all.

The virulent sea, which had taken so much from her, had this time brought her a miracle: a remarkable man who'd begun to lay claim on her heart.

Chapter 22

Standing in the drawing room, watching the storm while holding Amelia in his arms, Kip had had to fully admit to himself that he was in way over his head.

He had no actual identity in this time, no occupation, no income, no home, no family, no friends. He was growing exceptionally attached to a lady who should she allow herself to feel the same for him, would simply be adding to the troubles she already had.

Kip needed some answers, and he needed some idea of how to move forward before he ruined more lives than just his.

After seeing to their morning's work the next day, he convinced Smudge to go with him out to the lighthouse. Ivers hadn't shown himself to be the biggest fan of Kip, but he was knowledgeable about precisely the things Kip needed to know. It was he and his wife, after all, who had first indicated that there was a unique and significant aspect of Kip's situation that he needed to sort out. He now felt certain that what they had realized before anyone else was that he had traveled on the Tides of Time and didn't know it. Between Smudge, who understood the legends, and the Iverses, who clearly did as well, Kip might gain some idea of how not to sink entirely.

They spotted Ivers stepping out of the lighthouse, which saved them the trouble of trying to decide whether his house or his lighthouse was the best place to try first. Smudge called out to him using his given name, which told Kip they were already friends. That would help.

"Has him sorted it, then?" Ivers asked Smudge the moment they were within speaking distance.

Smudge laughed. "Thick as molasses not to have done so sooner."

The tiniest sparkle of amusement entered Ivers's expression, though nothing in it changed noticeably. "And how's him bearing up under the weight of it?"

"Better than expected. Better than the last few."

"Few?" Kip had heard about only Smudge's grandmother.

"As I told you, my granny cried for weeks. Captain Travers, who came this way not long after her did, was one of the tide travelers. Stayed here to the house, from what I remember being told."

Someone else who had been brought here through time. "Anyone else between them and me?"

"Probably," Ivers said. "Somewho might've washed up closer to Loftstone. Or might not have been found in time and drowned in waters hundreds of years out of their time."

That was not a very comforting thought.

"My grandfather says the tides swirl in other places, too, not just on this shore of England. There's whispers of a spot in Ireland, an inlet like this with an island placed just right. Makes the storms spin and the lightning turn green. I heard somewho say them thought it might happen off the coast of Spain as well."

A globe dotted with these pockets of water that twisted time into clumps and whirlpools. He would say that misery loved company, but knowing other people had gone through what he was going through wasn't proving very comforting.

He'd not heard anyone use the terms "time travel" and "time traveler," so he assumed that meant they were too modern. "Smudge here has warned me that I need to be careful what I say and what I tell people about my origins."

Both men nodded in perfect, emphatic unison.

"Travelers over the tides are brought to a place them weren't ever meant to be," Smudge said. "That begins a ripple."

"Are they always brought backward?" Kip asked.

Again, both men shook their heads at the same time.

"Then it's the ones pulled into the past that have to take care. A person going from the past into the future wouldn't have that problem."

"I suppose not," Ivers said in his usual gruff tones.

"Lucky me," Kip muttered.

They walked along the edge of the shore. It wasn't as miserable a walk as he'd taken that first day. He was better dressed for it now, and the shoes he'd found in the trunk of clothing fit well enough and were surprisingly more comfortable than they looked. Nothing else about the clothes he had could be described that way.

"If I'm not meant to be in this time and there are things I might say or do or reveal that could change time, doesn't it stand to reason that *anything* I say or do will change things? I can't just hide in a cave and hope not to starve to death."

"There aren't any caves on Guilford Island," Ivers said very matter-of-factly.

Kip opened his mouth to explain that he was being metaphorical but stopped at the well-hidden laughter in Ivers's eyes. He was proving more enjoyable company than Kip would have guessed.

"My granny was careful not to tell we about things that hadn't been invented yet or important events that were coming," Smudge said. "Her said it was likely important that her not ever be a person of importance. Keeping to her quiet corner, living a quiet life was, to she, the safest approach."

"But that quiet life involved raising a family. She was never meant to be here, but she came here by accident and, as a result, had children who had children who, I'm assuming, will have children." Kip shook his head. "If she was never meant to be in the time she found herself, then couldn't it be argued that all her offspring also weren't meant to exist? Including you?"

Far from bothered, Smudge shrugged. "If I had all the answers, I'd be a scholar somewhere, impressing people."

"I don't know who I am in this time and place," Kip said. "Classes are divided and determined so differently in the future. Divisions still exist but not in the same way."

"All of we assumed you were Quality when you first arrived," Ivers said. "That's what you feel like to the people of here and now."

"But isn't an important part of standing in Society the connections a person has?" That had come up in *The Beau* all the time. "I have no connections, at least none that will exist for another two centuries."

Man, he missed Malcolm. He was Kip's best friend, like a brother to him. He'd become family when Kip had had none. And Kip was never going to see him again. Never. The weight of that would never fully lift off his heart. It couldn't.

"I suspect Miss Archibald will let you stay here until you've sorted at least some of these questions," Smudge said. He then turned more toward Ivers. "Which brings us to another difficulty. Her has a heap of work to do here, more than can be managed by the hands her currently has doing it. You and your missus need to keep manning the lighthouse, and heaven knows that takes up all a person's day."

Ivers nodded his acknowledgment.

"Mick and I need to go back into the village, see if us can convince a few to come out and lend a hand. Them's nervous about the water, and I can't blame they. But it's calm just now. The storm last night didn't keep the sea road covered, and it's sitting above the waves. It's the best time to bring folks out, if them'll come."

"Them used to come quite often," Ivers said. "When there was last a family in residence, as long as the water was calm and the road sat high, them'd come out and work or visit. And there were quite a few employed at the house from the village back then." An edge entered Ivers's voice. There was no mistaking that whatever he was about to say was both important and coming from a place of frustration. "When the house was lived in, it employed a great many people. It was a boon to the village and important to their ability to survive. And when the house was lived in, the family would have visitors who would go to the shops in the village, and the pub, and would hire on temporary help from the village. The house was a source of income for the people of Guilford Village but also a source of pride. That it's been left to rot very much feels to the locals like them have been left to rot as well."

An uncharacteristic heaviness had entered Smudge's face as Mr. Ivers had gone through the recounting.

"The villagers cite the water as their reason for not coming across the sea road," Ivers continued. "But it's not just that. Miss is leaving when her six months are over. Her'll leave, the house'll be empty, and the village will once more be left to rot. You'll not get they to come help if there's no hope that it will make a difference."

Kip could tell Smudge knew that Ivers's evaluation was accurate. It was the first Kip had heard of any reason beyond the fear of the water. Nothing could be done to change the position of the ocean, nor its legendary abilities. But this issue was potentially changeable.

"She will be leaving Guilford House either way," Kip said. "The house is her uncle's, not hers. She doesn't have the choice to stay or leave."

"I didn't say it was fair," Ivers answered, "only that it is reality."

"Miss's uncle isn't likely to make his home here," Smudge said. "Us wouldn't overly like he doing so anyway."

It felt too hopeless for Kip's peace of mind. He was already dealing with something he couldn't fix, didn't ask for, and couldn't escape. "I'm going to talk with Miss Archibald," he said. "If she knows this is part of the difficulty, she can set her mind to it more fully."

"You seem to have a great deal of faith in her cleverness," Mr. Ivers said.

"She's shown herself to be inarguably clever, resourceful, and determined. I'd be foolish indeed not to make certain her mind is spinning on this question rather than just ours."

And while he figured attitudes toward women in this era weren't always what they ought to be, neither man looked shocked or appeared ready to argue the matter. It made him feel better about being stuck here himself. He had to find a way to fit in, but if that required him to be a misogynist, he was never going to manage it. Apparently, there was room in 1803 for men who weren't total jerks.

Smudge stayed back with Ivers, and Kip suspected they were going to talk about him. He'd rather not hear what they had to say. Losing his entire life was humbling him to the point that he wasn't certain he'd ever feel sure of himself in any context again. Hearing less-than-flattering assessments of him would only add to that uncertainty.

But he felt sure of Amelia. She was a source of unexpected and welcome stability in a world that felt as unsteady as the sea during a storm. He needed a dose of that stability in that moment.

Though the most likely place to find her at this time of day was her book room, something pulled his feet to the iron gate in the wall of her garden. And he found her there. Standing at the open gate, he watched her as she carefully tended a row of flowers. He knew this was her happy place. He knew it was where she felt safe and peaceful and at home on this island surrounded by the ceaseless echoes of the sea.

When she eventually found a home of her own, he hoped it would have a garden she could make her own. For that to happen, they had to sort out the difficulty with Guilford and the village and her uncle. Though Kip didn't know what he would do with himself in the long-term, he was determined to do all he could to secure her the future she deserved.

Chapter 23

Amelia wasn't certain how she knew, but as she looked up from her flowers, she was absolutely certain she would see Kipling nearby.

He was walking toward her with the soft look on his face that he wore more and more often of late. It never failed to make her pulse pick up. He cared about her; she was certain of it. And she knew he liked her, which was wonderful enough. But she was allowing herself to believe, to hope, that he felt something deeper, just as she did.

"I hoped to see you at dinner tonight or in the drawing room this evening." She used her cane to get to her feet as he drew nearer. "I've had an idea that I'm excited to tell you about."

"I'm excited to hear it."

People hadn't generally been interested in her thoughts. She wasn't yet used to that. It was a rather lovely thing.

She pulled off her gardening gloves and tucked them into the pocket of her gardening apron. Then he held out his hand to her, and she set hers in it, using her other hand to manage her cane as they walked through the garden.

"I've been pondering my uncle's return to Guilford. I wish you could have been nearby while he and Mr. Winthrop were here. You could have served as something of a buffer. That was my entirely selfish reason."

He shook his head. "Every person is entitled to basic dignity and safety. Wishing for that isn't selfish."

"Would it shock you to know that I suspect those are very modern views? Though I don't doubt there are those in this time who agree with you, it is not a common thing. Ladies, in particular, are subject to the whims of the men in their lives, including those who simply stumble into them. The idea of being granted any voice in our own lives is a very foreign one."

"Then I shouldn't be looked at too askance for espousing the idea, as apparently my voice gives me away as being a 'very foreign' person." She could tell she hadn't offended him, and she appreciated that he was willing to give her the benefit of his good opinion when she wasn't entirely certain that she was expressing herself well.

"You've been very clear that I can't simply be staying here as an unattached gentleman in the home of an unmarried lady without that proving disastrous," Kip said. "So I am assuming you have thought of a means of getting around that."

She nodded. "It came to me while I was working in the garden this morning."

"This truly is your happy place, then."

Her happy place. She had not ever heard that term or phrase, but it was very fitting. "This *is* a place where I am happy."

Amusement entered his smile. "I suspect I am going to accidentally teach you a lot of phrases from my time."

"Am I expected to say them in your accent?" She pretended to be horrified at the possibility.

Kipling laughed. "I would love to hear you try."

"You must be desperate for entertainment," she said through her own laughter.

"Not desperate. I simply like spending time with you."

She smiled up at him. "You've said that before. I am beginning to think you mean it."

"I absolutely do." He squeezed her hand. "And I absolutely want to hear your idea regarding your uncle's next visit."

"I think it is a good one," she said. "What makes your presence here scandalous, should it be learned of, is that there is no one else here. Were a gentleman and his wife to visit or a gentleman and his mother or aunt or even sister, that wouldn't be scandalous. If I had a companion, provided she were a dragon of a lady and probably old enough to be my mother, then you being here would not be so horrifying to those who are eager to be horrified."

His smile grew broad once more. Now that she was no longer entirely thrown off her balance by the brilliance of his smile, she found she simply enjoyed seeing it.

"Smudge and Mick must know of someone," she continued, "a woman of the appropriate age to play the role, who would be willing to come here and pretend to be kin to you. We could make certain she was dressed for the part, though doing so would likely mean asking a seamstress to create a wardrobe of some sort. I have enough funds for that."

That he wasn't immediately objecting gave her hope enough to press forward.

"When my uncle returns, he will be told that you and your aunt are traveling the countryside, seeing the fine estates in the area, which brought you to Guilford. I suspect a few words of praise for it will be enough to garner my uncle's acceptance. And I think he will be eager to show it to advantage."

Kipling nodded as he listened. "Which would help you, as he would be forced to praise the things you have accomplished."

"While we wait for his return," she said, "we can go on as we have been, with the addition of finding a woman to play this role and making certain she has what she needs and the two of you deciding what your feigned connection and story are. When my uncle returns, we will be ready. And you won't have to go into hiding."

"I would actually appreciate that. While I can't see myself being on particularly friendly terms with your uncle or his uncomfortable friend, being resigned to exclusively my own company in my bedchamber would grow tedious should your uncle choose to extend his stay next time."

"I can't imagine your company ever being tedious."

Whether it was her sincere compliment or simply the impulsive amendment, Kipling kissed her hand. Men in the future really were more openly affectionate than they were now. It must not have been considered scandalous in whatever year it was he'd come from.

That was still such a strange thing to believe. She didn't truly doubt it, but she had to continually convince herself that it really was true. If not for the ample evidence he provided in his odd turns of phrase and views of the world, she might have talked herself back out of it.

"There is one hitch in your plan," he said. "I have only just learned of this complication, and I know it hasn't been communicated to you."

"What is it?"

"Don't panic," he said. "I'm certain we can sort out a way around it."

She set her shoulders once more, reminding herself that she knew how to weather storms, both figurative and literal.

"Mr. Ivers has explained an additional unspoken reason why the villagers have, thus far, been unwilling to come to Guilford and help."

"Something other than their fear of the Tides of Time?"

"That does make them nervous," he acknowledged, "but in years past, it hasn't been enough to stop them from making the journey across the sea road. When there was a resident family living at Guilford, it was kept up and fully staffed, mostly with people hired out of the village. The resident family did their shopping in the village and hired villagers to undertake various jobs. When they had guests, those guests would hire temporary help out of the village and patronize the shops and generally create stability and opportunity and income for Guilford Village. When the estate was abandoned, so were they."

Heavens, she hadn't thought of that. "Is it that they're angry with my family for that abandonment?"

"I didn't get the impression that it's exclusively, or even mostly, anger. It sounded more like hopelessness. A feeling that even if they came to Guilford and worked to bring it back to the state it was in before, when your time there is done, it will simply be empty again and go back to what it was. It will, as Ivers put it, 'be left to rot,' and that, to the people of Guilford, will feel like they have been left to rot as well. Unless they can feel some reason to even bother, you're unlikely to get them to come out and help do work that will simply be undone by neglect."

They walked on a moment, into the part of the garden she hadn't yet tamed. She had to be more careful where she put the tip of her cane.

"I haven't the right to stay here indefinitely," she said, "even if I felt I could endure the sea for the rest of my life."

"I did point that out, and Ivers seemed to think the village understood that."

"But it doesn't change the outcome for them."

"Precisely."

Tension was tiptoeing back over her once more. She'd had such a good idea, and it had felt like she'd made progress. Now she was back to feeling like she was swimming against a tide.

"I could attempt to convince my uncle, but I guarantee he will not be willing to move here. He has his own estate, and it's a grander one than this. Not to mention it is nearer to London, nearer to Society. Guilford House will be left empty for the same reasons it was before, and there's nothing I can do to change that."

"Unfortunately, unless we can offer the village some hope that you *can* change that, we are fighting an uphill battle."

There was some comfort in hearing him say *we*. He'd told her more than once that he didn't mean to abandon her to this struggle, but hearing him so easily and naturally acknowledge it was wonderful.

"Do you think your uncle could be convinced to sell Guilford?" Kipling suggested.

"It is entailed. He doesn't have that option."

She could tell by the immediate confusion on his face that he didn't know what that was. Perhaps entailments were done away with two hundred years in the future.

"There's great worry amongst the landed gentry that the estates and the land and the holdings that they've acquired over generations will be sold off and split up. Land is and always has been very important to distinguishing people of rank and importance. It also offers stability that doesn't exist simply through bank accounts. Land with tenant farms produces income, which builds wealth and stabilizes families. To make certain that land all stays together, they are made part of entailments: legally binding methods of passing an inheritance down from one generation to the next. They dictate in perpetuity that anything subject to the entailment has to stay together and can't be broken off. It can't be sold."

"Ever?" That seemed to shock him.

"I suspect there are instances in which an entailment can be broken, but they are few and far between. Land is power. My uncle is not going to give that up, even for a property he doesn't care about."

"But Guilford doesn't have any farmland, so it can't be producing any income."

That was true. Its value was more in the ability to say that the Stirling family had a vast number of holdings. It was a line on a ledger.

She stopped all of a sudden, an idea forming so wholly and instantly in her mind that for a moment, she struggled to pull in a breath. Kipling watched her, his eyes wide, with a hopefulness in his expression that told her he knew that she had thought of something.

"Guilford doesn't produce an income right now, which makes it less important to my uncle than his other holdings, but tenants are not the only way for land to be profitable."

Her cane slipped on a rut in the path, throwing off her balance. Kipling righted her without seeming to have his attention to her words be disrupted at all.

"Families that have extra estates," she continued, "more than they might need for their children to use, especially if those estates aren't producing an income, often make them available to let."

"Oh, brilliant," he whispered.

Warming to the idea, she spoke faster. "If we could restore the estate and make it inviting and appealing enough, my uncle could let it to a family or a gentleman, perhaps a recently retired sea captain who would like to live near the sea. The rent would give my uncle income. The funds to run Guilford are provided by my uncle's estate. The rent would be pure profit."

"And the villagers would not be left with an empty estate and empty pockets."

She nodded, her mind spinning furiously. "It would take many, many years of rental income for Uncle to make as much as he would gain by simply seizing half my dowry. But I don't know that he is so desperately mercenary that he is entirely set on that course. He cannot possibly be so very different from the man who essentially raised me. There was an indifference to him, but he never seemed a truly bad person. Surely, he can still be fair and reasonable. At least, I hope he can be."

"And," Kipling said, "if you have restored the estate sufficiently to offer it up for a fine family to call their home, then he certainly can't argue that you failed to put it to rights or that you have been a bad steward of the estate. That would be proof he couldn't argue with."

She turned to look at Kipling, hardly daring to breathe. "If we tell the village this, if they have this hope of a family living here again, and if they know that the only way it will happen is if we restore Guilford to what it ought to be, then they would have a stake in the success of this too. I think we could secure the help we need."

"You might secure so much help that you would struggle to organize it all."

She smiled broadly. "A difficulty I am willing to accept."

"I know you aren't allowed to leave the island, but I think between myself, Smudge, Mick, and Ivers, we can offer this idea to the village in a way that will create an alliance between Guilford Village and Guilford House."

She closed her eyes and breathed. For the first time in more than six weeks, she felt truly and deeply hopeful.

Chapter 24

Having only ever seen semaphore used in movies, Kip was admittedly fascinated watching Ivers use flags to communicate with the lighthouse farther up the coast. Ivers had agreed to go into the village with Kip, Smudge, and Mick but couldn't leave the lighthouse unmanned.

"Loftstone is in the keeping of the Pierce family, legends among lighthouse keepers. Them'll send one of the family down this way to keep watch at Guilford while I'm in the village."

And that was exactly what happened. A man in a heavy wool coat over a thick-knit sweater, a cap pulled tight over his head against the wind arrived by way of a rowboat. Ivers and the man exchanged quick and silent nods, then the new arrival made for the lighthouse. Ivers turned on a dime and began walking along the island path back toward the house. Not a word was exchanged and apparently didn't need to be.

Maybe that was why Ivers wasn't overly prone to talking. He was used to communicating in ways other than words.

It wasn't until Mick, Smudge, Kip, and Ivers, tucked tightly into the pony cart, made their way around toward the side of the house facing the sea road that the lighthouse keeper broke his silence. He jutted his stubbled chin in the direction of the house. "Miss looks nervous. Be'est a fine idea for you to hop up there and reassure she."

The snickers from the other two told Kip he hadn't mistaken the teasing he thought he heard in the man's suggestion. Though it wasn't exactly the style of teasing he'd exchanged with Malcolm, he appreciated it just the same. Kip was alone in many ways, and his entire future had disappeared in an instant. To have even the tiniest hint of what he'd enjoyed about his friendship with a man who had been like a brother helped.

And seeing Amelia standing outside the house, watching them with a look that was both hopeful and anxious, somehow helped too.

Smudge brought the cart to a stop and gave Kip an expectant look. Not needing any more encouragement than that, he hopped from the cart and rushed up the stairs on the side of the house that led to the small terrace where she stood.

"I know you're not fond of standing out here, where you can hear the ocean so clearly," he said.

"I hate that I am leaving the doing of these important things to others. It's not fair to any of you and makes me feel too . . . weak, I suppose. Helpless."

He took her hands in his. It was not something he'd really ever done in his own time, except as part of a scene in a television show or movie. But it felt so right with Amelia. "We're all well aware of the requirements of your grandfather's will. And we'll reiterate that to the village so they know you aren't dismissing the importance of what you're asking."

"There is something very frustrating about being charged with proving how capable I am but being required to do so under circumstances that prevent me from being capable."

Kip leaned closer. He lowered his voice. "I think that might have been the point, my dear. I didn't know your grandfather, but all I've learned of him and this arrangement tells me he probably wanted you to fail."

She lifted her eyes to him again, and only then did he realize how close he'd actually come to her, leaning in as he had. She was so near that he could see the nuances of color in her brown eyes, the tiny freckles that dotted her face, and the subtle variations of color in her auburn hair. He couldn't entirely keep his eyes from dropping to her lips. He didn't know all the customs of this era, but he suspected they'd been bent and twisted in *The Beau*. That show had involved a great many romantic entanglements, where torrid embraces and quite a lot more happened remarkably quickly and frequently and with few if any consequences. But he knew by instinct that as much as he would like to kiss Amelia, and kiss her rather thoroughly, he'd have to be patient and measured and come to a better understanding of a lot of things before even tiptoeing in that direction.

He took the tiniest step back, squeezing her hands. "We'll convince the village, I'm certain of it. I don't intend to leave until we do." But that brought worry to her face.

"You might not come back?"

That was not the message he'd intended to send. He lifted her free hand to his lips, absolutely certain he was allowed to do that. He lightly kissed her fingers. "I will always come back. But I don't mean to come back alone."

She blushed, and that was tremendously rewarding. Maybe that was one of the reasons for all the strict rules of this era. It made for more of a challenge, and the reward for making progress was all the sweeter for it.

"We don't yet know how the village will respond to your situation," she reminded him. "Please be careful. I couldn't bear it if something happened to you."

Man, there it was again: that feeling of elation at such a simple proof of progress.

He gave a quick nod. "I'll be careful. And I'll come back."

He was still riding high as they crossed the sea road and made their way into the village, something Mick seemed to enjoy immensely.

They were a motley crew, to be sure, wandering into the Rusted Anchor pub. A gruff and impersonable lighthouse keeper. A scamp of an orphan who wandered wild over the local island. Smudge, who'd grown up here but had also been one of the only people from the village willing to make the journey across the sea road. And Kip, dressed as a gentleman, professing to be one, but clearly not quite fitting in.

It would actually be a very interesting cast of characters in a murder mystery TV series. They could wander from village to village solving mysteries and having larks. Sometimes Kip had to actually remind himself that all this was real, that he was living in the time that he was used to seeing glorified on the screen. It wasn't nearly as much fun, and the stakes were exponentially higher in real life. But it meant Amelia was real. And that meant what he felt for her was grounded in something true and sincere. He didn't know if he'd ever had that with Giselle. Not even at the beginning.

"Smudge's back," the barkeep declared to the others in the pub, which elicited a quick cheer and words of welcome.

"Always good to see you, Ivers," the barkeep added.

The older man, who had identified himself as Smudge's grandfather during Kip's previous visit to the pub, motioned little Mick over and had the boy sit beside him. To the barkeep, he said, "See if you have a spot of tea for this little scamp."

This was going relatively well.

To the room in general, Smudge said, "I'll give the lot of you one guess what's brought our Mr. Quality back out to the village pub."

Looks were exchanged, at first solemn but slowly sliding into smiles. Those smiles turned to laughter. Even Ivers cracked the tiniest bit of a smile.

Into the chuckles, Smudge's grandfather said, "Finally sorted it, did him?"

Smudge nodded. "Gave me a list of all the proof him had been seeing. And that were *before* him realized what had happened. Can't say I'd ever imagined that a traveler on the tides wouldn't even notice him had been tossed hundreds of years out of time." Smudge emphasized the word *hundreds* in a way that brought more laughter around the room.

"I suspect this means the lot of you don't think that I've lost my grip on my faculties," Kip said.

They all shook their heads and kept chuckling.

Smudge's grandfather said, "Different people along this stretch of coast react to tales of the tides in different ways. And us've heard from those what've traveled that, in future times, the tales'll not be believed. But you're fortunate enough to have found yourself in this moment among people who know it to be true enough."

That was fortunate. He couldn't imagine what he would have done if he'd eventually sorted out the truth of things in a place where that would have seen him thrown into an institution or locked in prison somewhere. He might just survive it in Guilford. But that likely meant he could never leave. His future lay in this tiny corner of the kingdom.

"Guilford Village won't view me as an oddity," he said.

"Oh, them will, sure enough," Smudge said, slapping a hand on Kip's shoulder. "But most of we won't think you mad."

He would likely still be eyed with curiosity. He could endure that.

"Miss Archibald's had an idea," Smudge said. "I think the village ought to give it a listen."

And that brought the laughter around the room to a halt. Faces turned more pensive and wary.

"Worth listening to," Ivers added. That changed the hints of suspicion Kip saw into undeniable intrigue.

Ivers and Smudge both turned to Kip, watching him expectantly. Mick was too busy eating the Yorkshire pudding and gravy the innkeeper had provided him to be paying much heed to anything else.

It was for Kip, then, to relay Amelia's plan. He liked that. He liked that she had trusted him, that his newfound friends were trusting him, that the village was trusting him enough to at least listen.

Standing up there in front of them all, he decided this had best be one of the better performances of his life. He needed to be convincing without being arrogant or dismissive or seeming to run roughshod over them.

He recounted with as much enthusiasm as he felt appropriate her idea about restoring the house to the point that it could be home to a resident family. He explained that she hadn't the right to remain, that she would be kicked out regardless when her six months were over. And he told them that she also didn't want to see the house and the estate fall to ruin, and she wanted even more desperately for the people of Guilford not to suffer for the selfish choices of her extended family.

"A person can't choose their family," he said. "But Miss Archibald's choosing to help; she's choosing to try. And while I do think it is a fine idea and could prove an amazingly helpful thing in the end, she absolutely cannot do it on her own. She's trying so hard, but she's been given an impossible task. Her grandfather was not a kind man. He placed her in this situation to hurt her, and she's determined that his cruelty to her won't hurt any of you." His eyes settled on Smudge's grandfather, suspecting he held a great deal of sway in the village and needed to be the one he convinced. "She has a good heart. She knows what it is to be unimportant to people with the ability to neglect someone into ruin. She doesn't want that to happen here."

The older man held Kip's gaze for a moment, and Kip sensed he was being evaluated. Kip, as Amelia's spokesman and the only person there who could speak on her behalf, had to convey her trustworthiness by proving his own. His sincerity would be used to judge hers.

It didn't feel like a performance anymore. He was pleading for her future. "If she fails at this, just as her grandfather arranged for her to do, she will still have to leave Guilford. It will still be left in whatever state she's able to get it to. But she will lose her chance to be free of her uncle, the man who's going to neglect the house and this village once more. And her grandfather's will gives her uncle the right to force her to marry whomever he chooses."

"That cad who was with Mr. Stirling, I'd guess." The tension in the barkeep's voice was echoed on the faces around the room.

Kip nodded. "The rest of her life will be determined by what happens here. It could plunge her into abject misery forever." He was attempting to convince them, but stating her situation so bluntly started to worry him. "And yet her idea is one she hopes will help everyone in Guilford Village. She is a good lady with a good heart. Please help us help her so she has a chance to help you."

Smudge's grandfather stood slowly and with the authority Kip had sensed in him. He looked over the rest of the people in the room. "Miss wants to make Guilford House a boon to the village again. Us can help weselves and, in the doing of it, help a lady what's good enough to be thinking of we." He looked over their faces once more. Kip held his breath. "There's plenty enough of we in need of work or who could spare some time to jaunt out to the island. Us can do a good thing for a good lady and maybe save this village in the doing of it."

That set the whole room abuzz with conversations. Kip's eyes darted to Smudge, who was grinning broadly. Smudge did that all the time though. Kip needed reassurance from a source who didn't exaggerate, who didn't sugarcoat, who wouldn't hesitate to tell Kip he was an idiot.

So he turned toward Ivers. The man didn't grin or smile or laugh. He simply gave a single, lightning-quick nod. And Kip breathed again.

Smudge pushed Kip over closer to his grandfather. Lowering his voice, he said, "Us is in need of another favor."

"What's that?" his grandfather asked with narrowed eyes.

"Mr. Stirling's supposed to be returning to Guilford soon and will likely bring his miserable friend with he," Smudge said. "There's no doubt in anyone's mind that's the fella Miss Archibald's uncle means to force she to marry."

A look of distaste filled the older man's expression. Kip liked him all the more for it.

"Her'll be safer and less nervous if her isn't alone in the house, but Mr. Summerfield here can't simply be staying at the house, him being unmarried and her being unmarried and that being what it is."

The older man nodded his agreement and understanding.

"So, Miss had yet another idea."

"Clever, ain't her?" Smudge's grandfather looked genuinely impressed.

"Her suggested a lady from the village might be willing to come stay at the house for the remainder of Miss Archibald's term there and pretend to be Mr. Summerfield's aunt. The two of they would say that them was traveling about the area, looking at fine houses, which would put it in Mr. Stirling's mind that Guilford House could be considered a fine house. And it'd mean there'd be somewho else in the house keeping an eye on things: both Mr. Summerfield and whoever us'd send with he."

Smudge's grandfather looked directly back at Kip. "Do you think Miss Archibald's in danger from her uncle's friend?"

Kip didn't know the answer for certain. "I don't know that he would actually hurt her or even inopportune her. But she is very uncomfortable with him. She's painfully wary. It has been my experience that when a woman has that reaction to a man, it oughtn't be ignored."

"And the man who makes a lady that uncomfortable oughtn't be permitted to continue doing so," Smudge's grandfather added. "Her ought to be at ease in her own home, however temporarily it's her home."

"My thoughts precisely."

Smudge jumped in. "Mrs. Finch can mimic the way Quality speaks. And should anywho try to make Miss Archibald unhappy, Mrs. Finch wouldn't have any qualms reproving that somewho."

Smudge's grandfather laughed low. "That's true as the day is long."

"She sounds perfect," Kip said.

"So long as you realize," Smudge's grandfather said in a tone of warning, "her'll rebuke you too. And her won't be bothered at all by it."

Kip just smiled. "If I deserve to be denounced, I certainly hope she *would* do it."

And again, the old man looked impressed. It was an expression Kip had longed to see from his own father. Just the slightest, briefest moment of acknowledging that he might not be a total failure or disappointment of a person. He thought maybe he'd have seen a hint of that the first time he'd been cast in a production, or the first time he'd had a role on television. He'd even thought that when he'd been given a significant recurring role in *The Beau*, his father would at least have acknowledged that it was steady work. Never happened. Nothing had ever been good enough.

Kip was never good enough.

Eventually, it would be reported that Kipling Summerfield, well-known, award-nominated actor, had been declared dead after ending up missing for however long it took for that to happen. Would his father miss him? Would he regret the gap between them? Or would he simply shrug like he so often did and make some remark about how it could have been different if Kip had made better decisions?

Maybe it was a mercy that Kip would never know.

Amelia paced in front of the windows facing the sea road. She'd been there for nearly two hours. She tried to drown out the sound of the sea by humming lightly to herself but hadn't entirely done it. She was on edge.

Her grandfather was taunting her. But she managed to summon the endurance to peek out the window now and then to glance at the sea road, hoping to see the pony cart returning with Kip inside. He'd said he would come back, and he would. He'd also said he wouldn't come back until he'd convinced the village to help, and she believed that too. But how long would that take? Was it even possible?

Another circuit of the room brought her to the window once more. She summoned the courage to look out. The pony cart was approaching. She held her breath.

Focusing solely on the cart and doing her best to pretend she couldn't see the ocean on either side of the road, she studied the faces in the cart. Smudge, Mick, Mr. Ivers, and Kipling.

Kipling.

She pressed her hand to her heart and whispered a quick expression of gratitude. He'd come back so quickly. Soon enough, he would be in the house. He'd hold her hand. He might even hold *her*.

And on the heels of that thought, she spotted something she hadn't yet noticed: behind the pony cart were two more carts filled with people.

Chapter 25

Kipling and his marvelous team of champions had managed a miracle. The new arrivals from the village had been at Guilford for a week, and the change was already startling. Mrs. Jagger had transformed the instant everyone had arrived from the unsure and almost dottering woman she'd been in the weeks that Amelia had been at Guilford into a capable and authoritative housekeeper. Amelia felt as though she was getting a glimpse of Mrs. Jagger twenty years earlier. The housekeeper organized those who were to work as maids in the house as well as consulted with a woman of about her age who had come from the village willing to act as cook for a time, making certain she had a couple of hands in the kitchen to help when the time came.

Marsh had chosen a man from among the villagers to act as a footman, feeling they didn't need more than one in the relatively small house. The young man he'd chosen was also skilled at building and making repairs, so when not needed in household duties, he would be joining Kipling and most of the rest of those who would be addressing the damage of neglect and improving the state of things around Guilford.

Mr. Ivers had shown an unusual amount of excitement, which, for him, amounted to the tiniest lift of his eyebrows when Kipling had insisted some of the work ought to include repairing paths on the island and making certain those living at the lighthouse and the keeper's residence had what they needed. Mrs. Ivers, who knew the villagers well, had warmed instantly to the flood of people. She'd come up to the house every day since their arrival, bringing her little baby with her and not only being friendly with those who were now going to work for a time at Guilford but also offering Amelia insights into who they all were and what she knew of them.

A miracle. An absolute miracle.

As evening approached on the eighth day of this fully staffed version of the house she was required to live in, she found herself overcome with the gratitude she felt at all these willing and capable hands. She understood that they had come because it would be good for the village. She didn't begrudge them that, didn't resent it or think less of them for it. She was grateful to have been in a position to help and to offer these good people the hope she was clinging to for herself: a future. And even though those futures would pull them apart, she still felt a sense of belonging and camaraderie with them. And for the first time since being imprisoned here, she felt a touch like she was at home.

Mr. Ivers was uncomfortable anytime she tried to tell him she was grateful. Smudge always turned those attempts into a joke. Mick was too busy running about the island like the ragamuffin he was to sit still long enough to be told thank you.

It was to Kipling she was most desperate to offer her gratitude. She needed to tell him in a way that truly matched the enormity of what she felt. That, she suspected, was actually impossible.

All he'd done, the way he helped and cared about people, his kindness, humor, intelligence, that he treated her with respect, as an equal . . . Her feelings for him felt impossible to truly express, but leaving them entirely unspoken was proving unbearable.

It was likely an hour before dinner would be served. Kipling would be in his room, though likely not yet starting to dress for the meal. It was one of the few times she was likely to speak with him with any degree of privacy.

The house wasn't empty, and Kipling was very busy. She didn't see him often. She missed that, but she understood.

She reached his door and lifted her fist to knock, but it was actually slightly ajar. She nudged it open further and peeked her head inside. Before she could ask if he would mind her entering for a moment, she spotted him sitting on the floor beneath one of the windows. A leather-bound book lay open on his lap. He was bent forward. At first glance, he seemed to be looking at it, maybe reading it, but a closer study revealed there was something heavier in his posture. Something defeated. And sad.

"Is something the matter?" she asked from the doorway.

He looked up, and her heart dropped to her feet. His expression wasn't merely sad; he looked as though he'd been fighting tears and not entirely winning the battle.

Good heavens. What had happened?

She crossed to the window and knelt on the floor beside him, setting her cane next to her. She'd comforted her cousin when she'd been upset, especially when they'd been younger, but she'd never offered comfort to a grown gentleman when he was distraught, especially a grown gentleman she wasn't related to and had undeniably tender feelings for.

Hesitantly, unsure if it was the right approach, she set her hand on his. "What's happened?" she asked softly.

A quick sigh accompanied the further drop of his shoulders. "I've been trying very hard not to dwell too much on what's happened. But that means it hits me in waves, and it's—it's a lot to try to think about."

"The Tides of Time, you mean?"

He tapped on the book open on his lap. "This journal was in the trunk of clothes. The man who wrote it was also a traveler on the tides."

"It seems reading about his experiences isn't helping."

"It is in some ways, and it isn't in others." He shook his head, helplessness joining the heaviness in his expression. "I feel less alone. So much of what he talks about is what I've felt: confusion and not knowing what to do. Not knowing where I fit. Being desperate to get back to my own time and place but knowing that I can't."

Her heart dropped at that. He wanted to go back. Of course he did. She couldn't blame him for that. But the thought of him leaving her struck pain in her heart.

"Thinking about staying feels like I'm giving up on going home," he continued. "But I can't really be giving up if it was never possible to begin with." He snapped the book shut and lightly tossed it onto the floor beside him. "I think part of me thought I'd read this and find some magic fix he discovered, some trick to hopping back on those tides and riding them home again."

Amelia swallowed down the immediate plea that sprang to her lips. If he found a way to return to his own time, she would be devastated. Yet how could she be so selfish as not to want him to be able to go back to what was his home?

He looked over at her and attempted to smile. "I won't be gloomy all night, I promise. I'll be wonderful company. Even Mrs. Finch won't have reason to correct me." His pretended aunt had taken on the role with gusto and spoke to him very much the way an older, overprotective, mothering type of relative would.

But his reference to her and the humor they had both found in that behavior fell flat in the moment.

Amelia set her other hand on his. "I wish I knew how to help this feel like home to you."

He shifted his hand so that their fingers interwove. "And I wish I knew how to make Guilford feel less like a prison to you."

She had discovered in the weeks she'd known him that Kipling Summerfield changed the topic as a means of avoiding difficult conversations. Sometimes, it was the kinder thing to let him make the shift. But sometimes, like in that moment, she knew that continuing to push aside what weighed on him would only lead to more moments like this, when the weight was crushing him.

She reached up and gently touched his face. "In four more months, I will be able to escape this prison, but you will still be two hundred years out of your time. Please let me help you with that. Please talk to me. A burden doesn't become easier by insisting on carrying it alone."

He set his free hand atop hers, where it rested on his cheek. He slowly and gently turned his head until her fingers rested against his lips, and he softly kissed them. He then lowered their clasped hands to his heart and kept them pressed there. "I'm very fortunate that I was brought where and when I was. And that you were here."

"I've thought the same these past weeks. But that makes me feel a little guilty. You coming here has pulled you away from the people and places and time you would understandably rather be with and in."

"I knew who I was then. It is a horrible thing not even having an identity anymore. I don't even know how to create an identity in this time."

She didn't know how to help with that. They were making up a history for him to tell her uncle, but there was no substance to it. When everything at Guilford was settled and done, he wouldn't actually have family or money or connections.

"You must be very lonely," she said.

"I was often lonely in my own time as well. Except when I was with Malcolm and Jen."

Amelia adjusted so she was sitting more comfortably. "Malcolm is the one you said is a saint?"

He nodded. "And Jen is his wife." He adjusted them both, arranging them so that rather than sitting facing him with her hands in his, she was sitting beside him, with his arm around her shoulders, tucking her up to his side.

"I grew up in America, like I told you, but I moved to England when I was eighteen years old to go to university."

That wasn't surprising. He had the sound of a person who was educated, though she didn't know what that looked like two hundred years from now.

"I met Malcolm at university. We were both studying acting, starting in the same program at the same time."

"You were an actor?"

His eyes darted to her. "You say that like it's a bad thing."

"It is not a . . . respectable occupation."

"The 'tattoo' of jobs?" He was clearly making an attempt at humor, but his frustration rendered the effort flat.

"Neither, I'm guessing, are looked down on in your time."

He shook his head. "But I need to hide my tattoo and abandon the idea of being an actor in this time." The frustration rolling off him was palpable.

"Your friend Malcolm was also an actor?" Perhaps speaking of his friend would give him some comfort.

Kipling nodded. "We became the very best of friends not long after we met. Malcolm has felt like a brother to me ever since. Over the last five years, we've worked on the same show."

Show? Did he mean a play?

"Do theater productions often run for five years?" She hadn't ever heard of such a thing.

His face turned ponderous. "It isn't really a theater show, but that's probably the closet comparison in this time."

If she was this confused simply having a conversation with him, he must be overwhelmingly befuddled most of the time.

"I'm the one who introduced Malcolm and Jen, which I, without question, consider one of the greatest accomplishments of my life. They're very happy, and that makes me happy."

A question occurred to her that she likely ought to have asked quite some time earlier. And asking it made her undeniably nervous. "Are *you* married?"

He laughed. It wasn't at all the reaction she'd expected, yet it somehow set her mind more at ease than a simple denial would have.

"I am absolutely not married, Amelia Archibald. There was, for a time, a lady I was courting, but fortunately for me, that did not amount to anything."

"Did you discover you two didn't suit?"

"She discovered I wasn't 'good enough' for her."

"If she was bacon-brained enough to toss you aside," Amelia said fiercely, "then *she* most certainly wasn't good enough for *you*."

He bent and kissed her temple. "That is one of the nicest things anyone's ever said to me."

She was walking on clouds. Only by reminding herself that he was struggling did she prevent herself from simply floating away. "Will you tell me about Malcolm and Jen while you're here at Guilford? I would like to know more about the people who are family to you."

"It might help to talk about it. I don't think it'll make me miss them less, but maybe I'll feel less like I've lost them entirely."

There was a deep, aching loneliness in his voice, and it broke her heart. Every person he'd ever known was lost to him. That was, she didn't doubt, the reality crashing in on him. And she couldn't change that.

In contrast, his arrival had given her companionship and hope. She had gained a friend. She had gained someone wonderful in her life, someone she had begun to love.

But could he ever be truly happy in 1803—knowing he had lost Malcolm, who was like a brother to him, and Jen, who, though he hadn't said it, was no doubt family to him as well? Even if he learned to care for Amelia as much as she cared for him, would it ever be enough?

"I would love to hear all about your life," she said. "Whatever part of it you'd like to tell me." She truly did want to know more about him. And she hoped it would help.

"I've been warned by just about every person from Guilford Village that I have to be careful what I say about the future and what I tell people. There will likely be things I can't tell you."

"But surely there'll be some things you can." She wanted to give him hope that he wouldn't be entirely alone or have no one he could ever talk to.

"Eventually, I'll get the knack of it," he said. "But I'll probably always have to be careful and moderately guarded." That added a degree of exhaustion to his existing sorrow.

She hated seeing him this way. She didn't know how to ease the heartbreak that he couldn't escape. She turned, looking up at him. "I don't want you to be alone," she said softly.

"That's part of what's been difficult about this." Kipling dropped his voice as well. "I'm beginning to realize I will always be alone to a degree."

"Don't say that," she whispered, closing her eyes against the tears that stung.

"Amelia." He too whispered. She felt him take gentle hold of her face. "Amelia." With the second whisper of her name, his lips brushed over hers. It was the softest kiss, the most delicate of touches. She returned it with one of her own.

He abruptly pulled back. So abruptly, in fact, that she thought for a moment that someone had yanked him away. But opening her eyes, she could see that wasn't the case at all. He had moved several arms' lengths away from her.

He jumped to his feet. There was a stiffness in his posture that felt unwelcoming. "It'll be time for dinner before we know it," he said. "Best go get ready, or Mrs. Finch will scold the two of us for being late." He crossed to the door and pulled it fully open once more, though it had never been entirely closed. He stood beside it much the way a footman did when holding the door for people to pass through. The message was not difficult to decipher.

Amelia took hold of her cane and managed to get to her feet, despite her confusion. Every inch of her was tense, the thrill in her heart at his kiss had evaporated. Her thoughts were in complete disarray as his rejection wrapped ice-cold around her chest.

She didn't know what had caused the sudden change in him, but she couldn't ignore that it had happened. The connection she'd felt between them had gone from something she had simply hoped for to something so real and tangible and undeniable.

He'd kissed her, but the moment she had returned that kiss, he'd pulled away, and not just physically.

ECHOES OF THE SEA

She couldn't look him in the eye as she stepped from the room and into the corridor. Her cane thunked against the wood as she moved with what speed she could to her own room. Only when she stood on the other side of her closed door did she let herself name what she'd seen in his face after having laid bare her heart to him: disappointment.

Chapter 26

Nearly twenty-four hours after kissing Amelia, Kip knew it had been the most amazing, incredible, terrible mistake he'd just about ever made. He'd enjoyed every second of it. And he'd known in an instant that the connection he felt to her was unlike any he'd felt before. It had changed everything and, in so doing, had brought a horrible truth crashing down on him.

She'd kissed him in return, with too much feeling for him to doubt any longer that his was not the only heart on the line. She felt this pull and this connection just as much as he did. And that was a problem.

Kissing her as he had, alone in his bedchamber, was considered unacceptable in this era, no matter that *The Beau* had pushed those boundaries to the breaking point over and over again. But that wasn't the reason he was castigating himself now. He wasn't an acceptable match for her. That plotline had played far too often in various episodes and seasons for him not to know it was going to be a problem now.

He'd kept his distance from Amelia since that moment in his bedchamber. He'd kept quiet during dinner and had gone directly back to his bedchamber afterward. He had thrown himself wholeheartedly into his carpentry work the next morning, and he was now standing in his bedchamber, donning one of the new sets of clothes Mrs. Finch had arranged to be made for him "posthaste." She'd taken one look at his wardrobe and declared that no one with any degree of observational skills would ever think he was a gentleman of means taking a tour of the countryside dressed as he was. Just as she'd had clothing made for herself that made her seem the aunt of a gentleman of means, she'd seen him provided with enough pieces to at least begin the act.

He was wearing a complete set of them just then, the sort a gentleman would wear during the day in just such an estate as this. And Mrs. Finch was eyeing him rather too critically for his peace of mind. He'd seen that expression on the faces of costume designers and casting directors when they weren't entirely certain they were equal to the needed miracle an actor was challenging them to conjure up.

"You at least look less like you stole your wardrobe off an abandoned clothesline." The dryness of that declaration made him grin.

"I only hope I play the role well enough to help Miss Archibald. That's my entire goal in all this."

"If you'd really like to be a help to she, then quit being so buffle-headed."

He was taken aback but only for a moment. Mrs. Finch had a knack for shocking him with the declarations she made, but she always delivered them in a way that forced his shocked silence into an immediate burst of laughter. He wished he were truly a gentleman of leisure and could adopt her as his aunt and travel around the country, listening to her snarky commentary. It would be an "absolute lark," as Tennyson Lamont would have said.

"Do you love Miss?" Mrs. Finch asked with her usual frankness.

He'd learned to return her bluntness with bluntness of his own. "It doesn't matter if I love her or not."

"Love always matters. Only the bitter say otherwise."

He shook his head. "I'm not saying love doesn't matter. I'm saying what I feel for her doesn't change the reality of our situation. Nothing can change it, and I need to remember that."

Mrs. Finch turned to grab the top hat from his dressing table. As she did, she muttered, "Seems to me, men in the future are cowards."

Again, a moment's shocked silence led immediately into a burst of laughter. "I think that's kind of unfair."

She spun back and held the hat out to him. "My parents didn't much care for my late husband when him was courting me, but him didn't simply shrug and abandon the effort. That courage meant us had twenty wonderful years together before I lost he. Us would've missed out on that life if him'd been as easily defeated as you are."

He set the hat on his head, knowing Mrs. Finch wanted to see how it looked on him. "This hasn't defeated me *easily*, I assure you."

"But you have let it defeat you," she said. "Are you not worth fighting for, Kipling Summerfield? Is Miss not worth fighting for?"

"Of course Miss Archibald is worth fighting for."

Mrs. Finch eyed him, gave a quick nod, and then waited. But waited for what?

After a moment, she said, "You didn't answer the entirety of my question."

The bit about if *he* was worth fighting for. "I'm nobody. In this time and this place, I am literally nothing."

"In your own time and place, who were you? Who were you before the tides?"

Kip pulled the hat back off and tossed it onto the table. "According to my father, I have always been nobody. Worse than that, I was a nobody plagued by stupidity."

She didn't look moved by the recitation of his family misery. "Doesn't matter what him or anywho else said you were. You need to decide who you are and if who you could be is worth fighting for."

"What if I don't know how to do that?" It was an admission he wasn't sure he would have made to anyone else. Probably to Malcolm. But no one else.

"I suspect Miss Archibald knows how," Mrs. Finch said. "A lady doesn't live as a poor relation in the home of a man like Mr. Stirling, where her is shown in countless ways that her's not worth fighting for, then grow into a lady who has worked tirelessly and planned and replanned and strategized and restrategized as much as her has since being here if her hasn't learned the trick of fighting for sheself when no one else thinks her's worth it."

"I won't burden her with this. I won't be a weight around her neck."

Mrs. Finch lifted an eyebrow and eyed him, but not with disapproval or the rejection he'd often seen on his father's face. It was disappointment, and that was infinitely worse. "I suppose that answers the second part of my question."

Feeling both offended and defensive, he said, "I already told you she was worth fighting for. She absolutely is."

Mrs. Finch didn't so much as wince. She held his gaze and said firmly, "Words are empty if there's no action to fill them. If Miss is truly worth fighting for, then you'll fight. And if her's not, you'll stoop your head and say there's nothing to be done, that nothing can be fixed, and you've given up."

"You make it sound very simple."

"And you make it sound overly complicated."

"Which part of this doesn't feel complicated to you?" He'd have paced if he weren't certain that wasn't what a gentleman of 1803 would do.

"What bit of it is feeling insurmountable to you?" Mrs. Finch asked.

"All of it." He threw his hands up in the air.

"Name one part at a time." Her bluntness was perhaps less endearing in that moment, but it also was exactly what he needed.

"A gentleman who could claim a place in Miss Archibald's life wouldn't have a profession; he'd be a gentleman. But for a gentleman to survive, he either has to have money or connections, preferably both. I have neither. So either I try to get a job—the only usable skill I have is carpentry, which would put me irrevocably below her station—or I try to assume the role of a gentleman in order to have some claim to the rung she occupies, but with nothing to live on and nowhere to lay my head."

"So pick."

"Pick *what*?"

"Which path you want to take. You could be a carpenter in this era and move forward with that."

"Without her?"

Mrs. Finch shrugged. "Perhaps."

He didn't like that idea. But he also didn't like the idea of starving to death.

"Or," Mrs. Finch continued, "decide you want to attempt to find a place in the world of gentlemen."

"A person doesn't just simply join that set."

"Brummel did."

If Kip didn't keep his wits, Mrs. Finch would convince him of impossible things. "Brummel had connections to trade upon."

"You have one in this very house," Mrs. Finch said.

"You mean Miss Archibald?"

She nodded.

"Her station in life comes through her uncle, who doesn't have her best interests at heart. Beyond that, I don't think she has any significant connections in Society."

"Not yet," Mrs. Finch said. "But her does know that world. Miss may have ideas, but you're so determined not to burden she that you won't let she help you. It'll tell she pretty clearly that you don't think having she in your life is worth fighting for. That you won't even make a decision about a path forward, even if you have to change that path because it doesn't prove the right one, tells me you believe your father more than you believe Miss Archibald. I've seen the way her looks at you. Her doesn't think you're nothing."

That comment hung in the air between them, and Kip began to feel a shift in the waters he was navigating.

But before he could ponder it even the tiniest bit, Jane rushed through the doorway, a panicked look on her face. "Mr. Stirling's carriage has been spotted on the sea road. Him's on the way to Guilford."

Chapter 27

Amelia watched the approach of her uncle's traveling carriage with greater confidence than she had felt during any of his previous arrivals. Guilford was sufficiently staffed. The villagers had worked hard and made incredible progress. Kipling wouldn't have to hide. And she had a plan to present to her uncle that he would directly benefit from but which more or less required him to treat her and her efforts with fairness and honesty. There was no guarantee, and he still had the upper hand, but it was a chance. And that chance gave her hope.

She waited in the drawing room, knowing Marsh would fulfill his role as butler with precision and impressiveness. Her uncle, accompanied by whichever of his companions he'd chosen this time—it might be the solicitor, it might be Mr. Winthrop, it could even be her aunt or cousin—would have reason to be impressed from the moment he was greeted. By the time Amelia heard footsteps approaching, her posture was precise, her appearance was proper, and she was ready to face him.

They had decided that whenever her uncle did arrive, Kipling and his "aunt" wouldn't be there immediately, wanting to give the impression that they were exploring and visiting, just as their story said they were. That meant Amelia would greet her visitors alone. But she was equal to it.

She'd not had to face Kipling and the disappointment he'd so clearly displayed after their kiss. Even with that disaster hanging in the air between them, she trusted him to keep his word and help her. He wasn't unkind or untrustworthy. She knew he cared about the village, and they deeply cared about him.

She turned from the window and faced the door as she heard Marsh step inside.

"Mr. Stirling and Mr. Winthrop, Miss Archibald." Marsh stepped aside and allowed the two visitors to enter.

Mr. Winthrop. Amelia froze. She had suspected her uncle would bring the would-be suitor with him. Seeing him step into the room filled her with greater dread than she would have predicted. But Kipling would be there, and in a role that allowed him to keep a vigilant watch. That would help.

"Welcome back to Guilford, Uncle Stirling." She dipped a curtsy, which was returned with the appropriate bow. She turned to Mr. Winthrop, forcing herself to appear unbothered by his presence. "And welcome back to you as well, Mr. Winthrop."

If he noticed her curtsy wasn't quite as deeply executed as the one for her uncle, he didn't let it show. It wasn't truly a slight; her uncle was a person of more significance in her life and certainly could be considered to warrant greater respect. But she felt better with the knowledge that she had made what little stand she was able to without rocking the boat overly much.

"You appear to have been busy since we were last here," her uncle said. "This room alone has received a deep cleaning and a good polish. And the pathway to the front of the house was neatly trimmed. The stone wall near the sea road has been repaired."

He'd already noticed improvements. That was encouraging. "Yes, I've managed to secure more staff and some talented workmen from the village. They've done excellent work. I anticipate the house being put to rights by the time my six months are concluded."

That brought a conflicted look to her uncle's face. Conflicted was better than aggravated, which was what she had anticipated. Mr. Winthrop made no effort to hide that her success did not meet with his approval. She would address that as she was able. At the moment, she needed to allow what she'd said to simply percolate and move forward without pressuring her uncle to feel one way or the other.

"It's a blustery day today," she said to them. "Would either of you care for some tea?"

"Yes, please," her uncle said.

Amelia turned to one of the maids they'd hired from the village, who had, thankfully, been extremely well trained by Mrs. Jagger. She stood near the doorway awaiting the instructions that the kitchen had likely already anticipated. To her, Amelia said, "Please have Cook send up tea and a few things to refresh our visitors after their journey."

The maid curtsied an acknowledgment and turned.

"And make certain there is enough for our other visitors as well," Amelia added. "I suspect they will return from their jaunt shortly."

"Of course, Miss Archibald." The maid quickly slipped out.

Casual as anything, Amelia walked to a chair and sat, leaning her cane against the arm of her chair. She indicated her visitors should do the same. They were both watching her with abject curiosity. Not wanting to draw attention to the fact that she had made certain to let them know there were others in residence, she chose a different topic altogether. "How fortunate that the weather has held today. Mr. Ivers, at the lighthouse, suspects we'll have a storm in the next day or two." She tried to pretend like it wasn't actually a shame that the storm hadn't come already and rendered the sea road unpassable.

As she could have predicted, her uncle did not allow her to remain on the subject of weather. "Do you have other visitors, Amelia?"

She smiled softly and gave a small nod. "A Mr. Summerfield and his aunt. They are embarking on a tour of the finest estates in this area of England. They wished to visit the Little Sister of Mont-Saint-Michel. I hadn't realized how legendary Guilford actually is in some circles."

"It *is* a very unique place," Uncle said.

Amelia nodded. "How grateful I was that we had made as much progress on the house as we had before their arrival. I think the gentleman and his aunt are impressed with what they've seen. And they've enjoyed exploring the island. I will have grounds workers set to the task of repairing more of the walkways that traverse the shoreline and the cliffsides. None of them are in complete disrepair, but some are rather precarious. Fortunately, the workers I've secured are good at what they do and work very hard." Leaving that to spin about in her uncle's brain, she turned to Mr. Winthrop. "I confess, I had not expected you to return a second time with my uncle. I assumed your own estate would be calling to you."

"My estate is efficient enough to more or less run itself. I'm not needed there constantly."

"How very fortunate for you." She was rather proud of how little of the snippiness she felt made it into her tone. "Has your estate been in your family for long?"

He puffed up, just as she'd expected he would. Keeping his attention focused away from Guilford and, by extension, away from *her* seemed a good strategy. "The Winthrops have lived in this area of the world for generations and will do so for generations to come."

"It's a fine thing to put down roots," she said.

Mrs. Jagger stepped into the room on the heels of that pronouncement, followed by the footman carrying a tray laden with tea things. Behind him was the maid Amelia had sent to deliver the message to the kitchen. She was carrying a tray of foodstuffs. It would be a perfectly acceptable offering without being a grand one, which is what they had all decided would be best. If her uncle got the impression that she was trying to impress him, he would wonder what she was covering up and what other deficiencies she was attempting to distract him from. Having things run smoothly and unexceptionally was wisest.

She had brought many of those who had come from the village into the discussions about strategy. Their futures were on the line as well, after all. And having a few different ideas was never a bad thing.

Everything was in order, and the servants had slipped back out just as Kipling and Mrs. Finch stepped into the drawing room.

It was a testament to how well both were dressed and carried themselves that her uncle and Mr. Winthrop immediately rose to their feet. Mrs. Finch had convinced them without a word that she was a lady. And Kipling fit the part so well that no looks of confusion or consternation flitted across either face.

Amelia rose more slowly but also with more dignity, a reminder to her two newest visitors that she was the lady of the manor at the moment and worthy of more consideration than either of them had given her on their past visit. "Mr. Summerfield, Mrs. Summerfield.

"This is my uncle, Mr. Stirling of Parkwood Manor outside of Tunbridge Wells, and Mr. Winthrop, whose estate is, I understand, not terribly far from here."

Bows and curtsies flitted about the room. Kipling and his "aunt" were seated among them, and Amelia began pouring out tea for everyone.

"How far is your estate?" Mrs. Finch asked. "Perhaps it is one we have visited. We have been all over this part of the world, seeing the finest of places."

Amelia wasn't certain she would ever not feel some amusement at hearing how well Mrs. Finch mimicked Kipling's accent. It wasn't identical, but it felt enough the same that one would absolutely believe it was simply the way Americans spoke in the area of America they were supposed to be from.

"Norwich Manor is approximately thirty miles inland from here," Mr. Winthrop said.

That pulled Kipling's attention. Whether it was his acting his part or something that held significance for him, she didn't know.

"I don't believe that one has been recommended to us." Mrs. Finch turned to her "nephew" with a curious look. "Have you heard mention of it?"

He smiled at her with the exact fond, indulgent smile a nephew would with his slightly eccentric aunt. "I don't believe it has, but perhaps we should add it to our list."

"Where is it you two are from if this is not your country?" Uncle Stirling no doubt had noticed their accents were slightly unusual, but she suspected he was trying to take an approach that felt less rude than simply telling them they sounded strange. She hadn't done that when she'd first met Kipling, which she was embarrassed to think back on.

"From America," Kipling said. "Though my aunt was born in England and lived here until she was nearly twelve years old. She wished to return to her homeland, and I couldn't resist the opportunity to come with her."

"Have you returned with an eye to remaining?" Mr. Winthrop's question might have been posed to either of the American visitors.

It was Mrs. Finch who answered. "Yes. I've longed to be back. And Kipling is such a delightful addition to any society in which he is part. I believe England will be all the better for having him." She reached over and patted his hand.

Amelia was grateful that she had a teacup in front of her mouth so no one could see the laugh she struggled to hide. Before long, Mrs. Finch would be cleaning his face with her handkerchief and indulgently attempting to ply him with sweets. Uncle Stirling and Mr. Winthrop would have very little trouble believing she was a doting aunt with a nephew she still struggled to view as a grown man. It was a rather perfect dynamic, really.

It was going well. For that, Amelia was grateful.

And she managed throughout to avoid meeting Kipling's eyes, for which she was deeply, deeply relieved.

Dinner that night was the perfect balance of food fit for a fine estate and an offering that felt like a family dinner rather than a formal gathering. They wanted Uncle to get the impression that this was a family home so that when she suggested to him that they prepare it to be let to a family, it would feel like a natural fit. If he set his mind to that idea, his stubborn nature would push him ahead with far more enthusiasm than any logical arguments from her could ever manage.

Upon reaching the drawing room after their meal, with the gentlemen remaining behind, as was customary, Amelia turned to Mrs. Finch. "I believe it is going well," she said quietly.

Mrs. Finch nodded. "Your uncle appears to be pondering all he's seeing and hearing." She kept to her assumed accent and manner of speaking, no doubt on the off chance that their visitors should catch them unawares. "Mr. Winthrop clearly recognizes that he's not making the progress he wants to and that he might be slightly losing his ally. But nothing is so obviously confrontational that they can truly object to anything."

Amelia nodded. It was what she had felt and seen as well. "And you seem to be enjoying your role of slightly eccentric American aunt."

Mrs. Finch grinned more broadly than Amelia had just about seen anyone do. "That Kipling manages not to laugh over any of it is so astonishing that I find myself enjoying it all the more. He told me that in his previous life, he was an actor. If it weren't such a scandalous thing in this time, I'd suggest he take it up again. He's very good."

"I imagine he misses it," Amelia said. "He misses a lot of things."

"He does. More than that, he doesn't know who he is without those things. I think he's more lost than he lets on."

Amelia had seen that in him the day of their kiss. It had broken her heart almost as entirely as his abrupt pulling away from her. It was a painful thing seeing him struggling and not knowing how to help or if she could. Or if he even wanted her to.

At the sound of the gentlemen's voices, she and Mrs. Finch assumed expressions and postures that spoke of a simple, friendly, unexceptional conversation. They needed her uncle to believe that Amelia was managing everything with ease rather than worrying and scrambling as much as she was. Pretending that she wasn't pretending was exhausting. Kip might have enjoyed being an actor, but she didn't think she would have.

"You have actually visited Chatsworth?" Uncle said as the gentlemen stepped inside.

"It isn't in this area of the country," Mr. Winthrop pointed out, sounding as though he had caught Kipling in a lie.

"We have been in your country for quite some time," Kipling said. "And this is not the first tour of grand estates we have undertaken. It's simply our most recent." He was unshaken, personable, and welcoming. There was a competence that didn't lean toward arrogance. He could navigate the objections and the difficulties even without warning. It was rather remarkable.

She pushed all those thoughts from her mind and offered a welcoming smile to the gentlemen.

"Have you planned any particular entertainments for this evening?" Mr. Winthrop asked her.

She couldn't tell if he was attempting to catch her out at having not planned something, was trying to sound as though he were bowing to her as the mistress of the house, or was simply wondering what came next.

"As I wasn't at all certain how weary you might both be from your journey, I have opted to allow this to be a quieter evening. Whatever everyone feels equal to can be undertaken, even if that is something as simple as reading a book and then retiring early." Could they hear that she very much hoped they would choose that?

"Perhaps you would play the pianoforte for us," Uncle suggested. He turned to Mr. Winthrop. "She plays well, if not expertly. Enough to quite pleasantly entertain people for an evening."

ECHOES OF THE SEA

Obviously, she hadn't entirely turned her uncle's thoughts away from a match with his questionable friend. That left her with something of a dilemma. Ought she to agree to play but do so poorly so as to give Mr. Winthrop second thoughts, knowing that might irritate her uncle? Or ought she to play as well as she was able in order not to upset her uncle, knowing that might further convince Mr. Winthrop of the wisdom of pursuing this match or, worse still, make him wonder if she was trying to impress him?

She didn't mind puzzles, but sometimes, a person needed a moment of simplicity.

Mrs. Finch turned to Amelia with a look of absolute maternal concern. She even reached over to her and placed a hand very lightly on Amelia's arm. "Oh, I can see you're going to agree in order to be a good hostess, but I simply cannot let you neglect your own well-being."

"Her well-being?" Kipling stepped closer, looking genuinely concerned. Whether this was more of his good acting or he was actually worried, Amelia didn't quite know.

"She hid it well during dinner," Mrs. Finch said, "but I finally wriggled out of her while you all were having your port that she has had a touch of a headache today. Nothing serious," she quickly added, looking at the other two gentlemen in a way that said any decent person would be suddenly quite worried, "just a hint. And we all know that the tiniest of headaches can grow into something absolutely unbearable if one is not careful."

"Oh, we certainly wouldn't wish for Miss Archibald to cause herself distress when we are all perfectly capable of entertaining ourselves for an evening." Kipling turned and looked at her uncle and Mr. Winthrop. "I cannot imagine the expectations of gentlemanly behavior are so different in England than they are in America that any of us would insist she remain and cause herself pain."

They couldn't object after that without seeming like cads. It was remarkably well managed.

Mrs. Finch very quickly ushered Amelia from the room, then made quite certain her felicitous declarations could still be heard in the drawing room.

Once they were in the corridor that held Amelia's bedchamber, Mrs. Finch dropped the act. "I realize you don't necessarily want to spend the entire evening alone in your bedchamber, but I think it would serve your purposes grandly if those two men what just arrived today are reminded that them haven't the right to bullyrag you. And you not being nearby for your uncle to parade in front of his irksome friend wouldn't be a terrible thing either."

"You and Kipling are a force to be reckoned with. I would not ever want to find myself on the opposite end of any endeavor as you both."

"Us *are* rather remarkable."

Amelia laughed as she was deposited in her bedchamber. Mrs. Finch smiled at her once more. The maternalness of it was still there, though it felt more real and more sincere now.

"You allow yourself a moment's rest. Think through how you mean to approach the remainder of their visit. Kipling and I will keep they occupied tonight and make sure their thoughts turn the way us needs they to."

"Thank you," Amelia said.

Long after she climbed into bed, pondering her next day and her most important tasks, thoughts of Kipling kept weaving themselves in. He was helping her and helping the village. She sensed he'd found family in Mrs. Finch, and whatever path he meant to take after Guilford, the dear woman would remain part of it in some way.

Amelia was happy for him. While part of her heart still longed to feel like she might be a fellow traveler on that path, and the broken part of that heart wished the kiss they'd shared had ended differently, she could still be happy for him. They would get through this visit. She would hold out hope that they would convince her uncle. And through it all, she would find a way to guard her heart against the pain of loving him when he didn't feel quite the same way.

Chapter 28

Mrs. Finch's voice refused to leave Kip's thoughts. She'd wondered aloud how it was that men of Kip's time were so cowardly. She'd more than implied that he didn't care enough about Amelia if he wasn't even going to try to build a life with her.

It wasn't that, he'd repeatedly told himself. He just didn't have the answers. Any of them. Until he knew what future he could possibly have, he needed to prevent her from getting entangled in it. He wouldn't cause her pain if he could avoid doing so.

Kip had kept his distance since their kiss, hoping to prevent that pain. But he missed her.

When his path crossed Amelia's the next afternoon as she was making her way back toward the house from the lighthouse, he knew he had a rare opportunity to talk with her away from Mr. Stirling and Mr. Winthrop and away from the listening ears of the villagers.

Amelia moved slowly on the rickety path he had taken to Guilford House on his first day on the island. She was very pointedly not looking at the sea beside and just below her, but she could not help but hear it crashing against the rocks below. They were not so high above the water here as at the lighthouse. The drop-off grew less drastic as the path wrapped toward the sea road. But for one who was as afraid of the sea as she was, getting closer to it might have actually been a more intimidating sight than being dozens of feet higher.

"Good afternoon," he said, unable to keep the nervousness from his voice. His acting skills were failing him.

She gave a quick nod and a flash of a smile, but it fell flat. It wasn't a dismissal, but it also didn't feel like a warm welcome. It was what Jen had once called mixed messages, the way she'd described a rough patch when she and Malcolm had been dating and he'd been feeling particularly unsure of himself. Kip had talked sense into his friend then, but Malcolm wasn't here to help him navigate this now.

"I need to apologize," Kip said to Amelia, "for two nights ago. Before dinner. In my room." He wasn't being very eloquent. "I made something of a mess of things, and I—" How did he explain? He wanted to get it right, and perhaps begin to make up for how wrong he kept getting things.

Amelia continued walking along the path. She carefully placed her cane with each step, and she didn't look at him. "You don't need to apologize. I sorted out that the people of your time are more free with their affection than we are in this time. I have to remind myself of that, but I do understand. I won't let myself believe again that there is more in these things than you likely mean by them."

"It isn't that."

Except there was some truth to what she was saying. In modern times, sharing a kiss like they had was a lot more acceptable than it was now. Ignoring the portrayals so rampant in *The Beau*, he knew that the very personal moment they'd shared in a very private setting would have likely been grounds for engagement, whether they'd wanted it or not. He'd pushed their relationship further than he should have. And that was probably adding to the "mixed messages" they were navigating now.

"I won't cross that line of propriety again," he said, "assuming you would rather I not." If there was any chance she would not entirely object, eventually, he didn't want to close that door completely.

Her cane wobbled on a patch of loose gravel. "I may not be as experienced with such shows of affection, but I do have ample experience recognizing when a person is disappointed. It is not something I generally care to repeat."

Disappointed? Did she think he'd found kissing her disappointing? Part of his panic had been that it was anything but.

A crash of thunder sounded overhead, pulling both of their eyes skyward. The storms really did arrive very quickly in this part of the coast. There never seemed to be any warning.

"Good heavens." Amelia's gaze jumped forward, not down at the waves, as he would have thought. "Some of our workers go back to the village toward the end of the day. What if they're on the road? What if they've not made it across and the sea surges?"

She rushed down the path, no doubt intent on stopping anyone attempting to make the crossing. She hadn't been entirely steady while moving at a slow pace.

"We haven't restored this part of the path," Kip said. "It's too dangerous to—"

A bit of the path gave way. She stumbled against the crumbling rock barrier, and it, too, gave way, tumbling her off the side.

"Amelia!" The wind carried his voice away.

He tore off his jacket and threw it over a large rock, tossing his hat there as well. As he reached the edge and looked down, he held his breath. What in the world would he do if she was lying lifeless below? Or if the sea had carried her away already?

She was just out of reach, clinging to a jutting rock at the bottom. Wave after wave battered her as he scrambled down the jagged rocks, trying to reach her, all while trying to determine how to get her back to safety.

"Don't let go!" he shouted.

He didn't know if she could actually hear him, but if there was any chance she could, he meant to keep talking to her, to keep assuring her that he was coming, that he wouldn't leave her there.

The moment before he found a sufficient foothold close enough to her to reach for her, a wave tore her away from her anchor. He plunged into the water as well and grabbed hold of her, pulling her back to the shoreline. The sea was angry and strong but not as powerful as it would be once the storm built. If they didn't both get out of the water as quickly as possible, they might not ever do so.

It was painstaking and slow going, but they managed to climb up the rocky terrain. Pain seared over Kip's right shoulder blade. Blood ran from a cut above Amelia's eyebrow. He hoped she didn't have a concussion or other serious internal injuries. It might not have been the twenty- or thirty-foot drop by the lighthouse, but it was still no small fall. And she'd been battered by the waves as well.

On the path once more, he snatched up his coat and wrapped it around her, though it was wet from the falling rain. The wind had carried his hat off. They would be shivering long before they reached the house. Kip kept an arm around her and moved slowly. Not just on account of the precariousness of the terrain but also because she wasn't moving very well. Her cane was gone, and she was likely in pain.

On top of all that, she had been plunged into the terrifying grip of the one thing in the world that frightened her the most. The trauma of that was likely only beginning to set in.

He held her as closely as he could. "We'll be to the house soon," he said. "You'll be warm there. And you're safe."

He repeated that again and again until they arrived at the side entrance to Guilford House. When the staff spotted them, a mad scramble took over. Her appearance was alarming, and he suspected his was too.

Her uncle and Mr. Winthrop came upon them as he and the footman helped assist Amelia up the stairs.

"What's happened?" Mr. Stirling asked.

"There's a portion of the path that's not been put to rights yet. It grew slippery in the rain, and she took a tumble."

"Off the side of the island?" Mr. Winthrop asked. "Into the sea?"

Amelia made no indication that she had registered his question or was hearing anything being said, and though the cold was starting to get to Kip and his mind was spinning with pain and exhaustion, he had just enough clarity of thought to know that for reasons he couldn't bring immediately to mind, he needed not to reveal that bit of what had happened. Whether it was another aspect of proper behavior or simply something that would be embarrassing, he couldn't remember, and he couldn't ask Amelia in this moment or look to her to answer. He simply knew it was time to lie ever so slightly. "I can understand why you would assume so, as we're both soaked. But you'll notice, if you glance out any window, that it is raining quite hard. I attempted to guard her against it with my coat, but even that wasn't enough."

They were making very slow progress. And she was starting to whimper. He could only imagine the pain she was in and the terror she was feeling.

"Where is her cane?" Mr. Stirling asked. "She struggles to walk without it."

"I'm not certain," Kip said. "Lost in her fall, likely."

They reached the corridor where her room was and came upon Mrs. Finch.

"Mercy, what happened to the two of you?" she asked.

"She slipped on the wet footpath and took a tumble onto some rather unforgiving rocks."

"It looks as though you did as well." Mrs. Finch lightly touched his shoulder, not exactly where it hurt but very close to it. He looked over his shoulder and could see just enough of the back of his shirt to spot blood.

They'd reached Amelia's room. Kip helped her inside, where Jane was waiting. Fresh clothes were already laid out, and Jane was setting a thick folded blanket on the edge of the bed.

Kip and the footman gave Amelia into Jane's keeping.

"Your mistress has been through a horrible ordeal," Kip said. "Please look after her. Make certain she rests, and her wounds are tended."

"Of course, Mr. Summerfield," Jane said.

Amelia spoke for the first time since her plunge into the water. "Make certain your wounds are tended to as well," she said weakly. It was so very like her. Not forgetting the needs of others even in her own distress.

"I will."

He stepped out of her room. A little nervous that Mr. Winthrop would cause her distress, Kip closed the door behind him. Nearly all the staff had gathered in the corridor, watching him with concern and worry. Their eyes darted between him and the door.

"I am not a physician, by any means," he said, "but she can walk, her words are lucid and well formed, and though she has sustained injuries, they do seem superficial. I suspect if she's kept warm and allowed to rest, she will fully and quickly recover."

They all looked immediately relieved but also quite determined. The people of Guilford Village were good and kind. And Amelia had so quickly won them over. She had allies whether she realized it or not.

"The staff seem very fond of Amelia," her uncle said as he walked alongside Kip down the corridor.

It was time someone pointed a few things out to the man. Kip knew he needed to tread carefully, but he thought it might be a good time for the man to realize what he had been ignoring. "My aunt and I have visited a great many homes and seen how they are run and how those who are so crucial to the success of those homes view the people who stand in positions of authority and ownership. I can say we have never seen a mistress of an estate more dedicated to the well-being of those attached to it, nor have I seen a staff or a local people so entirely devoted to the head of an estate. You must be very proud of her."

Mr. Stirling didn't immediately say he was, but he did look ponderous. Kip was full-on shivering by the time he reached his door.

But Mr. Winthrop, in typical fashion for him, made things more difficult. He stood in front of that door and blocked Kip's way inside. "You are exceptionally attentive to Miss Archibald."

"I didn't realize that, to English gentlemen, offering assistance to a lady after she has sustained injuries is so unusual as to be deemed 'exceptional.' Apparently, that is one way in which Americans differ from the English."

Mr. Winthrop ruffled up at that. "There is a marked difference between bringing her back here as a matter of ordinary kindness and giving yourself the right to look after her."

"I gave her over to the care of her abigail. I am not the one looking after her." More was the pity, really. He'd hated to leave her there when he suspected the terror of what had occurred had not yet fully settled in.

"What is your design here?" Mr. Winthrop demanded.

Feeling rather put out with the man and exhausted himself, Kip said, "At the moment, my design is to change out of my wet clothes before I develop an inflammation of the lungs."

Mr. Winthrop still didn't budge. "I have secured her uncle's approval and cooperation for this match. I will not be the last of my line. I refuse to be." An unexpected deviation from the topic. "Miss Archibald is young enough to produce an heir," Mr. Winthrop continued, "and unlike other young ladies, she can't refuse if her uncle agrees."

In a tone as dry as he wished his clothes were, Kip said, "How romantic."

With a look of disdain, Mr. Winthrop said, "You have now hit upon something that is different between English and Americans. We do not embrace such sentimental nonsense."

"And Americans know better than to leave a watermark." Kip motioned at the floor growing wet beneath him. He hoped his indifferent tone was believable. If Mr. Winthrop saw Kip as a rival, the gentleman could likely make things very difficult for Amelia. Simply shaming Mr. Winthrop into behaving was the better approach.

It must have worked to some extent. Mr. Winthrop gave him one last look-over, punctuated by disapproval, and stormed off.

Beginning to feel very sore and chilled clear to his bones, Kip opened his door and stepped inside. The Guilford footman and Mrs. Finch were both inside with dry clothes and thick blankets ready for him. Thank goodness.

Mrs. Finch crossed to Kip's door and closed it once more. "I'll not put you to the blush," she said. "I'll look the other way while your man here helps you change out of them sodden clothes. I simply wanted to see for myself that you've not torn yourself to pieces."

The footman helped him undress, which was a good thing because his fingers were so cold he couldn't work the buttons himself.

"Checking to make sure I'm alive?" Kip said. "Watch yourself there, auntie, I might think you care about me."

"All of we care about you," she said. "Might be I care more, but that's what family does."

He smiled at that. "Are you claiming me as family?"

"I haven't any of my family left since losing my husband," she said. "Though I've friends aplenty in Guilford Village, I miss belonging to somewho. If you'll claim me, I'd like to be family to you."

"I'd like that," he said. "And not just because I also don't have any family."

"That settles that, then," Mrs. Finch said firmly. "Before you get new shirt sleeves on he, Jimmy," she said to the footman, "us had best take a look at whatever it is that's bleeding."

"The shirtsleeves are all that I've left to pull on," Kip said. "Now's the right time for taking a look."

"I'll warn you, Mrs. Finch, he has a . . ." Jimmy dropped his voice to a whisper. "Tattoo."

Mrs. Finch waved that off. "I've already seen it. Horrid-looking thing." But there was a twinkle of amusement in her eyes when she glanced at Kip after saying it.

"I'll have you know it's considered quite fashionable in my time."

"*This* is your time now. You belong here whether you realize it or not."

He hoped that did prove to be true in the end. He needed to find a way to belong.

Mrs. Finch moved to stand at his side, eying the painful spot high on the back of his right shoulder blade. "It doesn't look too awful."

With some twisting, he could see a fraction of it himself. A decent cut, but he didn't think it went beyond that. "We'd best sanitize it so it doesn't get infected."

Mrs. Finch and the footman exchanged confused looks. Did people at this time not understand infections? He felt certain they'd touched on the topic in *The Beau*, discussing how wounds could kill if they turned putrid. Maybe that needed to be the word he used.

Or maybe it was the idea of "sanitizing" that was baffling to them. Was that something he could safely explain, or was that going to ruin something?

If they didn't know about the necessity of cleaning wounds, Amelia was at great risk of infection. He had to say something, but what could he safely say?

"I cannot tell you why, only that I have reason to know . . ." He gave them pointed looks, hoping they understood that he was referencing future knowledge. "We need to clean this wound thoroughly. Get out any bits of debris or dirt, even *unseen* dirt that might be in it. Very thorough cleaning. And if it shows the tiniest hint of putrification"—he was proud of himself for recalling that from a script several seasons ago—"some brandy dabbed on the wound can help." Alcohol could be a disinfectant, but it was a harsh one that he didn't particularly want poured all over his one wound, let alone Amelia's many. "We need to communicate to Jane that it is of paramount importance that all of Miss Archibald's injuries be thoroughly cleaned as well. I cannot overemphasize how deeply important this is."

To his relief, they didn't argue or press. And they believed him.

His wound was cleaned and bandaged, and then he wrapped himself in a thick blanket over his blessedly dry clothing. He sat in a chair near the roaring fire in his bedchamber, ever more grateful that the people of Guilford knew the tales of the Tides of Time and so readily accepted them. It had allowed him to help safeguard Amelia without having to reveal things that he ought not.

He'd been warned so extensively and so intensely about the possibility of changing the future by revealing things in the past. And Mr. Winthrop's presence had already filled his mind with a horrifying possibility.

Malcolm was a Winthrop, and his family had lived in this area for generations. Every interaction he had with Amelia's would-be suitor came with a risk of changing the future of the Winthrop family.

And Malcolm was that future.

Chapter 29

Amelia hadn't let herself think about what had happened little more than an hour earlier. The monumental task of limping back to the house and changing out of her wet clothing, followed by Jane painstakingly cleaning every cut she had, under instructions from Kipling, and then dressing once more had distracted Amelia's mind sufficiently. But there were no more distractions.

Alone in her room, wrapped in a warm blanket and dressed in dry clothes, hearing the storm rage outside, she could only listen to her heart thud against her ribs as her mind spun with terrifying recollections: Her cane slipping out from under her as the ground itself shifted. Her twisted foot betraying her. Tumbling over the edge. Excruciating pain as she scraped against rocks on her way down while frantically grabbing for anything she could cling to. The bite of being submerged in cold water.

She shook all over again, trembling as the terror returned anew. She'd held on to an unforgivingly jagged rock there at the shore, searching with her feet for something solid beneath her.

The ocean had continued to pummel her, continued snatching at her, trying to pull her into its inky depths.

She took in a deep lungful of air, hoping to reassure her spinning mind that the ordeal was over and that she was on dry land, safely inside the house. It didn't help.

Amelia was not one for crying and weeping. She couldn't even remember the last time she'd done it. And yet she couldn't hold her tears back any longer.

She cried at the cruelty of a grandfather who was forcing her to live in the one location in all of England that would make her the most miserable, under terms that meant an accident as harrowing as she'd just endured could cost her the inheritance that he had dangled in front of her. She'd left the island, no matter that she hadn't done so on purpose, and that might very well be considered a violation of his requirements.

As if that weren't enough, her tears also fell because she'd fallen so entirely in love with Kipling. Again and again, she had declared herself grateful that the Tides of Time had brought him into her life. And that made her feel every bit as cruel as her grandfather because Kipling had lost everything and everyone he knew, and he was lonely and heartbroken.

Though she hardly remembered her parents, thoughts of them flooded over her. And she wept for them too. She wept for her own loneliness. She wept for the neglect she'd known. She wept for the uncle who had changed so quickly at the promise of money. And she wept at the thought of Mr. Winthrop and the life she would likely be expected to build with him.

It was too much. She was a woman of strength and determination. She was capable and determined. She was also overwhelmed.

The door to the mistress's dressing room opened. On the other side of the dressing room was a small bedchamber, where the lady of the estate's abigail would likely live, which also had a door to the servants' corridors and access to the servants' stairs. It would be very convenient for the servants, but in moments like this, when the lady of the house longed for privacy, Amelia thought it more of an inconvenience.

She could hear the slight clink of what sounded like dishes on a tray. Cook had sent up food.

How could Amelia be annoyed at the interruption when the good people who'd come to help her with Guilford were looking after her still?

She rose carefully, using her chair to steady herself. Turning fully to the window allowed her to keep her face hidden. "You can place those on the table." She was impressed with how steady she kept her voice. She hadn't turned around, so whoever among the staff had brought the food likely wouldn't realize she'd been crying. That would give her time to pull herself together before she had to face anyone.

"It is quite a labyrinth getting in here through the servants' stairs." *Kipling.*

Amelia turned toward him; she couldn't help herself. She was always drawn to him when he was nearby.

He was focused on setting items from the tray onto the table.

"I wanted to come check on you, but I didn't want your uncle to think that he had an open invitation to do so. And definitely not Mr. Winthrop."

She just nodded, feeling unequal to actually saying anything.

"I asked Mick to show me the trick of getting here unseen, he being an expert at slipping about the place. He was all too happy to—" Kipling's story ended very abruptly as he looked up at her. His brow pulled in tight. "You've been crying."

She didn't intend to lie and insist she hadn't been, so she made a valiant attempt to wave it off as though it were only a small thing, and he needn't be concerned.

He crossed the rest of the way to her, never looking away. His expression was one of concern but not pity, and somehow that combination undid her. The tears came again, flowing unchecked once more. In an instant, his arms were around her, holding her so kindly and so tenderly.

Even as the tears flowed, the words spilled from her. "I was in the sea, my worst nightmare. I was living the horror, and I didn't know how to get out. And I'm in pain and sore. I've lost my cane. I'm still cold. I have to stay here, surrounded by the ocean, for months yet. My uncle doesn't seem entirely convinced of anything. And Mr. Winthrop has begun looking at me with a possessiveness that makes my skin crawl, but I'm not in any position to make him leave. I was tired before today's ordeal, and I feel so exhausted now that I don't know how I will ever even function again."

Kipling didn't offer any platitudes or dismissals. He simply held her, managing to embrace her in a way that didn't add to that pain. It was gentle enough to take into account her injuries but strong enough to give her strength.

"If you hadn't helped me, the sea would have taken me away." She couldn't summon more volume than a whisper. "I ought to feel relieved, but . . ." She took a shaky breath.

"But what?" he asked softly.

"I was off the island, Kipling. My grandfather's will is very specific. Should I at any point not have at least one foot, one hand on the island, then I have violated the terms of his will." It felt like such a petty thing to be worried about when she had almost died, but she did have to worry about it. "No exceptions were made for accidents."

"Mr. Winthrop asked if your fall had placed you in the water when we came into the house. You were in such a state of shock that I didn't think you heard. I wondered at the time why he asked, as he doesn't seem the sort to be concerned with others' welfare."

Amelia leaned back enough to look up at him. This very important conversation had not even brought her to her senses that night. She had been too far gone with the horror of the moment. But if Mr. Winthrop knew, then her uncle knew. And if her uncle knew, then everything they had been working for was undone.

Kipling's smile was reassuring and not the least patronizing. "I told him that you stumbled onto some particularly unforgiving rocks off to the side of the path, which I'll point out is true. We were both soaked, I said, because it was raining incredibly hard, which was also true. I will hold to that story to my dying breath, Amelia Archibald. You need simply tell the same one."

Some of her distress began to ease. "I wish my uncle could be trusted to be fair about my accidentally 'leaving' the island. But I don't know that he can see past the possibility of claiming half my inheritance."

Kipling gently stroked her face, managing to avoid the cuts she had sustained there. "I will tell you, because I suspect you were too pained and in far too much residual terror to have paid much heed to the people we encountered as we returned to the house, but your uncle did look genuinely worried for you and sincerely relieved that you had emerged from your ordeal relatively unharmed. I don't think he's as far gone as we have worried he might be."

"And Mr. Winthrop?" she asked, more calmly than she'd spoken even an instant earlier. Kipling was setting her mind at ease and soothing her battered heart.

"Oh, Mr. Winthrop is still a definitively horrible person. Indeed, the more I know of him, the more I suspect we don't even realize what a dastardly villain he probably is."

"And he is the man my uncle will insist I marry if I fail here at Guilford. That undermines your insistence that my uncle is redeemable."

Kipling's confidence didn't seem to waver, which helped hers remain strong.

"After all you have been through, other than keeping your wounds clean and resting, one of the best things you can do is make sure you take nourishment."

He kept an arm around her as he helped her sit once more at the little table where he'd set the tray. He saw her seated, then studied her a minute, the sort of perusal that a person generally undertook when hoping to discover that someone they worried might be unwell was, in fact, well enough. After a moment, he looked satisfied with what he saw.

"While you eat," he said, "I need to make a confession."

She glanced at him nervously.

He smiled, and her heart flipped about, as it always did with his smile. "I'm not about to tell you I've done something horrific." Kipling stepped back and set his shoulders. He didn't mean to confess to past crimes, but apparently, whatever he did intend to talk about was not a small thing. "Please do eat while I talk," he said. "It will be good for you, but it will also give you something to do other than look at me like I'm a complete imbecile."

"*Are* you a complete imbecile?" She asked the question a touch dryly, and just as she'd hoped, he laughed. She would always love the sound of his laugh and would remember it long after they parted ways.

She began eating, just as he wished her to, but he had her full attention regardless.

"I was attempting to explain to you today, out on the path, before everything happened, that I'm something of an idiot."

It was such an unexpected thing for him to say that she smiled despite herself. He did briefly as well.

"Before that day in my room, when I—" He looked self-conscious, maybe even embarrassed.

Feeling an odd surge of boldness, she said, "Kissed me?"

He tossed her a pointed and theatrically arrogant look. "Kissed you rather expertly is probably the phrase I would use."

She shrugged as if it were nothing. It absolutely had not been nothing. But humor, she was finding, helped him when he was overset, and it was easing her mind as well.

"You've said you realize that in my time people are more affectionate on far less grounds than now, and that's true. But it doesn't mean that kiss wasn't powerful or revealing or didn't have depth or meaning behind it. I—" He shook his head and paced away. "I realized in that moment how quickly and entirely I—I had—" He ran a hand through his hair, which proved a rather mesmerizing thing. He turned back to look at her. "I've fallen in love with you, Amelia Archibald."

She pulled in a swift breath. *Love.* He was in love with her?

"I've had my head turned now and then over my life," he said, "but I've never . . . I've never felt like this, and that made me panic."

"Panic?" She managed the two syllables despite the pounding of her heart making words difficult.

He held his hands up in a pose of supplication. "I don't know who I am now. So much of who I was in the future revolved around my profession and who people perceived me to be. I knew my place in that time and in that world. But now?" He dropped his hands and resumed his pacing. "Falling in love is a foolish thing to do when I don't know if my fate here is as a poverty-stricken member of the lower classes, which means I have no right to even imagine a place in your life, or as a counterfeit member of the upper classes, inventing a life for myself and trying to make enough friends who would be willing to give me a place to stay and food to eat, which is also unworthy of you." The look of deep humiliation in his eyes undid her.

She rose with some difficulty from her seat. He was near enough that she needed to take only one step to reach him. She set her hand over his heart, though she didn't know what to say. He set his hand over hers and held gently to it.

"I had intended on the path today to simply tell you that I hadn't meant to hurt you or cause confusion or make things worse. I'd meant to tell you that I was determined to sort out what I could be in this time so that I would know what I could offer you, so you could decide if there was a place for me in your life."

With his free hand, he brushed a strand of hair from her face.

"The sea took away everyone I cared about," he said. "For a horrifying moment today, I thought it was about to again." His voice broke. "I don't know where our paths will take us, Amelia, but I'm asking if you'll let me be part of your life while I sort out everything." Emotion abruptly cut off his words, and he dropped his gaze. "In the end, circumstances might tear us apart regardless, but I'm hoping you'll let me stay until then."

"We don't have to have all the answers right now," she whispered.

He looked at her once more, uncertainty warring with hope in the depths of his beautiful eyes.

"We know we want to find the answers," she said, "and maybe that's answer enough."

"One step at a time," he said quietly.

"As long as that one step is headed in the opposite direction of a crumbling seaside cliff," she said.

His smile inched back. Did he realize how wonderful it was that they could speak of difficult things, could be worried and sorrowful but still lighten each other? She meant to hold fast to this connection, trusting it wouldn't be severed in the end.

"While I'm sorting out my path, we'll find a way to convince your uncle of the brilliance of your plan for Guilford. And we'll sort out what's to be done about Mr. Winthrop."

She studied Kipling. "There's uncertainty in your voice when you speak of Mr. Winthrop. That's new."

"I think he might be my friend Malcolm's however-many-greats grandfather." Kipling didn't appear to like that he'd discovered that. "Same surname. Malcolm's family has lived in this area of the country for centuries. I feel like I'm playing with fire every time I interact with the man."

"The villagers have warned you about changing the future."

Kipling nodded. "Changing Mr. Winthrop's future feels especially dangerous. Malcolm is part of that future. I don't want to change who he is or, worse yet, do something that means he'll never exist."

Amelia hadn't thought of that. He would never return to that future he had been part of, but the possibility of erasing it must be horrifying.

He pressed a gentle kiss to her forehead. "We will sort all this out, Amelia. I'm certain of it."

"So am I." Questions hung over everything, but she wasn't feeling crushed by them.

"I will leave you to eat." He stepped back but kept hold of her hand, walking back with her to her chair and seeing her settled at the table again. He raised her hand to his lips and kissed it softly and tenderly. "Please rest."

"I will."

He made his way back toward the door leading to her dressing room and would, no doubt, make his way through the labyrinth again so no one would disturb her.

"Kipling?"

He turned back from the threshold. "Yes, my dear?"

My dear. She very much liked that.

"Promise me you'll rest as well."

He dipped his head in a bow that no one could ever mistake for anything but the gesture of a gentleman. "I give you my word."

He didn't entirely know where he belonged, but she knew one thing for certain: They belonged together.

Chapter 30

The storm had been a significant one. Walking back along the island trail, Kip spotted broken tree branches scattered about. He'd taken a peek that morning at the sea road; it was entirely underwater once more. Mr. Stirling and Mr. Winthrop wouldn't be leaving anytime soon. In the meantime, he meant to see to it that the trail that had nearly cost Amelia her life was made safe as quickly as possible.

"This entire section here looks a problem to me," one of the workmen said. He'd come up from the village along with all the others a couple of weeks ago and had almost immediately taken over the exterior efforts.

"It was along this stretch here that Miss Archibald had her accident," Kip said. "I don't want to see anyone else hurt."

The man nodded and turned to shout instructions to some of the others about reinforcing that entire stretch of the path, which was a relief.

Were Kip to point out *precisely* where Amelia had fallen, it wouldn't be difficult for people to ascertain that she'd been plunged all the way into the sea. No one could know that but the two of them.

A bit farther back, closer to the lighthouse, another section of the trail, one every bit as precarious, ran beside an outcropping. If someone slipped there, they would land among the rocks but not off the cliff. It was a good fit for what he'd told Mr. Winthrop had happened.

Kip made his way there, double-checking that it would work for his story. He leaned farther and glanced over the cliffside. While she most likely would have been caught before plunging all the way, had she somehow rolled off the edge here, he didn't know that she would have survived the fall. Walking along such treacherous terrain with her cane and her often fragile balance was dangerous. It was further testament to her late grandfather's cruelty that she was required to live here.

He slowly walked along the path, looking for any places where the workmen ought to focus. He knew the Iverses took this path up to the house. He didn't want anything happening to any of them either.

Unfortunately, his focus on helping was disrupted by the arrival of the very person he wished could be tossed off the island. Mr. Winthrop was studying a stretch of the path almost exactly where Amelia had fallen. That was reason for caution.

"Is this where Miss Archibald had her accident?"

Kip shook his head and, turning, pointed behind him. "It was up the trail a pace. Closer to the lighthouse, where the rocks jut out even more."

Mr. Winthrop eyed him doubtfully. "It seems if she'd fallen from that height, she would have been hurt far worse than she was."

"If she had fallen all the way off the island, I think she almost certainly would have died. Fortunately, as I said, she tumbled onto the rocks beside the path. They're jagged enough to do a great deal of damage even if not fallen on from a great height."

Mr. Winthrop still didn't look convinced. Indeed, he was studying the rocks below them. "I believe I see a scrap of fabric down there, a torn piece, stuck to that bit of rock."

Kip thought quickly. "I lost my hat as I was helping her up off the rocks. Miss Archibald lost her cane. Do you see either of those items down there?"

Mr. Winthrop looked back at him with a pulled brow.

Kip shrugged and pressed onward. "Since you are apparently convinced that I don't know where the accident *that I witnessed* happened and are further certain that a small piece of fabric possibly torn from Miss Archibald's coat or dress could not have been moved about at all in what was obviously a very rough storm last night, then my hat and her cane must be right there as well. Precisely where they would have fallen."

Smudge was standing nearby and clearly got the gist of what was being argued. "There's a right big tree branch down there as well. Odd thing, since there are no trees growing in that spot, and nothing could possibly have been brought there by the storm from somewhere else." Smudge shrugged, almost making the gesture seem sincere and authentic rather than a sarcastic indication of how ridiculous Mr. Winthrop was being.

Of course, Smudge didn't know that Mr. Winthrop was actually correct. Amelia had fallen very near to this spot, and somehow, a scrap of fabric torn from her dress hadn't been carried away by the storm.

Mr. Winthrop's eyes darted about, a few of the other villagers working nearby barely holding back their grins of amusement. A flush of embarrassment stained his cheeks. If he weren't such a blowhard, Kip might have felt sorry for him. The man could stand to be humbled.

Kip suspected, even if the villagers knew where Amelia had taken her fall and that it had plunged her into the ocean, setting her at odds with her grandfather's requirement, they would have lied through their teeth to make certain no one knew. She'd struggled at first to gain their cooperation. In the end, though, she'd won them over entirely.

Mr. Winthrop stomped off, more petulant than a grown man ought to be. He likely didn't even realize how honestly pathetic he really was. More than that, Kip suspected he didn't really care. He was at Guilford with one purpose in mind: securing for himself a biddable and controllable wife.

"What do you think Miss Archibald will do after her leaves Guilford?" Smudge asked after their unwanted interruption had begun making his way back toward the house.

"Can't say for certain, except that I have no doubt she will head somewhere away from the ocean."

"And what'll *you* do?"

With a grin he knew likely revealed the whole truth of it, he said, "I'll go wherever she does, if she'll let me. And if I can manage it. I don't fit in the world of either gentlemen or tradesmen. I don't imagine this time and place allows for much straddling of the two."

Smudge half nodded, half shrugged. "If you stayed in and around Guilford Village, you could. Us knows who you are and when you're from. Us'd find a way to help you sort it out."

"The village would let me be a gentleman tradesman?" Kip laughed.

But Smudge didn't. "The villagers like having you around. You might not be the usual sort, but us isn't the usual village. All of we would like having you nearby."

Until he heard Smudge say it, Kip hadn't realized how much he'd needed to hear words of welcome. He hadn't fit anywhere since before arriving at Guilford. He'd lost his place among his colleagues and in a world that had been his for years. And he'd had very little to do with his family.

He had been searching for home for far too long.

"You and Mrs. Finch are pretending to look at local estates," Smudge said. "Maybe you ought to do some actual looking. Might be there's a place near Guilford Village that would suit you."

"To buy an estate, a person has to have money. I don't have a single pound to my name."

Smudge acknowledged that with a nod. But in trademark Smudge fashion, he also didn't look deterred. The man could make a person believe almost anything was possible.

Kip continued down the path, searching for spots that needed attention. He trusted the workers to find them, but the sight of Amelia plunging over the rocks was too fresh in his recollection for him not to feel anxious that nothing was missed. The path took him past Amelia's garden, and he peeked inside. It had sustained damage in the storm but nothing, at least as far as he could see, that couldn't be cleaned up with relative ease. No trees appeared to be toppled. The stone wall was still entirely intact. He'd have to tell her that and set her mind at ease. She was likely worried, and heaven knew she had plenty enough to be worrying about.

He eventually came upon Mr. Stirling. Kip offered a brief bow, one with a degree more deference than he'd offered Mr. Winthrop. Amelia's uncle didn't seem entirely past redemption.

"It was quite a storm we had last night," Mr. Stirling said.

Kip nodded. "The grounds workers are assessing the damage. They are all dedicated to making certain the island paths are as safe as they can be. We are very fortunate your niece was not injured more severely than she was."

Mr. Stirling nodded absentmindedly. His brow was drawn in a look of contemplation. "Mr. Winthrop told me he suspects Amelia was plunged into the ocean, not merely tossed onto some rocks."

"I am assuming I don't need to explain to you why he is hoping that was true," Kip said, "even to the point of putting forth the story despite the fact that it means he is implying that a gently bred young lady is lying."

To his credit, Mr. Stirling looked a touch uncomfortable.

Kip pressed onward. "Even if Mr. Winthrop's erroneous claims were true, I would hope that as both a gentleman and family to her, you would feel an increased compassion toward her, an increased concern, a desire to make certain she is well and whole. *If it were true*"—he emphasized the word *if*—"you must ask yourself what kind of gentleman suspects that a lady has been through an absolutely harrowing ordeal and expresses not the tiniest bit of compassion for her."

"It isn't as though he and I are the very best of friends," Mr. Stirling said defensively.

"What your connection might have been previous to your bringing him here is of very minimal consequence when taken in the context of *why* you've brought him. Whether you knew what he was before isn't nearly as significant as the fact that you now know what he is and still you mean to resign your niece to building a life with a man like that. Before you knew his character, it could be excused as ignorance. Now that you do know, it is intentional."

"He truly does *want* to marry her." Mr. Stirling emphasized the word *want* as if that would convince anyone listening that there was some tenderness of feeling.

Kip gave him the driest look he could manage. "Mr. Winthrop told me directly that what he wants is an heir and a wife over whom he will have complete and total control. If he is willing to admit to that with no shame and no hesitation *before* securing a marriage, it isn't difficult to imagine how he would treat her after."

To Kip's relief, that seemed to give Mr. Stirling significant pause. They reached the door to the manor house.

Kip paused long enough to offer one last thought to Amelia's uncle. "Your niece has formulated a rather brilliant plan for Guilford. You would do well to listen to her, as its entire focus is the benefit it can bring to you. Even as her future has been at risk, even as you have contemplated forcing her into a match where the best she can hope for is a husband who relishes the idea of browbeating her mercilessly, she has been pondering ways that she can help *you*."

"I'm not so terrible a person as this makes me seem." Mr. Stirling didn't allow much beyond the slightest lift of a shoulder.

"Ask her about her idea for Guilford. You might find that neither of you needs to make room in your lives for someone like Mr. Winthrop."

"He's selfish and not as gentle-spirited as some, but I don't think he's as terrible as you are believing him to be."

"And I think," Kip countered, "you are trying very hard to convince yourself that you haven't invited a fox into the hen house."

Chapter 31

Though Amelia was still exhausted from her fall the day before and still in pain from her injuries, she dressed for dinner that night. She would give her uncle no reason to declare her a failure as a hostess or neglectful of her duties. Further, her distrust of Mr. Winthrop made her nervous about being alone in her room, not knowing where he was.

After a quick knock, Mrs. Finch poked her head around the door. "Dressed for dinner, I see." She stepped fully inside, closing the door behind her. "I told Kipling you would decide to join everywho for the meal."

"Has he underestimated my stubbornness?"

Mrs. Finch nodded. "But the rest of we didn't." She produced from behind her back a long, sturdy stick with a bend at the top. "It isn't a proper cane, but the workmen scoured the island looking for something that would make a decent substitute for you."

"How thoughtful." Amelia was truly, deeply touched.

Mrs. Finch set the "cane" in Amelia's hand. "Them smoothed it down so it won't give you splinters."

"The people of Guilford really are wonderful."

"A feeling us has for you and Kipling as well."

Amelia tested the cane and found it to be just the right height, not overly heavy, and sturdy enough for leaning on. "I do hope my uncle and Mr. Winthrop aren't being unkind to anyone."

"Other than *you*?" Mrs. Finch gave her a pointed look.

"A few more months and I can be free of them both." She set her shoulders, grateful for the friendship of this wonderful woman and the kindness of the people of Guilford. "Shall we go endure an evening with the two of them?"

"Our Kipling will be there." Mrs. Finch hooked an arm through Amelia's. "That'll make the evening far more enjoyable."

"He is rather lovely, isn't he?"

"Quite lovely."

They were nearly to the end of dinner, having spent much of the evening on the sort of pointless, mundane discussions that tended to punctuate awkward meals. Into that pointed awkwardness, Uncle quite suddenly introduced a topic of great importance to her.

"Amelia, Mr. Summerfield tells me you have an idea for Guilford that I am likely to find myself quite in favor of."

She looked to Kipling. He nodded encouragingly. Most of the gentlemen she'd known would have simply shared the idea themselves. It wasn't entirely a matter of putting themselves ahead of a lady on such matters but that they recognized that many of their fellow gentlemen would be more likely to listen to a man.

But Kipling had managed to navigate both difficulties with a great deal of acumen. He had primed her uncle to listen to her and had given him reason to believe that he ought to. That significantly increased the odds of her being heard. He was, without question, exceptional.

"Guilford is a very nice estate, and its nearness to the sea would make it intriguing to many people." Just not to her. "I am determined to see it ready to be lived in again."

"Are you hoping to live here?" her uncle asked.

With perhaps more fervor than she'd intended, Amelia said, "No." Just the thought of living here permanently sent a shiver of horror through her. "But there's no reason it couldn't be made an appealing and exciting place for a family."

Uncle seemed genuinely intrigued. "The house is entailed."

"I wasn't going to suggest that it be sold," she said. "You could find a family of standing in Society who could make their home here. Then the house wouldn't be empty, you could have income from it, and it wouldn't fall back into disrepair."

To her delight, she saw his eyes brighten. He hadn't dismissed the idea out of hand.

"I am working very hard to organize those I have hired from the village. The progress they are making has me increasingly convinced that it is an entirely possible and sensible approach."

"Restoring Guilford is requiring funds from the Stirling estate," he acknowledged. "Should it deteriorate again, those funds would have been wasted. But I am not going to abandon my home in order to live here and look after the place."

"Of course not."

"You think it could be made ready for a family to take up residence?"

She nodded. "I believe I could have it ready by the end of my six months. And since the ordinary needs of Guilford are already accounted for in the expenses of your estate, whatever you charge the family to whom it is lent would be profit."

A slow smile spread over Uncle's face. He was not merely considering her suggestion. He seemed to have already begun embracing it.

Amelia hazarded a glance at Kipling, wanting to see if she was misjudging her uncle's reaction but also not wanting to give away her hopeful nervousness. Kipling offered a very subtle smile that, while she certainly hadn't missed it, she didn't think would undermine anything.

She made the mistake of letting her gaze wander the tiniest bit to Mr. Winthrop. He, far from looking pleased or intrigued, appeared legitimately livid. So much so, in fact, that she involuntarily recoiled.

"You may have stumbled upon something worth pursuing, Amelia," Uncle said.

"My nephew and I have seen quite a few homes throughout England," Mrs. Finch said. "Several of them were let to families who paid rent to live there. It is not merely a common arrangement; it is also a wise one. An estate that sits empty is far more likely to fall into disrepair. It is also far less likely to be visited by those looking to be impressed by the holdings of otherwise impressive families."

Uncle nodded, though whether he realized he did so wasn't clear.

They had finished the last of their meal, and Mrs. Finch rose. She didn't generally break with protocol, which told Amelia that she felt it wise, for some reason, to leave the gentlemen without delay. Perhaps she felt Uncle Stirling was more likely to do some pondering if he didn't have to do so with ladies present.

Amelia took hold of her already-beloved cane and stood as well.

The gentlemen all got to their feet. Mr. Winthrop stomped away, apparently upset enough to be uncivil.

As Amelia passed Kipling, he smiled fleetingly. How she wanted to stop and throw her arms around him. She kept herself to proper decorum, though, and made her way from the dining room.

Out in the corridor, far enough from the room not to be overheard, Mrs. Finch said, "I believe you are very near to convincing he. Hold steady a bit longer."

Amelia felt that same hope.

Mrs. Finch slowed their forward progress, studying Amelia as she'd taken to doing since the previous day's misadventure. "You're aching again, I would wager."

There was no point denying it. "I suspect I am going to be in pain for some time."

"I'll find Jane and have she make certain the fire in your room is built up so you'll be warm when you return there. And I'll fetch you a warm shawl as well."

"Thank you," Amelia said.

She received a fond smile in response. "Us're watching out for you. Don't ever doubt that." Mrs. Finch hurried off in search of Jane.

Amelia made her way slowly toward the stairs leading to the drawing room. But her eyes happened upon the front windows. It wasn't so late that it was truly dark out. She could see a figure near the sea road. Surely everyone was well aware that it wasn't traversable yet. Wandering in that direction would be dangerous. Whoever it was needed to be warned.

She stepped through the front doors and out under the portico. She would make quick work of the swift reminder to wait for the sea to retreat, and then *she* could retreat back into the house. But first she had to reach the person, as the wind was too strong for her voice to carry to him.

She was within a few yards of the sea road when she spoke to him. "It isn't yet safe. You need to—"

He turned, and she froze.

"Mr. Winthrop. Why aren't you in the dining room with the other gentlemen?"

"Your uncle promised," he said. "I offered him a portion of your dowry. I sacrificed what would have been mine by rights. And he *promised*." Anger flashed hot in his eyes.

"His promise always depended on my success or failure here." She backed up carefully, too afraid to turn her back on him but too unsteady on her feet to rush. "I'm not failing at Guilford. He has to honor the terms of—"

"He will not break his word to me." Mr. Winthrop moved surprisingly quickly, placing himself in her way.

"My uncle alone doesn't determine what happens to my inheritance. The solicitor must be in agreement with him."

Her attempt at countering his anger didn't help. Mr. Winthrop didn't speak, didn't move. Indeed, there was something about his expression that told her his thoughts had suddenly jumped far afield. But he was still too much in her way for her to get around.

"Please allow me to pass." She spoke as firmly as she could manage. Her speed was not sufficient to escape on her own; he would have to permit her to do so.

He grabbed her arm and yanked her in the opposite direction of the house—toward the water-covered road. Toward the sea.

She pulled backward, resisting his efforts, ignoring the pain he was causing her. Only the day before, she'd been torn on rocks and tossed into the ocean. She tried to hit him with her cane, but he held her too near him. She couldn't manage the right angle.

He dragged her farther from the house.

"The sea road is still underwater," she said. "You cannot get to the village yet."

"I don't have to get you to the village," he said through tense teeth. "You simply have to be off the island."

Off the island. He meant to force her to break the terms of the agreement.

She pushed back as hard as she could, but she was weakened, and he was bigger than she.

Closer and closer he pulled her. Sea spray lashed her face and her hair. The wind off the water chilled her to her core. He would have her in the water. It was so close. All she could hear was the angry crash of waves.

A flurry of limbs suddenly pounded into Mr. Winthrop. *Mick.* He'd arrived out of nowhere, without warning, as he so often did, and was fighting Mr. Winthrop fiercely. His efforts freed Amelia from Mr. Winthrop's grasp, but in the next moment, the man flung Mick, who tumbled toward the sea. She lunged for the boy, horrified at the idea that he might be carried away.

But before she reached him, Kipling flew past.

He shouted back at her, "Stay on the island!" He grabbed the brave boy and pulled him to safety.

Mr. Winthrop made to reach for Amelia once more. She swung at him with her cane. He was yanked back by Smudge. Jane placed herself between Amelia and her would-be abductor. Mrs. Jagger and Marsh joined in the efforts. Others from the village did as well. Kipling, holding fast to Mick, reached her side. They'd managed to stay out of the water, but Mick would be bruised and sore, just as she was.

Kipling put an arm around Amelia and tucked her up close. She leaned against him, relieved and a bit shaken.

"I think it's time *this* was off the island." Smudge shoved Mr. Winthrop forward and toward the missing sea road.

"Toss him in." Mr. Ivers spoke from his rowboat, glaring thunderously at Mr. Winthrop. "Us'll not wait for the sea to retreat. Him's leaving now."

One of the groundskeepers tossed Smudge a length of rope, which he used to tie Mr. Winthrop's hands behind him. They apparently were taking no chances of him putting up a fight. Smudge strong-armed Mr. Winthrop into the boat and jumped in with him.

"What do you think they are going to do to him?" Amelia asked.

"It might be best if we don't know."

"Likely, them'll just make certain him don't come back and bother you," Mick said. "The people of Guilford are protectors, not murderers."

"It's a shame we can't, with any degree of confidence, say the same of Mr. Winthrop," Kipling said. "Isn't it, Mr. Stirling?" He looked just beyond her, in the direction of the house.

Amelia followed Kipling's gaze and found her uncle standing there, looking horrified.

"Once he had his money and his heir, what do you think he would have done to her?" Kipling continued. "If he was willing to do what he just did *before* getting what he wanted?"

Uncle Stirling looked around at them all, uncomfortable.

"But at least you would have gained a rentable estate and some extra money in your pocket," Kipling added coldly. "Is that what constitutes an honorable trade in England?"

"I didn't realize he was this horrid," Uncle insisted.

"*This* horrid?" Mrs. Finch scoffed. She tucked an arm around Mick. "That you knew he was horrid at all and still meant to move forward is despicable."

Kipling kept his arm around Amelia and walked with her back to the house. The villagers took up the procession and followed.

Once inside, Amelia breathed a heavy sigh of relief, one that shook with the enormity of all that had happened.

Kipling pressed a light kiss to her temple, "You are remarkable, you know."

"You saved Mick," she said.

"And he helped the village save you."

Amelia looked over her shoulder at all of them before stepping inside. "Thank you," she said. "Thank you all."

"Us don't want to lose you," Mick said, looking embarrassed at the sentiment yet speaking it firmly. "Either of you."

For one who had never really been wanted before, it was deeply touching.

Kipling took her to her book room. "If your uncle decides to go looking for you, he likely won't start here. You may have more time to yourself."

"A good plan." Her words shook despite herself. She was safe now, but two days in a row of being threatened with the ocean had taken a toll. "I only wish I couldn't hear the waves in here."

"We are, without question, going to get you away from the ocean the moment it's possible. I don't think I can endure watching you plunge toward the water a third time."

"Perhaps there is a home somewhere near Guilford Village but not on the water. We've found family here."

He grinned. "*We*. I like that, Amelia Archibald."

She smiled as well. "We could be the eccentrics of the area: a lady who wields her cane like a sword and a gentleman with a surprising knack for carpentry."

He wrapped his arms around her. "I like the sound of that."

She looked up into his beloved face. "I can't leave for months yet."

He leaned his forehead against hers. "My aunt and I will simply have to scout the area in the meantime to see if we can't find the perfect place."

"And you will keep coming back to tell me what you find?"

"Always," he whispered.

Chapter 32

Tentative music floated out of the drawing room as Kip approached it. A week had passed since Mr. Winthrop's forcible removal from Guilford Island. Mr. Stirling had remained until that morning but had finally made his departure as well. The house was likely to be peaceful now. It would, Kip hoped, begin feeling more like home.

Mrs. Finch stepped out of the drawing room just as he reached the door.

"I think I'll retire early tonight," she said, winking a little too pointedly. "Now that us is rid of Mr. Stirling, I'm wanting a spot of peace and quiet."

"And you don't think you'd find that in the drawing room with Amelia and me?"

"I'd hate to risk it."

He smiled; he couldn't help himself. "In the . . . theatrical production I participated in before the tides brought me here, chaperones were *constantly* abandoning their duties. I didn't think that was permitted in this time."

Mrs. Finch shrugged. "It's not."

"You do things your own way, don't you?"

"Always have."

"We're going to make a very interesting pair, you and me. Eccentric aunt, subtly odd nephew."

"England might never recover." Her smile was a laughing one as she made her way down the corridor, away from the drawing room.

Kip was in good spirits as he stepped inside. He left the door open as a nod to the rules they'd broken over and over on *The Beau*. Mrs. Finch was willing to bend things marginally to give them some time together, but Kip wasn't willing to get into the habit of fracturing those rules.

Amelia was at the pianoforte, a sheet of old-fashioned music in front of her. Except, unlike his first time in this room, he now knew it wasn't actually old-fashioned. It was now-fashioned, for want of a better descriptor.

"It is good to hear you playing again, Amelia."

Kip pulled a chair over and set it beside the stool she sat on. He slipped his arm around her waist.

"I do have a complaint to lodge against you, Kipling Summerfield." The laugh in her tone took out any sting.

Indeed, he found himself grinning as he tucked her even closer. "What's your complaint, my dear?"

"You said you would teach me 'Heart and Soul,' but you haven't so much as played it again."

He tipped her a crooked smile. "Teaching you to play a tune would require that I stop hugging you."

"I'm betting on you being willing to do it again in the future."

"A safe bet." Making a show of doing so under duress, he pulled his arm back again. "The best thing about 'Heart and Soul' is that it is most enjoyable when played as a duet."

"Truly?"

He nodded. "I'll teach you one part, then I'll play the other. You'll enjoy it."

"As much as you enjoy hugging me?" There was unmistakable mischief in her eyes.

So he offered his most roguish grin and was rewarded with a fierce blush.

Amelia proved a quick study. She had her part of "Heart and Soul" learned in no time. Once he felt certain she had the rhythm of it, he played the other bit. The two merged perfectly, creating the iconic tune. Well, what would, in a hundred fifty years or so, be an iconic tune.

"Oh, that is diverting. The two parts sound so wonderful together."

"Many people in the future know how to play one of these two parts on the pianoforte but literally can't play anything else."

"Little wonder, then, that you were so shocked that I hadn't heard of it."

He smiled at her. "But we probably need to never play it in front of anyone else since it's a future thing. We'd hate to accidentally erase the Beatles or something."

"Would erasing bugs be such a terrible thing?" she asked with a laugh.

"According to a movie I saw, yes."

She mouthed the word *movie* with mingled confusion and amusement.

"You might very well decide, Amelia Archibald, that being in my company is not worth the constant bewilderment."

Amelia looked at him with so much tenderness that it stole his breath for a moment. "There's something else I've wondered about you, Kipling."

"What's that?"

"You've told me that you are speaking with an assumed accent so that you won't stand out so much."

He laughed. "An accent, which I was told often when I first arrived is very strange."

"How did you speak in your own time, when you weren't portraying someone else?"

She wanted to hear his American accent? Why did he find that so touching?

He had to think for a moment to let go of the accent he'd been using. It had become so ingrained after weeks and weeks of only ever speaking with that accent that it was now his default.

Finally wrapping his mind around the shift, he spoke in his American accent. "Not everyone in America talks like this, but a lot of them do. I grew up in the western part of the United States and a lot of us out there sound similar."

Her eyes pulled wide. Her mouth pulled into a tight *O*.

"Don't like it?" he guessed.

"You sound almost like you're from Cornwall. Not exactly—no one would ever think you actually were—there's just some similarities."

"You still haven't said if you like it or not."

"It would take growing accustomed to, but I don't dislike it."

"And I don't dislike the way I've been talking since arriving here. That would probably be easier in the long-term, as fewer people would ask us potentially precarious questions."

Amelia leaned nearer. "I do like hearing you say 'us' in any accent, Kipling." She lightly brushed her lips over his.

He slipped his hand behind her neck and wove his fingers into her luscious auburn hair. "And I like saying it." He kissed her softly, lingeringly.

Her fingers slid along the tip of his collar, sending shivers over his neck. His heart thrummed.

"Oh, Amelia. We might need to ask Mrs. Finch not to make an early evening of it again, lest I forget there are rules now."

He could feel her laugh softly, and it eased some of his tension. She leaned against him, and he set his arms around her, breathing and grinning and silently thanking the mysterious tides for the havoc they'd wreaked on a life he'd not intended to leave behind but which he'd traded for a life he meant to treasure.

Chapter 33

The final day of Amelia's six months on Guilford Island arrived. Kip and his aunt were in the Guilford book room, seated unobtrusively off to one side. Amelia sat next to her uncle, both facing the desk where her late grandfather's solicitor sat reading out the details of her inheritance. Kip had gained a better understanding of what value money had in this time, enough that when the solicitor read out the total that she had received, he didn't entirely manage to keep his expression neutral. She perhaps couldn't rival the royal family, but she would never want for anything. And she most certainly could afford a home of her own.

All the necessary papers were signed, and everything was put in order.

"Congratulations, Miss Archibald," the solicitor said. "Your grandfather set you a rather difficult task, and you managed it."

Though her expression and smile were of the soft and demure variety expected of a lady of this era, Kip knew her well enough to see the pride shining in her eyes.

"I am very pleased to hear that my uncle will, in fact, be able to offer Guilford House to let. That was my aim, and it is always a fine thing when one's efforts prove fruitful."

She hadn't taken full credit for the idea, though she certainly could have. Societal expectations were a complicated thing to navigate. Kip felt more confident moving forward knowing she would help him with that navigating.

Though *The Beau* had been an amazing experience and had brought him closer to Malcolm and had in many ways helped him manage this strange permanent role he was taking on, there were aspects of life in 1803 that it had very ill prepared him for.

"If your grandfather had thought to make the house suitable for letting," the solicitor said, "you might not have found yourself with quite so much work to do here."

"But then," Mr. Stirling said, "my father might simply have given her a different task entirely."

Amelia's eyes darted to Kip very briefly. "It has been difficult, but I'm grateful to have been here these past months."

Kip smiled at her, resisting the urge to wink. He'd discovered winking at ladies was not really the done thing in 1803, but it made Amelia blush in such an adorable way that he couldn't always resist the urge.

The solicitor remained behind to gather his papers. Mr. Stirling accompanied his niece from the room, and Kip accompanied his aunt.

As they walked down the corridor, Mr. Stirling said, "I do hope you are proud of yourself, Amelia. I will confess, when my father's requirements for you were first read, I didn't think there was any chance of success. I was quite certain the ocean alone would drive you away before the end of the six months."

"I worried about that myself," she said. "And then Mr. Winthrop made the island almost too uncomfortable to remain."

"That blaggard tried to toss you off the island entirely," Mrs. Finch said dryly.

Mr. Stirling hadn't become truly at ease with Kip's aunt's tendency toward blunt speech. Kip thought it was brilliant.

"He spent a good amount of time pouting over all that," Mr. Stirling said.

Kip ignored how dismissive the choice of wording was. At least Mr. Stirling wasn't still trying to manipulate his niece into a life of misery. "But I heard through a mutual acquaintance that he recently initiated a search for a distant relative who is in line to inherit from him. He seems to have given up on securing his own heir."

A different part of the Winthrop family might make this area home. Kip didn't regret preventing the horrid Mr. Winthrop from marrying Amelia—he would have done so again if given the chance—but it had weighed on his mind, knowing his interference might change or erase Malcolm's eventual existence. It was entirely possible that the distant family who inherited from Mr. Winthrop was the line Malcolm would come from.

More than that, it meant that Kip being there in 1803, preventing the tragedy of Amelia being forced to marry such a horrid person, would be what actually brought Malcolm's direct ancestors where they needed to be so that Malcolm would someday make the world a better place.

Perhaps Kip's being thrown back in time didn't threaten to ruin things but held the promise of making at least some things right.

Their traveling trunks were tied to the carriage that would take them across the sea road. Mr. Stirling was remaining on Guilford for the night, but Kip, Amelia, and Mrs. Finch were not remaining a moment longer than required.

The matter of Amelia's inheritance was settled. Her time on this island, surrounded by the ocean, had come to an end. Mrs. Finch had a good friend in the village with whom she had lived in the years since her husband's death who'd offered lodging to them all, which they had readily accepted.

Kip reached over and took hold of Amelia's hand. "I realize you're likely eager to reach the place you'll be staying for the next few days, but if you've a bit of time and energy you're willing to expend, my aunt and I have something we'd like to show you."

"Today, I'm eager to see anything and everything that is away from this island." She turned to Mrs. Finch. "I hope you realize this isn't meant to be a reflection on anyone who helped make these last months bearable and successful. I will be forever indebted to the people of Guilford Village, and if there is any possible way that I can find a place to live nearby, it would be a dream come true."

Mrs. Finch shook her head and waved that off. "Every last one of we knows how eager you are to put some distance between yourself and the sea. Us don't begrudge you that."

Amelia looked relieved. "In that case, I would love to see whatever it is you two wish to show me."

Kip grinned. "Excellent."

Kip watched Amelia as she studied the estate they were visiting. Elegant, well-maintained, sizable without being overwhelming. She held his hand as they walked along a path made of carefully laid paving stones. Her cane didn't appear to slip at all.

She looked back at the house, then at the expanse of lawn and tall trees in the landscape. "It is beautiful."

He and his aunt had done a decent amount of traveling in the area around Guilford. That had allowed him to make the acquaintance of a few gentlemen his same age who had proved fast friends.

He had a better grasp on that area of the country and the expectations of this era. And the day they had visited this estate, he'd known almost immediately that he wanted Amelia to see it as well.

"You've not seen the best part." Kip led her to the arched entry to a walled garden. He held his breath as he stepped through with her.

"Oh, Kipling," she whispered.

"Is that a good 'Oh, Kipling' or a disappointed 'Oh, Kipling'?"

She turned to him. "It isn't overgrown or in disrepair, but it also isn't complete."

He nodded, watching and waiting.

"Though you haven't said as much," she said, "I suspect we've come to visit here because this estate is available for purchase, and you think it might be a good fit for us."

Us. Hearing her say that would always thrill him. "I've spoken with the gentlemen who've become my friends these past months, and they all assure me the asking price is more than fair and well within your means."

She set her hand gently on his cheek. "*Our* means, Kipling."

He set his hand over hers, shifting it to his lips and kissing her palm.

"How far are we from Guilford Village?" Amelia asked.

"Less than thirty minutes walking."

She looked around once more, turning and studying the garden. She closed her eyes and held very still. Kip, standing behind her, set his arms around her just as he'd done months earlier at a window of Guilford House as a storm had broken overhead.

Amelia leaned back against him. "I can't hear the ocean," she whispered.

"I wouldn't have even brought you here otherwise," he said. "You deserve to live where you feel safe and where you aren't afraid."

She turned in his arms. "Would you live here as well?"

"I wouldn't be anywhere else." Kip kissed the tip of her nose.

"I think we could be very happy building a home here, my darling Kipling," she said.

"I would be happy anywhere in the world with you, my Amelia." He bent closer and, in the instant before kissing her, whispered, "I traveled centuries to find you, and you are home to me."

Acknowledgments

The amazing *Seeking Persephone* movie team for welcoming, encouraging, and patiently teaching me as I've shifted into the world of film.

My editor, Sam Millburn—We got this book done in time, which was more of a miracle than anyone will ever know. Thank you!

My agent, Pam Pho, who found a way for me to keep writing in the midst of one of the most horrendous years of my career. You are incredible.

Ginny and Jesse, fabulous proofreaders.

Katherine and Paul, invaluable team members. Can't wait to see what's next!

Indispensable Reference Resources:
- Feltham, John. *A Guide to All the Watering and Sea-Bathing Places; with a Description of the Lakes* (1813).
- Nicholson, Peter. *Practical Carpentry, Joinery, and Cabinet-Making* (1826).
- Orchard Halliwell-Phillipps, James. *A Dictionary of Archaic and Provincial Words, Obsolete Phrases, Proverbs, and Ancient Customs* (1847).

About the Author

SARAH M. EDEN is a *USA Today* bestselling author of more than eighty witty and charming historical romances, which have sold over one million copies worldwide. Some of these include 2020's Foreword Reviews INDIE Awards gold winner for romance, *Forget Me Not*, 2019's Foreword Reviews INDIE Awards gold winner for romance, *The Lady and the Highwayman*, and 2020 Holt Medallion finalist, *Healing Hearts*. She is a three-time Best of State gold-medal winner for fiction and a three-time Whitney Award winner.

Combining her obsession with history and her affinity for tender love stories, Sarah loves crafting deep characters and heartfelt romances set against rich historical backdrops. She holds a bachelor's degree in research and happily spends hours perusing the reference shelves of her local library.

Sarah is represented by Pam Pho at Steven Literary Agency.
www.SarahMEden.com
Facebook: facebook.com/SarahMEden
Instagram: @sarah_m_eden

Enjoy All the Books in the

Storm Tide Romance Series

BY

SARAH M. EDEN

Available wherever books are sold

FALL IN LOVE WITH A
PROPER ROMANCE
BY
SARAH M. EDEN

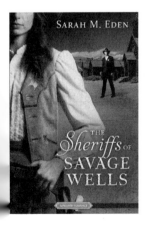

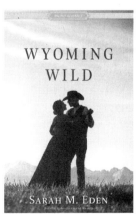

Available wherever books are sold

PROPER ROMANCE

READY TO FIND YOUR NEXT ROMANCE?

LET US HELP.

◎ @shadow_mountain

◎ @properromanceseries

f Proper Romance Series

The Proper Romance series is a collection of sweet romance novels from award-winning authors, with strong heroines and handsome heroes.

SHADOW MOUNTAIN